podium perfect

LEXI RICHARDS

PURPLE SECTOR PRESS

First published by Purple Sector Press in 2025
Copyright © 2025 by Lexi Richards

This is a work of fiction. Any references to historical events, real people, or real locales are used fictitiously. All characters and events in this publication, other than those clearly in the public domain, are fictitious and any resemblance to real persons, living or dead, is purely coincidental.

Cover Design: Sam & Deb | Ink & Velvet Designs
Editor: Britta Jensen with Yellow Bird Editors

Identifiers:
Trade Paperback ISBN - 979-8-9990323-0-0
Ebook ISBN - 979-8-9990323-1-7

For every woman who needs an escape to a world of glamour, travel, laughter, and happily ever after.

prologue

LOS ANGELES, CA
Silver Racing Headquarters

Avery took hold of the steering wheel and pushed down on the accelerator, the car biting back immediately. She eased up the hill as a lifesize view of the Circuit of the Americas appeared on the screens in front and all around her like a 3D movie theater. She played it safe her first lap, trying hard to keep it clean and avoid any crashes, while Teddy leaned on the doorframe, watching with a sly smile.

"What was my time?" she asked, as she crossed the finish line.

"2:30:22," Alan answered back. "Damn, I didn't know you could drive!"

Avery grinned. "Ehh, not good enough. Let's go again." Teddy's laps had been in the 1:40-1:45 range. She knew she wouldn't get there, or she'd be driving in F1 Academy, the women's series, but she knew she could go faster.

Avery rolled out her wrists, stretched her neck side-to-side. "I'm going for 2:15 this lap," she looked back at Teddy, who nodded at her.

She braced the steering wheel again, nodded to herself as much as to Teddy and focused, pressing the balls of her foot into the pedal, doubly glad that she hadn't worn heels today. Wouldn't have been able to do this, that's for sure. She pushed down on the accelerator even harder, easing up a tad as she rounded turn one. Crunch. The car whipped back. Into the gravel it went.

"Shit," she shook her head, looking back to Teddy to see his reaction.

"It's alright, bella. Happens to the best of us, go again," he nodded.

Bella. He'd called her that in Italy too.

"Try steering into the turn using a wide racing line," Alan coached her through the radio.

"Yes, again," she took a deep breath.

She started up the hill, again. "NOW, steer left now," Alan shouted through the headset. Crunch. Gravel. Again.

"Damn it," she took her fingers off the wheel and exhaled. *Frustrating.*

Teddy had a coy smirk on his face.

"Here, let me show you," Teddy offered from his spot on the wall, striding up to the left side of the fake car setup. "Like this," he leaned over, and put his hands on top of hers.

Avery felt heat rush up her neck at his touch. His hands felt warm and strong, steadying hers which had involuntarily begun to shake.

"Okay, start accelerating," he instructed her.

She pushed down on the pedal.

"More," his voice was deep, commanding.

Avery pushed down again, nearly bringing it to full throttle as the car zipped up the hill.

"Okay, now don't let up but put your other foot on the break," he explained. His face was so close to hers she could feel the breath from his words, like a tickle, a very serious tickle. There was no lightness when it came to Teddy Ross and mastering a race corner.

He pressed down harder on her hands, generating an almost electric heat between them. Did he feel it too? That chemistry she felt with his hands splayed out above hers? What would it feel like to have the rest of his capable body pressed up against hers? Her crush, her body, momentarily distracting her from the task at hand, while Teddy took control, firmly, but quickly whipping the wheel to the left, before allowing it to straighten itself back out.

"Ohhh," Avery breathed. "So that's how it feels?"

Teddy smiled satisfactorily, and leaned in closer, his lips almost grazing her earlobe. Avery's pulse quickened. If she turned her head, their lips would be a mere inch apart. She didn't dare, there's no way she'd be able to resist the temptation of leaning in even closer, seeing if he was feeling that same magnetic pull.

"That's how it feels when you don't hold back. When you take control," he whispered into her ear, before letting go of her hands and pulling back, his eyes assessing her as if he had just *really seen her* for the first time.

"Now try it again, by yourself," he nodded, resuming his coaching stance by the wall. Avery remembered that they weren't alone, her cheeks warmed at the thought that Alan and a handful of engineers had witnessed that moment on their screens, and had probably thought Teddy was whispering something much more risqué in her ear. Not that what Teddy had said, hadn't affected her. *Like a bolt of lightning down my spine.*

Avery shook off the remaining heat from Teddy's hands, tried to free her mind from thoughts of Teddy's lips, his hands, and felt the oxygen return to her lungs as she took a deep steadying breath.

I've got this.

one

Four months earlier

People moved around Avery in every direction, like a human beehive, or that famous intersection in Tokyo. Her body buzzed along with the activity around her as if the crowd's excitement was rising up from the asphalt and entering her body through her feet. Or maybe it was the heat? A bead of sweat trickled down her neck, and she grabbed a ponytail holder from her wrist and pulled her long, jet-black, curly hair up into a messy bun on top of her head. Was Bahrain always this hot in April? Avery had been to this race track before, but she didn't remember the desert heat being quite this intense. It was going to be a three shower kind of a day.

In exactly thirty-two minutes the first Formula One race of the season would be underway, and drivers were trying to make their way to their respective cars and garages while being mobbed by photographers, reporters, and VIP fans during the pre-race grid walk, one of her favorite race day traditions. It was absolute chaos, but she relished every second of it.

Throngs of VIPs were taking selfies with the drivers and cars, thinking that the absurd amount of money they paid for grid walk access for ten minutes before the race entitled them to get in the way. Avery cringed at the poor reporters, their shirts soaked through and stuck to their backs, and who were jamming microphones in celebrities' faces, mostly being ignored by these noobs who didn't actually know anything about the cars or the sport.

As much as she was enjoying taking in the spectacle, Avery needed to get back to the Silver Racing garage, where her dad, Michael Silver, the majority owner of the team, was waiting for her. But her feet were glued to the ground beneath her as she took in the scene one last time as a fan before she had to report for duty as an *official employee* of the Silver Racing Charitable Foundation.

She hadn't made it ten feet through the chaos before two huge dudes stopped in their tracks, blocking her path.

"Bro, that's him, for sure," she overheard one say. She stood on her tiptoes to see what they were looking at.

It was the Prince of Wales. Fair enough. He and his cousin, an over-dressed princess, appeared to be giving their best wishes to Cody Davis, the rookie driver on the Archer team. She reached into her bag for her phone to snap a picture since she didn't see a photographer capturing the moment. A million cameras and not one pointed at senior members of the British royal family? Weird.

"Cody, over here!" she yelled. They'd met a few times before. Hopefully, he'd recognize her voice. He somehow managed to hear her over the blaring techno music and the roar of helicopters overhead, and posed, putting his arm around the princess. Only a blonde-haired, blue-eyed American would be so bold as to casually embrace a bonafide princess.

She'd send the pic to Josh, who did PR for the Archer Automotive team, one of Silver's rivals on track. He was standing behind the driver and royals, his brown skin glistening in the sunlight, and wouldn't have been able to get a pic from that angle.

Josh's gray eyes lit up when we saw her, and she waved. Josh and Avery had briefly dated for a semester in college after bonding over their obsession with motorsports. They broke up when Josh graduated, but had remained good friends. Her family's introductions had helped him land his first job in the sport.

He managed to make his way over to her, nearly rubbing shoulders with the prince as he squeezed past.

"I got a pic of Cody with the royals for you," she said proudly.

"Thanks! How are you? How was your off-season?" he asked.

"The usual, mostly," Avery was grateful she didn't have to explain what she meant by the 'usual' to Josh. He knew she'd spent the time off with her family in Los Angeles. *My mom parading me around at holiday parties in front of Hollywood's most eligible bachelors.* Even though they had been squarely in the "friend zone" for a long time, it didn't seem right to share that bit of information.

"*But*, I do have one piece of news to report. My dad offered me a job opportunity I may or may not be qualified for," she jiggled her new employee ID badge hanging from the lanyard around her neck.

He looked at the badge. "Director of Silver Charitable Foundation. Congratulations, you'll be perfect for it," he grinned. "And now we both get to work with young drivers whose reputations precede them. What do you make of your dad's new young gun?"

Josh was referring to Teddy Ross, the driver that her dad and his partners had hired in the off-season.

"I've never spoken to him, so I don't know," she said, shrugging her shoulders. "I think everyone calling him the future of Formula 1 is a bit premature."

Could he live up to the hype? Avery had seen so many promising drivers flame out after a season or two, so she wouldn't get too excited yet. Teddy would have to prove himself to her, and to everyone else, with results on track. Especially because despite a successful rookie season the year prior on Alpha Fuerte, Teddy was infamous for an epic meltdown a few years ago that had cost him the championship in Formula Two, Formula One's version of the minor leagues.

Regardless of his performance, she was grateful that she'd get to work with a new driver, one who would be able to see her as a professional, not just the kid who had been hanging around the garage for years, the way Teddy's predecessor had. That is, if she ever had a chance to have a real conversation with him. He had the benefit of many years of media training, and in every interview she'd seen of him, he was perfectly polished, a master at skirting a reporter's question, always giving an obviously rehearsed answer.

"I better go deal with that," Josh nodded his head to reporters trying to get a last word from Cody before he slipped on his helmet and got into his car. "Good to see you, Aves," he said quickly as he trotted off after his charge.

Avery knew she should hustle to the Silver garage with the race start drawing nearer, but she allowed herself to take a second, to breathe in the scent of the rubber and tar and sweat as a fan one last time. Because today, as soon as she walked into the garage, everything would change. Everyone would be counting on her to do *real work*, or at least she hoped so. All eyes would be on her to see if she was up to the task, or if she was just another nepo-baby.

two

SAKHIR, BAHRAIN

Three men stood huddled around a computer screen in the Silver garage. Her dad's imposing figure was impossible to miss, his sport coat sticking out like a sore thumb in a sea of dry-fit polos. *Good,* her first opportunity to show him her professional side. Brandon, the team principal, gestured to something on the monitor. The third, Teddy Ross, man of the hour, was frowning, his chocolate brown hair curling out from beneath a ball cap, and his race overalls unzipped to the waist, revealing his tight-fitting undershirt underneath. *Holy abdominals.* She'd seen him from a distance countless times before, but up close she noticed how tall he was, especially for a F1 driver, and broader across the shoulders than most too.

Not that she would pay any attention to how cut he was, how she could see the hard lines of his muscles as his broad shoulders narrowed into a trim torso. *Avery, get it together. We do not check out the talent*. It was time to roll up her sleeves and be her most professional self.

"Hello, sweetheart," her dad called, looking up from the screen and waving her over.

Sweetheart? No one was going to take her seriously when the boss called her sweetheart. Avery joined the huddle, trying to duck away from her dad's arms, outstretched for a hug. He wouldn't hug his other employees, would he?

"Hi, Dad. Hi, Brandon," she said, in her deepest, most adult-sounding voice. She turned to Teddy and stuck her hand out, trying to appear much more confident than she felt. *Fake it 'til you make it they say*.

"Hi, I'm Avery Silver, Director of Silver Charitable Giving."

"I know who you are, Avery," Teddy replied quietly, his British accent tinged with a hint of a Scottish brogue. "But it's a pleasure to officially meet you."

He knew who she was?! Teddy, who had more followers than a Kardashian, knew who she was. She was surprised, and a bit flattered, if she was being honest with herself.

"Oh. Okay, cool," she replied, her voice rising. Avery looked down at her outfit and tried to smooth the creases that had already formed on her shirt. Why did she suddenly feel self-conscious wearing a staff polo, athleisure skirt, and sneakers? Every member of the staff was wearing some version of the same outfit, and she was trying to blend in, wasn't she?

"Welcome to the team, and good luck out there today," she managed to squeak out, her deep professional voice long gone. She hadn't been this flustered by being in close proximity to a driver since she was a silly, hormonal, pubescent girl.

Maybe it was the combination of his movie-star looks and her nerves. Or maybe Teddy Ross had this effect on all women.

That would explain why he was often swarmed by female fans who were more interested in his megawatt smile and chiseled cheekbones than how fast he could drive a car.

Teddy nodded seriously at her and put the earbud that had been dangling around his neck back in his ears and turned and walked toward the car.

Was he listening to rap?

EDM?

Why do I care? His music taste had nothing to do with the team's big end-of-season fundraising event, one of her main responsibilities in her new role.

"Should we go take our seats?" her dad asked, interrupting her thoughts.

He pointed up at the five red lights on the overhead gantry that had just turned on, indicating there were five minutes until the race. Now it was really time for everyone, except for essential personnel to get out of the way. She saw Brandon and the race engineers slip their headphones on and take their positions in front of their huge array of laptops and screens. They would be monitoring everything from the weather radar to the tire pressure on the cars, calculating and recalculating strategy.

"Let's do it!" she replied. Her insides were vibrating in anticipation of schmoozing with the sponsors and VIPs in the exclusive seating area above pit lane while she talked up the company's charitable work and community involvement; the team's responsibility to use F1's newfound popularity to help the next generation. Most drivers who made it to F1, the pinnacle of motorsports, came from very privileged backgrounds, not unlike her own. And one hundred percent of them were male. She wanted to do what she could to level the playing field and give all kids, especially minorities and girls, an opportunity to pursue their dreams in sports.

The roar of the engines filled her ears as the drivers turned on their engines for the formation lap. Around her, other spectators put in their earplugs to turn down the sound. But not Avery, she relished the noise, even if she'd regret it later on when she needed hearing aids. It drowned out every nagging thought in her head, allowing her to succumb to her fandom. Would this be it? The year her beloved Silver team finally won the constructor's championship, the award given to the team that earned the most points over the season? With "Zippy" Zack Maimon and the newly intriguing Teddy Ross driving, anything felt possible. Avery was on her feet, leaning as far over the glass railing as she could without falling over, as the cars weaved back and forth across the track, warming up their tires.

The starting lights turned red one by one. One. Two. Three. Four. Five. Avery held her breath until lights out. The Formula One season was officially underway.

three

SAKHIR, BAHRAIN

The sun had set, leaving Avery and her dad clouded in darkness that matched her mood as they drove in one of the team shuttles back to their hotel from the track. Teddy ended up in the bottom ten of the twenty racers, and only the top ten drivers earned points for their team. His teammate, Zack, had predictably ended up in the top five, earning some points for the team, but didn't quite make it on the podium. Avery sank back into the leather seat—this was not the start to the season they'd wanted. It was only the first of twenty-plus races that spanned the nine months-long F1 season, but the loss stung anyway.

"I'm going to call it a day and head up. What time do we need to leave for the airport in the morning?" she asked her dad. She was going to hitch a ride on the team's chartered jet back to Southern California with the staff and the car itself, where the team's engineers had their work cut out for them. They'd have to work from dawn to dusk all week to improve the car's speed before the next race, which was merely a week away.

"How about one drink before you head up?" her dad asked, his face shining. "We can catch the last few minutes of the Lakers game at the bar, for old time's sake?"

"Okay, one drink," she said. "For old time's sake." Avery smiled, remembering fondly the nights from her childhood when she was allowed to stay up late with her dad to watch Kobe.

They found a table in the lounge with a view of the TV. Her dad sat down on a couch facing the screen, and Avery grabbed a seat on the opposite sofa, facing him. Avery couldn't remember the last time she and her dad got to hang out, just the two of them. The rare alone time would be nice, a chance to show her dad how much she'd grown up.

"Michael, nice to see you!" a gray-haired gentleman interrupted.

"Ron, this is my youngest daughter, Avery. Avery, Ron runs partnerships for Aurelia Strap Watches, who you, of course, know is one of the team's biggest partners. Ron, please, join us."

So much for that one-on-one time. She could practically hear her crisp hotel sheets calling to her. But getting up from the table now, when one of their biggest sponsors had sat down, would not only be rude, it would be bad business for the team, and for the foundation.

Avery's attention and eyes wandered back to the hotel's entrance where another Silver branded vehicle was pulling up. Maybe Stacey, the team's physical trainer, who also was her closest, *only*, female friend on the team, was back, and could rescue Avery from this conversation. Avery and Stacey's friendship went back generations. Stacey's grandfather had been one of the first Australian F1 drivers and an early investor in the team that Avery's father later bought. Neither of the young women could escape the siren call of motorsport.

But it was Teddy who emerged first. Avery had never seen Teddy in street clothes before. He was wearing wide-legged designer jeans, Golden Goose sneakers, and a clean, short-sleeved white v-neck tee, giving her a glimpse of biceps. The smooth tan arms that had been hidden by his racing suit earlier made her breath hitch. A middle-aged woman spotted Teddy and shrieked with excitement, alerting the whole lobby to his presence. The woman ran up to him, waving her camera phone in his face, and a small queue formed in front of him.

Avery cringed. There would be no sport without the fans, but it seemed like more and more often the fans forgot that the drivers were real humans, who may want a little personal space.

Teddy patiently stood in place for each selfie, flashing a megawatt smile. *Wow, he really is handsome.* But he probably had a huge ego like all the rest. It came with the territory, she supposed, being one of the twenty best drivers on the entire planet, insanely fit, with women of all ages throwing themselves at you no matter where you were around the globe. Normally, she'd completely ignore this type of scene, roll her eyes at a driver who hammed it up for his fans, but she kept watching. There was something about Teddy that was different. Between his big smiles, his face turned serious as he greeted each fan. He didn't wave them off. Instead, he shook hands and thanked people for their support. It was unusual.

"Teddy, come over here, there's someone you need to meet," Michael shouted over the high-energy lobby.

When Teddy finally reached their table, after being stopped for photos several more times, they all stood and Michael proudly introduced his new driver to their wide-eyed, star-struck sponsor.

"Teddy, sit, and I'll get you a Perrier so you can hydrate," Michael insisted.

Teddy accepted the invitation and looked around for a seat. Any driver who had made it this far knew the importance of building relationships with the money guys. Formula One was a multi-billion-dollar business, after all. She had long ago accepted that driving was a small percentage of the drivers' actual week, but how did Teddy feel about it? Had he been disappointed to learn that his dream of making it to Formula One included so little time in the car?

His hair, which had been mostly tucked away under a ball cap or helmet earlier, now spilled out over his ears. It was longer than she'd expected, but still neat. It looked damp from the shower and probably smelled fantastic. *And here I am, still coated with dried sweat and in the same ugly outfit as earlier.*

"May I?" Teddy asked, cocking his head at her.

Right, the only open spot at their table was next to her on the leather couch, which she suddenly realized was more of a loveseat. Awesome. *The super-hot race car driver who I have to work with is going to think of me as the girl with the B.O. for the rest of time.* But there was nothing she could do now without being rude, or worse yet, awkward.

"Oh, uh, yes, sure," she scooted as close to the armrest as she could.

She looked away as Teddy sat down next to her, and despite her wiggling over, their thighs touched, sending a little burst of heat up and down her legs.

"I'm sorry you finished out of the points today, I'm sure it's

21

not how you imagined your first race with Silver," she said softly.

"Not ideal, but we knew going into today that the car didn't have the pace for a win, but at least Zack got some points for the team. And now we will look ahead to next week," he replied in his very polished, rehearsed way.

She nodded at him, holding back an eye roll. He'd probably said the exact same things to reporters as soon as he'd gotten out of the car.

"Well, that's a very nice way to look at it. But, I'm not a reporter, Teddy." She angled herself toward him, no easy feat sitting side by side on the loveseat. "You're among teammates here, you don't have to give me the party line," she challenged him. Was this guy a handsome robot? Or was there anything underneath all that floppy hair?

He blinked his eyes, which she noticed were a warm hazel now that his face was literally inches away from hers.

He cleared his throat. "Are you planning to come to many of the races this season?" Teddy asked her, quickly changing the subject.

Not going to open up, then.

"Yes, definitely," she answered. "One of the best parts of working with the Silver Foundation is that I have an excuse to travel with the team when there's a chance to raise funds or highlight our causes."

"Well," said Teddy a bit coyly, "Do let me know how I can be of service, Avery."

"I certainly will," she said, her heart beating faster as neither one of them looked away. His seemingly flawless face from a distance was perfectly imperfect up close: slightly stubbled rather than clean-shaven, and a white scar cutting across his bottom lip. Avery fought the urge to reach out and touch it, and then trace the outline of his heart-shaped lips.

"I have one large Perrier," a waitress chirped, interrupting their prolonged eye contact.

"That's for me, please," Teddy replied.

"Oh, wow, yes, you're welcome." The poor woman nearly tripped over herself as she realized who she was serving.

Teddy took it in stride and gave the flustered woman another one of his dazzling smiles and winked as she unscrewed the top and started pouring, staring in disbelief at Teddy. Avery rolled her eyes. *Good grief, if she doesn't take her eyes off Teddy and focus on her job she's going to miss the glass entirely and pour the bottle all over him.* The whole interaction was so cheesy. She knew being gracious with fans was part of the job, like taking the time to talk to an owner and a sponsor.

Teddy reached for his glass.

"How about a toast to the season ahead?" Teddy suggested, returning his attention to the men across the table.

"Here, here," her dad said, tapping his glass with Teddy's, then Ron's before taking a sip. *What am I, invisible?*

"Teddy, what did you think of the car's new side pods today?" Ron asked, hoping for some inside scoop. "Do you think the team should stick with them or go back to the drawing board?"

Teddy launched into a rather technical explanation of the strengths and weaknesses of the current car design, toeing the line between giving an important sponsor the VIP/insider treatment he so clearly wanted and not giving away so much information that any trade secrets were divulged to someone not on the team payroll.

"What about Alpha Fuerte's design with no side pods? Is

that something we should look at?" Avery interjected, trying to insert herself into the conversation.

"Say, next time in SoCal, do you think I could get on Teddy's simulator?" Ron asked before anyone could respond to her. "That's about as close as I'll get to experience what Teddy here is describing."

Avery took a deep breath. She was used to it by now - men like Ron tuning her out when it came to the technical side of the business. Sure, she was Michael Silver's socialite daughter, someone they recognized from the society pages. But, she also knew way more about motorsport than a guy who sold watches for a living. It made her blood boil.

"Gentlemen, if you'll excuse me, I have an early flight tomorrow," Avery announced politely.

Her dad stood and gave her a quick hug, "Sleep well, sweetheart." *Again with the sweetheart, no wonder men like Ron don't take me seriously.*

"Good night, Dad. Ron, nice to meet you. Teddy, see you again soon?"

Teddy stood up, "I'll walk you to the elevator. My trainer probably has some disgusting shake for me to drink before I call it a night. Ron, a pleasure to meet you. Michael, I'll talk to you soon."

"Avery, shall we?" he gestured toward the elevators.

Avery was hyper aware of the space between their bodies as they walked side-by-side around the corner.

Teddy looked back over his shoulder. "What a wanker," he said quietly in Avery's ear.

Her chest expanded with validation. "I know, right," Avery said enthusiastically.

"Thank you for giving me an opening to exit that conversation. I doubt he'd let me go before I promised him my first-born child."

Avery giggled, "No, thank *you*. I... it... can be lonely being the only one my age on the team," she paused. "And I'm glad you were there tonight."

The elevator doors chimed and slid open before them.

"After you," he said as his hand hovered over the small of her back. Even so, Avery's spine tingled with his phantom touch as they stepped inside.

She was certainly intrigued by him. The drivers had always thought of her as a kid sister, and the rest of the team as the boss's daughter. But maybe Teddy could be something else entirely—an ally, someone to share a knowing look with when the boomers said something inane. *That is if I can ignore how attractive he is, how my heart rate picks up and skin tingles every time he gets close to me.*

four

LOS ANGELES, CA

"Let's go with the checkered-flag option for the save-the-date, but with the red text," Avery directed the graphic designer over the phone.

"I will have it to you by Friday at the latest," the graphic designer promised. "Thanks, Avery."

Avery hung up the phone and took out her earbuds. She was at her desk in the family office near the beach in Santa Monica plowing through her to-do list, and her heart jumped as her calendar reminded her of her next call - the annual grant-making meeting of the Silver Racing Foundation board of directors. Namely, her mom, dad, brother, and brother-in-law. It had the potential to be life-changing... or soul crushing. *Ready or not, I'm about to find out.*

She stood up from her desk and placed one hand over her heart while she drew in a big breath. *In, two, three, four, five. Out, two, three, four, five.* The image of Teddy's abs in his undershirt filled her mind as she tried to relax. *So much for lowering my heart rate.*

Her parents had always stressed the importance of giving back to the community, but when it came to dispersing the foundation's funds, they were happy to just rubber-stamp the same grants year after year. Which were all perfectly reasonable causes, but not particularly inspiring. Sure, funding a new lecture hall at USC was a nice thing to do. But it was so indirect. And Avery wanted to help kids now. Not maybe help kids who might benefit at some later date if they happen to go to that school. Plus, she suspected that her parents really did it because they liked seeing "Silver Racing Lecture Hall" in big bold letters whenever they were on campus.

And now was her chance to shake things up. She was a college graduate and the paid director of the foundation. This was her job. She'd devoted every working hour she could since she'd gotten back from Bahrain weeks ago putting together a proposal that they would vote on today. Hours of researching programs and visiting with non-profit leaders had led to Avery crafting a vision for the future of the foundation. A future with a clear mission: supporting diversity and equity in sports. *And since I'm the only one in the family who seems to care about doing the actual work, maybe they will let me make some actual decisions too.*

She walked to the office kitchen to shake off her nerves. She was too jittery for caffeine. She'd have to let the adrenaline coursing through her body keep her sharp.

She grabbed a sparkling water out of the fridge, the office so quiet she could hear the refrigerator's hum. The only person in the office today was Caroline, their executive assistant, and one of her closest friends. Avery made it a point to work in the office at least a few days a week when she was in town, but her parents and older brother rarely did. It had been a gargantuan task to find a time the whole family could meet via video call. Ben, her older brother, lived near their parents in the San Fernando Valley suburbs with his husband, Adam, and their daughter Sadie. Ben had gone all in on his suburban stay-at-home dad life, and Avery couldn't blame him.

Adam, her brother Ben's husband, was the first to join the call, dialing in from his law office in Sherman Oaks. His diplomas and State Bar license were prominently displayed behind him on the screen.

"I can't believe we haven't seen you since Bahrain! How was it?" he asked cheerfully.

"Bahrain feels like a thousand years ago already," Avery replied. "I'm just glad the team recovered from that disaster of a weekend." After the disappointing results from the first race, Silver had managed to snag some points in the following two races in Saudi Arabia and Japan. Avery had reluctantly stayed in LA instead of criss-crossing the globe to watch those in person, spending most of her time preparing for today's meeting.

"Seriously. But what I really need to know is whether Teddy is as gorgeous in person as he is in photos? I hear he's a shameless flirt and has women following him wherever he goes."

"Yes, Teddy is equally attractive in person," Avery replied. *Smoking hot was more like it. And I've thought about him about once an hour since we met.* "Dad and I saw him at the hotel bar after the race, and he really worked the room. I think I actually saw his teeth sparkle and heard that cartoon winky sound when he winked at every woman between the ages of 18 and 80."

Adam snickered in response, "Oh my god, he sounds like a cartoon character."

"Oh, looks like Ben is logging on," said Avery. "Hold on, Dad is texting me. He and Mom can't find the link to join the meeting"

"Hi, everyone," added Ben. "I only have about forty-five minutes until I have to pick up Sadie from pre-school and take her to ballet, so let's get started." Avery squeezed her fists in her lap, knowing that the camera was centered on her face. She loved Ben dearly, but it was just like him to think that the world revolved around him. As if it would be the end of the world if Sadie were five minutes late to ballet. *As if my own time isn't more valuable than a three-year-old's extracurricular activities.*

Avery emailed her parents the link to the meeting once again, and a moment later she could see the top of their heads, her dad's jet-black, closely cropped hair and her mom's honey-colored highlights, as they crowded around the computer in their home office. *Finally.*

"Mom, lower the camera so we can see your faces and then we can get started," Avery said, attempting to get the meeting started in a timely fashion so they could maybe get through one proposal before Adam got interrupted by a client or Ben left for baby pilates.

"Honey, are you saying something? I can't hear you. This isn't working," her mom yelled.

"Ugh," Avery groaned to her brother and brother-in-law. "They probably have the volume turned down and don't realize it. Type in the chat box that they need to turn up the volume from their keyboard."

"Yeah, I don't think they know to look at the chat box," added Ben. "I'll call them and describe what they need to do."

Avery took a deep steadying breath. This was really going to use up all of her patience today. Five frustrating minutes later, Michael and Sharon Silver had both video and audio components settled, and Avery felt steam coming out of her ears, "Dad, how do you run a successful business and a racing organization with over a thousand employees, yet you can't figure out how to log on to a video call!"

"I think I do just fine and have provided a pretty nice life for you kids without any of this new gear," answered Michael a bit defensively, his frown lines showing. "I didn't hear any complaining about my management style when I took everyone to Lanai over the holidays."

Avery rolled her eyes in her mind again, "Okay, fine, now that we are all here, can we get to work?"

It was her first time leading the annual grants meeting; she'd always been a vocal participant before, but now she was running the show, and she wanted her family to take her, and her proposal, seriously.

She tugged on one of her curls and set it behind her ear before she cleared her throat and began.

"As you saw in the annual financials on page one of the deck I sent yesterday, last year Silver Racing Foundation gave away nearly $750,000 to worthy causes. About $300,000 of this was raised from the annual gala, and the rest came from the company, and our family's bottom line," Avery said. "I anticipate we will have approximately the same amount to disperse after this year's gala."

Her dad nodded along from his corner of her computer screen, while her mother's eyes had already glazed over at the first sign of math. Adam had already turned his camera off, his square black.

Avery took a deep breath and picked up the squishy, dumpling shaped stress ball she kept on her desk. She squeezed it through her fingers, trying to shake off her aggravation with her family's lack of attention.

"Given that we will likely have $750,000 to give away again this year, as the director of the foundation I recommend we allocate our funds this year as follows..." she suggested, her voice shaking.

She ran through the slides highlighting the organizations she thought they should support: Women in Motorsport Scholarship program, and the construction of a new gym at the Southside Youth Sports complex. No one said a word as she explained how the scholarships would benefit young women trying to break into their male-dominated sport and how many kids would benefit from the new construction.

She got through her points and let out a big exhale, "Sound good?"

"Darling, those are nice ideas. But, I don't see a line item for the annual gift to the Screen Actors Guild Museum? Or the Motion Picture Retirement Fund?" Sharon asked, squinting at the screen down her nose through her reading glasses.

Avery tried to ignore the crushing blow of rejection that her mom's easy dismissal sent through her chest. "That's because they aren't there this year. I think now is the time to turn over a new leaf and really focus on mission-driven gifts."

Sharon pursed her lips. "Well, they are counting on us, and we can't just leave them high and dry after supporting them for over fifteen years. It wouldn't be a good look," her mother cocked her head in that way that sent Avery through the roof.

"How we'll look? Mom, come on, aren't there more important things than what people think of us?"

Sharon harrumphed in response. "Well, when you've received the LA Times Philanthropist of the Year award, then you can tell me what's important in this town. As for the guest list, don't forget to invite the new tennis director at the JCC and the rabbi," she continued, either oblivious to or choosing to ignore the increasing tension. "And you can assume Daddy's and my list of friends is the same as last year. Ben, do you want to invite the admissions directors at the schools Sadie's applying to for kindergarten? And what about any new personal guests? Avery, are you bringing anyone *special* this year?" Sharon asked, as if the donation conversation was over. "I just met this adorable up-and-coming director. I can get you his number?"

A DM from Adam appeared in the chat box:

> Here we go! Outburst from my darling
> husband in 3...2...1...

"Mom, just stop. We don't have time for this. Adam works 60+ hours a week and took time out of his busy day to serve OUR family's foundation and you want to use it as an opportunity to grill Avery about her love life, and pressure her into dating some douchebag actor," Ben's voice was getting louder and louder as he angrily paced around his sparkling white living room. "And did it ever occur to you that Avery might have life goals beyond bagging a husband?"

Avery felt the blood rush to her head as she fed off Ben's anger. She completely agreed with her brother. Her mom's intense interest in their personal lives, and complete lack of interest in their work lives was beyond annoying, but unlike her brother, that was the least of her grievances at her mother at the moment. Why did her mom get to decide where all the money went? She'd never lifted a finger to earn a penny of it.

"Wait, so that's it? We're done talking about what we want to accomplish with our money?" Avery asked, frustrated. "We're just going to give our money away to Mom's friends' pet projects so she can get invited to movie premieres and get more awards?"

Above Adam on her screen, Avery could see her dad shaking his head from his little box.

"Now, that's no way to talk to your mother, both of you. She cares about you. Working together on this event is supposed to be FUN and HAPPY for our family," he shouted, working himself up as he went. So much for calming the situation.

Avery couldn't take it a second longer. She hated it when her family fought like this. She had to do something or she'd never get them back on track discussing her ideas.

"I have a date already!" she blurted without thinking, trying to get everyone to just shut up for a minute.

Her family fell silent. Regret bubbled up in her throat. Great, now she had to come up with a date, too.

"Who's the lucky fella?" Adam asked, wiggling his eyebrows. She could always count on him to lighten the mood.

"Well, uh, I can't say who it is just yet, but I will find my own date," she squeaked out. "Can we get back to the donations now, please?" she practically begged, blinking back the tears that were welling in the corners of her eyes. Three months of meetings, research, and crafting the slides. Had anyone in her family bothered to look at her proposal before they got on this call?

Her dad rubbed his temples. Ben and Adam were both looking down, probably at their phones as they conducted their own side conversation via text.

Finally, her dad nodded his head again. "Avery, you know how much I value my employees taking initiative. And I happen to agree with the point you make on page eight about aligning the business and non-profit initiatives."

Her dad's rare compliment helped ease the blow of defeat. She jumped on the opening. "And, I already met with the team's marketing team and they agreed we should really focus our giving on causes that directly relate to our sport. They're all in..."

Michael held up a finger, stopping her in her tracks from all the way across town. "However, your mom has a valid point. We have made commitments to our existing charity partners, and we can't just pull the rug out from under them. So, I'll tell you what - you're running the show on the gala this year. Last year we raised $300,000 at that event. Anything raised *over* $300,000 this year can go toward your projects. Does that seem fair to everyone? You raise it, you spend it how you like."

Avery tried to swallow away the lump in her throat. It wasn't at all how she'd thought this would go, but it was moments like this that reminded Avery how her dad had built his business empire. Her eyes darted around her screen, taking in her other family members' reactions - they all looked fairly indifferent, which was its own kind of insult.

"All in favor say, aye?" she asked, her nerve returning, as she looked each family member in the eye as best she could, daring them to reject the opportunity she'd just been handed.

The family responded in a chorus of 'ayes' and the meeting ended.

Avery sat at her desk, her head in her hands. She was so fucked. She'd already promised the Southside Youth Sports Complex the funds, and now she'd have to raise more than $300,000 before they got a single penny. She'd have to double the amount raised at last year's gala to cover her parents' projects and her own initiatives or go back on her word. There was no way their usual country club event could raise twice as much as years past. She'd have to find a way to reach a whole new audience. A new venue for sure to appeal to the sport's new, younger fans and some press to get other teams' attention and support. Maybe a celebrity to co-chair with her? At least that part her mom would agree with.

The next race was at Silverstone, near London, in a week and several teams had headquarters in the area. She could ask their marketing teams for meetings while she was there and give them the same pitch she'd given Silver's marketing team. *Maybe they'd buy tables at the gala and/or donate items for their auction? They wouldn't turn down a meeting with someone whose last name was Silver.*

She got to work, and by the time she came up for air at 6 p.m. she had secured meetings with Archer, Phoenix, and Alpha Fuerte and had rebooked her flight to London. She'd have to fly out tomorrow. But her usual packing list of team branded shirts and athleisure for the days at the track and business casual attire for meetings seemed depressing, especially when she thought about Teddy's effortlessly cool look in Bahrain. He was so polished, always looking like he'd stepped right out of a glossy magazine page. *Besides, I deserve a little retail therapy after the day I've had.*

five

LONDON, ENGLAND

Avery took her time as she strolled past the Diana Memorial Playground in Kensington Gardens, the sound of kids shrieking bringing a smile to her face. The magnolia trees were in full bloom, their pink blossoms making the whole atmosphere feel almost like a fairytale. She took a lap around the round pond, where she remembered seeing swans and ducks last time she was here. She sniffed the air. Not as charming as she remembered: swan and duck poop covered the path around the pond.

Back on the main thoroughfare through the park, the much faster joggers who were also taking advantage of the gorgeous weather, continually whizzed past in both directions. They all looked more-or-less the same to her in their spandex until she spotted a ridiculously fit couple round the curve who put the rest of the casual exercisers to shame with their quick pace. They were being photographed with an iPhone by a somewhat paunchy fellow who was struggling to keep up. *Poor guy, his boss or sister or whomever torturing him on what would otherwise be a perfectly pleasant afternoon.*

As the group got closer, Avery realized the fit woman with the blonde ponytail bobbing up-and-down was Stacey, not some influencer wannabe. And the guy she had mistaken for the boyfriend in the couple was Teddy. She almost hadn't recognized him so out of context, her eyes wandering down below his running shorts to his well-defined, lean calves.

She realized she was staring and pulled her eyes away before she was caught ogling him. *Before I embarrass myself.*

She wanted to give them a big, enthusiastic American wave, but held back and instead waited until they got closer before giving a much more subtle raise of her hand.

After a thumbs-up to the camera, Teddy looked back up at the running path and saw Avery's wave. He slowed his pace and waved back at her and smiled, coming to a stop when they reached her.

Avery felt butterflies in her stomach as she watched a bead of sweat drip down Teddy's forehead, his chest rise and fall as he caught his breath. Teddy noticed her staring and followed her eyes to his forehead. He rubbed the bead of sweat and his chocolate brown hair off of his face. Avery felt her cheeks burn. *He caught me this time.* She really needed to get a hold of herself.

"Avery, so nice to see you again. I didn't know you were here already." He took a long gulp from the water bottle Stacey handed to him without breaking eye contact with her, and she squirmed under his focus.

"No, I, uh... actually came a few days early for meetings. And London is one of my favorite cities in the world, so I was happy to have an excuse to hang out here for a couple of days before the race, so yeah," her voice sounded high-pitched to her own ears. It was like she forgot how to form coherent, adult-sounding sentences in his presence.

"Avery, you're here! Awesome!" Stacey squealed, finally joining the conversation after typing furiously on her phone. "Give me one second, I just gotta enter some notes about Teddy's workout before I forget."

"James, mate, you okay over there?" Teddy asked, nodding to the social media guy who had his hands on his knees and was still breathing heavily from the exertion.

"Not all of us have your physique, mate, but I'll survive. How about one quick shot of the two of you before I go?" James asked, gesturing to Avery and Teddy. "Team owner's family hanging out with the new driver ahead of his home race. The internet will love it - fits right in with our current social strategy trying to make the whole team look like one big, happy family."

"I'm rather sweaty, but if Avery doesn't mind my post-workout stink, I'm all for it," Teddy looked at Avery questioningly.

She usually tried to stay behind the scenes as her family would allow and let the spotlight shine on the causes she worked so hard to support, but her cheeks flushed at the thought of their bodies touching again, hopefully not as awkwardly as their thigh graze in the hotel lobby in Bahrain. She gave a silent little prayer of gratitude that she'd made the effort to fix her hair and put on a real outfit after landing this morning. "Um, sure, fine by me."

Teddy put his arm around Avery and she found that not only didn't he stink, she quite liked the manly, woody smell emanating from his direction, the weight of his arm on hers.

"Ok, on three - team Silver!"

James snapped the pic quickly, and Teddy removed his arm from around her shoulder, leaving Avery with a warm feeling where his arm had been.

"Thanks, guys. I'm going to post this on Teddy's story right now and then hit the showers," James lowered his voice, "And Teddy, don't forget what we talked about earlier, we need to offer up something better, and fast."

Teddy grimaced as James gave him a pointed look.

The back of Avery's neck tingled.

"Anyway, Aves! Hi! I'd hug you, but I'm almost as sweaty as this one after our workout," Stacey chirped, breaking up some of the tension.

"Yes, she smells far too good for the likes of us," Teddy added.

A rushing sound filled her ears. "Thanks, I showered when I got off the plane, so I guess that worked out for me," she tried to laugh off the compliment.

"I better go do that too," Stacey said, smiling. "But do you want to meet for high tea in the lobby later before we head to the track? I missed you the last few weeks and I want to hear about your work."

"Yes. I really need to fill you in." *And ask what the heck James had been talking about.* "Work is a lot."

Stacey's phone buzzed again and she looked down at it. "Teddy, your helmet with the new design for the weekend is about to be delivered to the hotel. I'm going to go meet the courier. Don't forget to stretch. Avery, I'll see you later this afternoon."

"Thanks, Stace," Teddy replied.

Stacey started jogging in the direction of the hotel, leaving Teddy and Avery alone in the garden, Avery's stomach fluttery.

"She's like the energizer bunny, isn't she?" Teddy asked after a beat of silence.

"That she is," Avery agreed. "She's been a force as long as I've known her." Stacey had always had the spirit of a high school cheerleader and was the best person in the world to talk to when you needed a pep talk, which Avery often did.

"So, when did you arrive?" Teddy asked, tilting his head to the side while awaiting her response. "I assumed you'd arrive later in the week with your dad."

Avery looked down, trying to hide her smile. He'd thought about her too.

"This morning. I have some important meetings tomorrow for the foundation. Now I'm trying to fight fatigue from the overnight flight by getting some sunlight and enjoying one of my favorite parks in the world."

"I'll walk with you," Teddy offered. "I need to cool down a bit after jogging at Stacey's pace for an hour while trying to look smart for the camera."

Before Avery could strike up a conversation, she heard giggles from behind her, as she and Teddy both turned around and found two teenage girls following them. *Following Teddy*.

Teddy, playing his part beautifully, beckoned them over.

"Would you ladies like a selfie?" he asked gregariously.

Avery shook her head as subtly as she could. It was hard for her to tell if Teddy's actions were a well-honed act or if he was genuinely that nice.

"OMG! Are you serious?" one of the girls squealed, bouncing up and down on her toes in her high-topped Air Jordans.

"Yes, of course. Come on over, don't be shy," Teddy offered back.

"Is she your girlfriend?!" asked the other, giggling as she nervously gathered her long wavy hair over one shoulder. "I thought you were single! I was going to ask you to my end-of-term dance!"

Her chest tightened. "No. No. I'm just his coworker? Friend?" Avery looked up at Teddy, silently pleading with him to rescue her from her own awkwardness. Though the perky teenagers obviously couldn't possibly know about her little crush on Teddy, her muscles tensed. He caught her drift and winked.

"I'd be honored to accompany you to your end-of-term dance. But unfortunately, the races that time of year are all in Asia, which would make it nearly impossible for me," Teddy interjected. "How about this instead... send me a DM when it gets closer reminding me who you are, and I'll record a video wishing you and your classmates a wonderful night."

The girls jumped up and down with delight, thanking him profusely, completely forgetting that he'd dodged their girlfriend question before they scampered off.

Wow, he really has an answer for everything.

"Do all the groupies get annoying after a while? Or do you enjoy it?" Avery asked, trying to gauge his authenticity.

Teddy rubbed his hands over the three-day stubble on his chin, "I know I wouldn't have this job and the opportunities it presents without the fans - so I do appreciate them. My mum reads all of my fan mail and keeps all of it in these giant three-ring binders. I know it makes her proud," he smiled sheepishly.

"Aww, that's so sweet," Avery smiled back. "I look forward to meeting her."

Teddy blanched momentarily before continuing. "Honestly,

women propositioning me is rather annoying. I need to be 100 percent focused on my racing. I don't have time for romance."

A bit severe. However, Avery respected his ambition.

"So many people are counting on me to get results on the track. But it's not about the expectations, it's about me. I want to be great. I want to win races. And I can't have anything, or anyone, get in the way."

Was it something he said to every woman he encountered to let himself off the hook if they were to develop feelings? Had he noticed the effect he had on her? She was usually a good judge of character, but so far she couldn't quite read him, even though this was the third time they'd met. *Not that I'm counting.* On the one hand, he'd seemed so genuine, but he was so quick to shut down, so quick to turn on the charm. It made her head spin.

They'd been standing and walking shoulder-to-shoulder, occasionally brushing each other's side, and Avery took a step to the side, creating some air between them. At least now she knew for certain that she had to play it cool around him and bury her little crush, since he would probably be annoyed to learn he had yet another starry-eyed admirer.

"I get it," she answered in a confident tone, trying not to hint at the twinge of disappointment she felt. "I know it's nothing like being in a car going 200 miles per hour, but the pressure I feel for the Silver Foundation gala is similar. So many organizations are counting on me to raise money. And I have to find a date for the event to please my mother, who unlike your mom, couldn't care less about my work. Instead, she's obsessed with my love life."

Her stomach quivered. She'd said too much.

But Teddy chuckled. "Your mom is obsessed with your love

life? I haven't had the pleasure of meeting her yet. Does she come to many races?"

"Her social calendar is too full to travel this much, but you'll definitely meet her at one of the US races," Avery shook her head and smiled wryly. "Don't say I didn't warn you."

"She can't be that bad, can she? I'm sure I can handle her. Didn't you see how I handled those girls back there? Or that waitress at the bar the other night?" Teddy smirked.

Avery smiled back but shook her head at him. He may be charming, but he'd never met Sharon Silver.

"She's about as judgey and easy to win over as those swans over there," Avery pointed to the unaffected creatures gliding along the water, completely ignoring the paddleboats and the kids splashing and wading at the water's edge.

"Then you better come up with a really fantastic date to please her, huh?" Teddy asked.

"You don't happen to know any fabulously successful, 25-30-ish celebrities willing to publicly date me and come to the gala?" Avery laughed. "Bonus points if they are Jewish or willing to convert."

She looked up at Teddy, and her breath hitched. He wasn't laughing back, he looked at her seriously, as if he were contemplating something.

It had been so easy to talk to him, but it had probably been inappropriate to talk that way with someone she worked with. That must be why he wasn't laughing anymore.

"Thanks for the cool-down walk, Avery. I should head back and shower before my strategy briefing. Are you headed back to the hotel too?" he asked, and Avery detected a note of hopefulness in his voice. Maybe he didn't want to end their conversation either.

"Yes. Are you staying at the hotel with the team?" she asked. Somehow it hadn't occurred to her that Teddy might be staying there too, given that he lived in London.

"Yes, I didn't want to change up my race week routine, even for my home race," he said. "And there are too many distractions at my flat."

"That makes sense," Avery said.

The light turned green.

"Now we only have to make it two more blocks back to the hotel without me getting recognized."

"Sounds like you need a decoy date as much as I do. Maybe teenage girls and waitresses would leave you alone if they thought you were in a real relationship," Avery joked.

Teddy looked at her again with that contemplative look. "That's brilliant," his hazel eyes twinkled with hope. "The public benefits of being attached without the commitment of an actual relationship."

"Have James post a few pictures of you with someone - surely he can make anything seem real on social media," Avery continued, only half joking now.

Teddy pushed the large glass doors to the hotel's lobby open, and a burst of refreshing air-conditioned air hit Avery, giving her goosebumps, as Teddy held the door open for her.

"All the other guys' wives and girlfriends come to nearly every race and post photos, so my 'girlfriend' would need to do the same for it to be at all believable," he said, following her into a light-filled lobby atrium.

This was starting to sound less like a joke, and more like the beginning of a real plan? She felt bristly at the idea of a faux-girlfriend following Teddy around at every race. She was really enjoying spending time with him, even if it was always going to stay in the friend zone. And some woman hanging around posing as his girlfriend would just be annoying.

"I don't really want some hanger-on following me around the globe for a few pics. That would be almost as bad as a desperate fan waiting for a selfie," Teddy continued as if he had read her mind, "But it would really help me out, more than you know."

"Well, then find someone who is more convenient. There are twenty teams and a traveling circus each week. Certainly, there's someone around here who could play the part," Avery suggested.

"There are hardly any women engineers or execs in this sport, and even fewer who are unattached. And I don't imagine anyone from another team would be interested in helping me out so that I can focus on beating their driver to the finish line each week."

"I guess that leaves me or Stacey," she offered up.

No we couldn't...could we?

"Would you consider doing it?" Teddy looked at her, daring her to say yes.

Avery's heart began beating so violently it nearly leapt out of her chest. She could barely squeak out a response. *Was this actually happening?* "Me? You want me to pretend to be your girlfriend?"

"Sure. It makes perfect sense, if you think about it," Teddy continued, his voice getting louder. "You are already invested in the team's success. You travel with us most weeks anyway, and I want to get to know you. Plus - we did already get our first photo together."

Avery began to play-out the scenario in her head – she'd do almost anything that was in the best interest of the team, and it's not like spending a little more time with Teddy would be torture. Pretending to be Teddy's girlfriend might be strategic too, if she could get him to help with the gala.

"Well, it does make sense, ya know, for the sake of the team. But I need something from you in return," she counter-offered, tugging on her curls. "Would you attend the end-of-season gala as my date? And would you and James help promote it in the weeks leading up to it?"

"Sure. That's easy. I just need one more thing. We have to let James tip-off a reporter that we are dating before we post anything on social media."

"A particular reporter?" she asked, her eyes wide. Was this what James had been referring to?

Teddy ran his hands through his hair. "I'm in a bit of a pickle, and yes, I really need to let it play out that way...that is, if we have a deal?"

Avery wanted to ask more, but Teddy was looking around the lobby to see who was in ear shot, so she knew not to push it, at least not now. "Deal," she agreed, sticking her hand out to shake his.

"If we are going to make this believable, I don't think a handshake will do."

He leaned in for a hug, wrapping his strong arms fully around her body. Avery leaned into him for a beat longer than was strictly necessary, enjoying the warmth of his strong chest and arms, before he gave her a peck on the cheek.

She tried to ignore the tiny itch of disappointment she felt that his kiss hadn't reached her lips.

"This is going to be fun," he whispered into her ear before removing his face away from hers.

Her ears felt hot from his breath, and his words.

And without so much as another look back at her, he bounded toward the elevator, rendering Avery completely speechless. *What have I done?* It was the most impulsive decision she could remember making in her entire life. On one hand, she was positively giddy – what was better than having an excuse to get close to one the most handsome men she'd ever met? But on the other hand she was keenly aware that this had the potential to end badly. Very badly.

six

LONDON, ENGLAND

"Let me get this straight. You're going to pretend to date Teddy? The incredibly buff, extremely sexy race car driver your dad pays me to train and assist?" Stacey's eyebrows were so high they practically reached her platinum blonde hair, "So that you can use him to raise extra money at the gala and get your mom off your back?"

They had just sat down to high tea, and Avery had told her about her impending fake relationship with Teddy. She could understand why her friend was so surprised. It was pretty out of character.

"I guess so? The opportunity sort of presented itself. I mean, if *you* think he's sexy, then you should do it."

"Not a chance. I already know way too much about him," Stacey poured hot water into her cup, her neon pink nail polish a stark contrast with the cream-colored porcelain teapot. "I could tell you his daily schedule down to the minute, every calorie he ingests, and what time he goes to sleep each night. He's like a science project to me. I couldn't possibly pretend to be interested in him like that."

"Fair enough," Avery nodded in agreement. "Plus, he said it would help him out too. What is his deal anyway? What were he and James talking about?"

Avery attempted to seem nonchalant by examining the finger foods on the tiered serving tray sitting between them while eagerly awaiting her friend's response. She finally selected a bite-sized fig tart and a cucumber sandwich.

Stacey opened her mouth to reply, then shut it.

Avery tapped her foot under the table, desperate for any information she could get about Teddy.

"He takes his job *very* seriously. He has a lot riding on this season. It's not only the pressure to perform for the team, he provides financially for his mom and his younger brother too after they sacrificed to support his racing career."

"I had no idea," Avery admitted. She took a bite of her tart and chewed slowly as she turned this new piece of information about Teddy over in her head.

Stacey glanced over her shoulder before continuing. "He didn't have a happy home life growing up—that's all I can say. And recently, a reporter showed up at his mom's door asking questions. James got the reporter to back off by promising a better story. I guess *dating you* is going to be the better story."

The muscles in Avery's neck and upper back tightened.

"I'm not sure if this fake girlfriend plan is insane or brilliant. But, whatever you do, don't actually fall for him," Stacey lowered her usually peppy voice, "He means it—he is one hundred percent committed to his career and his performance on the track and won't let anything get in the way of that."

Avery took another tart for herself without offering it to Stacey first. She knew Stacey, being a paragon of fitness and nutrition, wouldn't want it.

"I can handle it. I've seen too many girls get their hearts broken by race car drivers to get involved emotionally," Avery meant every word, and yet her stomach quivered.

"You have a good head on your shoulders, but I also know you pretty well and you turned beet red when I called him sexy. I don't want to see you get hurt," Stacey frowned, two little lines appearing between her eyebrows.

"I appreciate that. Really, I do," Avery put down her food and reached across the floral tablecloth to squeeze Stacey's hand, "But it's a win-win. If there's a chance it will bring attention to the gala, I have to try it."

"I know how much you want to prove your worth. But why are you putting so much pressure on yourself to do it all at once? Why not give yourself a year to learn the ropes?"

Avery scratched her forehead and sighed. *Because every year counts for a kid who wants to start karting and doesn't have the means to fund it.*

"Remember that year I spent living in the UK when I was twelve? When I convinced my parents to let me go to boarding school and enter some karting races?"

"Yes, it was like a semester abroad for a twelve-year-old, I was so envious," Stacey admitted.

"I learned two things that year: one, 12 is too late to get started in motorsport; and two, you have to be rich and male to get noticed. I raced against only a handful of other girls at races the entire year, and everyone else was rich, white, male or all three," she took a deep breath. "I have a chance to make this sport more fair. I have big plans to improve access to quality coaching and sponsorship for kids from underprivileged backgrounds, not just in motorsports, but in all sports. I want to do big things."

"Okay, that's admirable. But I don't think it's reasonable for you to think you can take down the race car patriarchy and prove yourself to your family in one year," Stacey raised her eyebrows.

"You're right. It might take two," Avery laughed. "But I have to start somewhere. And getting that gala as much press as possible is as good a place to start as any."

SEVEN

SILVERSTONE, ENGLAND

Avery held up the badge hanging from the lanyard around her neck and waited for the familiar 'beep-beep', giving her access to the paddock, the restricted working area for teams, sponsors, media, and officials. Avery entered the gates and hesitated: where to head first in her new alternate reality as Teddy's pretend girlfriend? Wives and girlfriends typically hung out on the sides of their drivers' garages or killed time in the multi-story team-branded hospitality suites. She had no clue who Teddy may have told about their new situation and how he would act when he saw her. Teddy and his engineers would be deep in their work reviewing data from the previous day's practices and working out their strategy. Would her presence in his garage be welcome? Or was that overstepping the nature of their agreement?

Probably best to go straight to the adjacent makeshift office area where staff would be holed-up working. It was qualifying day, and all hands would be on deck, and she needed to coordinate a few upcoming charity appearances with the media/PR department.

Her colleagues sat around a fold-out table, laptops out.

"Avery, pull up a seat," James called out, pointing to a stack of plastic chairs in the corner as soon as she walked in.

Avery breathed easier—at least one person considered her part of the team. She dragged a chair over as James scooched his, making room for her on his side of the table.

"We're reviewing Zack's and Teddy's interview schedules for the weekend. We may have overbooked them," he said, turning his screen to her.

She squinted her eyes. *Good, they hadn't cut the five-minute appearance/photo-op with the local girls' coding academy she'd asked for.*

She was scanning the rest of the color-coded lines of the spreadsheet, when someone approached from behind and squeezed her shoulders.

She turned around and looked up to see it was Teddy, and found herself unwittingly breaking into a grin. Whether *he* was acting or not, she was genuinely glad to see him. He was once again sporting the standard at-work look of all F1 drivers: race suit half-zipped with the top half hanging around his waist, exposing his long sleeve fireproof undershirt. He looked unbelievably cool. Avery couldn't help admiring the now somewhat familiar outline of his impressive physique under the tight-fitting top.

"Lads, I'm going to need to steal this one away for a moment, if that's alright," he said, to the four guys sitting there, who exchanged puzzled looks.

Avery stood up from her chair, and Teddy gently placed his

hand on her lower back, and guided her out of the work space. Her mouth went dry. *Is he just being a gentleman? Or is this it, our debut as a couple?*

He led her through the back of the team's office on wheels and to his personal dressing room. For all the times that Avery had been in a garage, she'd never been in a driver's private room. It was less glamorous than she had imagined. A small round table, a gray armchair, some shelves, and a portable clothes rack took up most of the space.

"Take a seat," Teddy gestured to one of two plastic chairs at the small table as he sat down in the other.

"You put on quite the show out there," Avery said. "So, has James told the reporter about us? Is the cat out of the bag?"

"Yes, it's done," he nodded his head and tapped his hands on his thighs.

"I should probably tell you that I told Stacey about our plan, but I trust her to keep it quiet," Avery wrapped one of her dark curls around a finger.

He shrugged. "It'd be nearly impossible for me to hide anything from her anyway. A driver's trainer knows him better than he knows himself in some ways."

"And I assume James knows the truth?" Avery asked.

Teddy nodded again. "He does."

"And I want to tell Caroline, my right-hand woman and dear friend, if that's okay with you. But I guess we should keep up the ruse at work, otherwise..." Avery paused, "You never know who has loose lips and could blow our cover."

"Agreed. The fewer in the know, the less likely there is to be a leak," Teddy added. "I won't tell anyone else on the team or in my personal life that we're not really together."

Did he have anyone in his life who he could confide in?

Though she often experienced some amount of loneliness spending so much time on the road, especially as a woman in such a male-dominated sport, at least she had Stacey. And her family's involvement allowed her to see her dad regularly. Silverstone was the fourth race of the season, and Avery had yet to see any close friends or family join Teddy for a race weekend.

"Alright then, I guess you and James will loop me into your schedule for the obligatory WAGs pics," she said using the internet term for 'Wives and Girlfriends' of professional athletes. "And I'll have Stacey and James add the gala and a few additional foundation-related appearances to your calendar."

There was a knock on the door, and Brandon, the Silver team principal, poked his head in. His eyes went wide.

"Oh, sorry Teddy! I didn't realize you had company in here," Brandon said. "But we need you in the garage. Q1 starts in 20 minutes."

"We were finishing up here. I'll be right out," Teddy said as Brandon quickly closed the door behind him.

"Well, I'm sure Brandon will mention seeing me in your dressing room. I'll have to tell my parents that you're the guy I've been 'secretly' dating and will be taking to the gala."

"Looks like we are really doing this thing, doesn't it?" Teddy raised his eyebrows at her. "Feel free to stay in here as long as you like, but please close the door behind you on your way out." He trotted down the hallway to catch up to Brandon.

Avery took advantage of a moment alone in Teddy's little sanctuary from the racetrack madness to see if there were any other clues lying about that could provide her a bit more insight into his state of mind. She didn't want to snoop, but she figured anything in plain sight was fair game since he had invited her to stay.

However, the small space was devoid of any personal items or flair. There were six race suits identical to the one he was currently wearing hanging from the clothes rack. And the shelves were nearly bare save for a basket of protein bars, energy drinks, and Teddy's current helmet, the unique design of which was the only hint of personality in the space.

Formula One drivers often worked with graphic designers to incorporate unique, personal elements into their helmet design, alongside the necessary sponsor and team logos. Avery carefully picked up Teddy's helmet from the shelf and inspected the design. The whole helmet was wrapped in a blue, yellow, and red tartan pattern, and a small Union Jack flag was printed on one side. It was a lovely homage to his Scottish roots and the race's location.

She made a mental note to ask Teddy if that particular tartan had a special meaning to him as she placed the helmet back where she found it and quietly slipped out of the dressing room, hoping no one would notice her. She wasn't eager to start dealing with the gossip that was about to spread like wildfire through the Silver ranks.

eight

LONDON, ENGLAND

The next morning Avery pulled her hair in a low bun at the nape of her neck; her hair was as good as it was to get. It was raining buckets outside. The Silvers had done fantastic in the sunny conditions during the previous day's qualifying rounds. Zack would start in third and Teddy in fourth place for the race today, a team second row lockout. But now the track would be wet, which could change everything. She always cared about the Silver team, but she'd never felt so personally invested in any particular driver as she did with Teddy.

She put on one of her larger pairs of diamond stud earrings, and swiped on a brighter-than-usual shade of lipstick. As a general rule, Avery didn't usually wear much makeup, but having grown up in the circles she had, and with her family's means, she generally kept up her appearance with regular facials and mani/pedis, which gave her a natural looking glow and put-together vibe despite her low maintenance nature.

Her phone rang right as she was about to nibble a bit of the avocado toast she had ordered up from room service. She picked it up, the acid churning in her stomach had killed her appetite anyway. She looked down at her phone: her mom was calling. She braced herself.

"Hi, Mom."

"Hi, darling. I just saw the article on ESPN. You and Teddy are dating?!"

I guess the article is now live.

"I'm a little offended that they got the scoop before I did. You know you can trust me to keep a secret."

Ha. Her mom, keep a secret? It was laughable. Sharon Silver was the last person on earth you should tell your secrets to.

"I'm sorry, I wanted to tell you," Avery apologized. "We were trying to keep it quiet as long as possible for the sake of the team."

"Not to worry. Really, I'm thrilled for you," Sharon said.

Avery winced, and moved her phone away from her ear. Sharon was obsessed with celebrities and her volume increased with her daughter confirming the news she was dating one. It would make for a great humble brag at the country club.

"Thanks, Mom. Appreciate the call. I've got to get going."

"Wait, does your father know?" Sharon asked, her tone turning from giddy to serious.

Her mom had a point. If anyone should have heard the news directly from her first, it was her dad. "I haven't told him, but I'm sure he knows. Teddy told Brandon—that's what the HR manual instructs."

"I can't imagine he will be too pleased that his shiny new driver is falling in love during the season. But at least it's you— he doesn't have to worry that you'll do anything crazy that could mess with his performance, like break his heart mid-season."

"No, Mom, he doesn't need to worry about his driver getting his heart broken mid-season." If she only knew. "Mom, the shuttle is waiting for me to go to the track; I really have to go. But, thanks for the call."

Avery grabbed her new trench coat instead of a logo half-zip sweatshirt and baseball cap. She took one last deep breath before she headed out of the quiet, safe space of her hotel room, ready as she'd ever be to hard-launch her faux relationship.

* * *

When she arrived at the circuit, James beckoned her over to where he was standing with Nora Maimon, the beautiful dark-haired wife of Zack, Silver's lead driver.

"Avery, let me get a photo of you and Nora together cheering on your other halves," James said.

"So nice to see you, Avery," Nora said in her velvety accent as she leaned in to give Avery an air-kiss on both cheeks, her large hoop earrings brushing Avery's hair. "Where would you like us, James?"

"Let's get you two ladies right in front of the garage there," he answered.

James got the shot fairly quickly and showed it to them for their approval. It seemed that as soon as they had both nodded their heads in agreement, the photo appeared on the team's social media with the caption 'The ladies behind the men of team Silver here to cheer.'

There was no hiding now. She ignored the tightness in her chest. Avery looked over and saw that Nora was already re-posting to her own account, tagging the brands she was wearing and adding the dancing girls emoji. *I guess I'm supposed to do that too.* She copied Nora and added the picture to her story, tagging Nora, Zack, and Teddy. She braced herself for the comments that were about to flood in.

Nora took her by the arm and led her into the hospitality suite. "Welcome to the club, you've got this."

Avery took her time saying hello to every big wig in attendance, talking up the work of the foundation and hinting at the fundraiser. She got lots of promises and had several sponsorship leads she would follow up on during the business week. But were they only talking to her because she was Teddy's new girlfriend or Michael Silver's daughter? Her stomach churned. This deal with Teddy wasn't exactly going to help her stand on her own two feet this year. *Eyes on the prize, Avery. It doesn't matter why they buy tickets to the fundraiser—as long as they come and donate.*

nine

MILAN, ITALY

Avery picked up her phone for approximately the 200th time that day, as if she could manifest a text message from Teddy. She hadn't heard from him since the race in the UK, twelve days ago. It had been lonely seeing the tabloid stories about them circulate, especially because she was trying to keep her promise to hide the real nature of their relationship. Teddy was the one person who was also living this same experience, and it would have been nice to process it a bit with him or at least roll their eyes together at some of the more outrageous headlines. Her personal favorite had been one that read "Avery and Teddy - Will This Romance Last Longer than A Ferrari Pit Stop?"

I mean, I could just reach out to him. It had been a recurring thought she'd had all week, but she hadn't yet taken the initiative. She didn't want to come off as needy or annoying, since the whole point of this fake relationship for him was to avoid the distractions of a real romance. But, she wanted to get to know him better: there was something about him, not only his chiseled abs, that piqued her curiosity.

She drummed her French-manicured fingernails on the desk in her hotel room. *Now that we're in the same city for the Italian Grand Prix it's not crazy or needy to check in, right?* She had a good reason at least. They were scheduled for a joint appearance at the AC Milan game that evening.

The event was an opportunity to check multiple boxes—she and Teddy would be seen together in public, plus Teddy would join the team's players for a meet-and-greet on the field after the game. It was the first time she had initiated an event with the team that wasn't strictly charity-related, and she needed it to go smoothly. If it garnered some positive press for the team, who knows what else they'd let her take on. She had tons of ideas for ways that the drivers could engage with fans and promote the team's (or least her) values of inclusion and opportunity.

She picked up her phone again.

> Hi, Teddy!

Nope. The exclamation point was too much. She deleted it and started again.

> Hi, Teddy.

There, that was professional, yet warm.

> Hope you had a great week! Your event brief for the soccer game should be in your email inbox, please let me know if you have any questions. Otherwise, I will see you soon.

She sent it off into the ether. Less than thirty seconds later, her phone buzzed with the sound of his reply, and she felt a jolt of electricity from her toes to the tips of her ears.

> Ciao, bella! I think you mean futbol game
> ;)
> And yes, I've got all the info I need. Look
> forward to seeing you there.

Avery smiled to herself. There were definitely worse ways to spend an evening than at an Italian futbol game with a handsome date, fake or not.

* * *

The decibel level was overwhelming in San Siro stadium, and Avery could feel the vibrations through the soles of her feet. It wasn't unlike the volume at an F1 race. She and Teddy were surrounded by a sea of fans clad in red who had stood all game long and were singing and chanting in Italian. Avery didn't understand a word except for "Forza, Milan" and "Goal!" The passion for sport, however, now that she could relate to. She turned toward Teddy to drum up conversation, and her eyes landed squarely on the thick bands of muscles of his wide neck, a key physical characteristic honed by every F1 driver to help them withstand the mega G-forces of high-speed racing. Despite the fact that their outing to the game was primarily a photo-op, she wanted to make sure he was enjoying himself and their time together.

She stood on her tip-toes so that her mouth could reach his ear, and caught a slight whiff of a spicy, woodsy scented cologne.

It suited him. She wished she could hold him right there and get a better sniff.

"How was your week? Did you come straight here after Silverstone?" she shouted over the cacophony.

"I'm sorry, I couldn't hear a word you were saying," Teddy leaned into her so that they were cheek to cheek, she could feel the prickle of his stubble. "Say that again."

She repeated her question as she inhaled, gulping in his scent. Did he always wear cologne or was it for her?

"I went home to Scotland for a couple days to see my mum and brother and got here Tuesday."

Out of the corner of her eye, Avery saw the flash of a camera go off, and then another. They had been spotted. Teddy met her eyes with a conspiratorial gleam.

He put his arm around her shoulder before waving and flashing his megawatt smile at the photographers. "We might as well give them a good show."

A *show, right*. It was all for show. If only she could convince her overactive nervous system of that when it insisted on going into hyper-sensitive mode whenever Teddy was nearby.

Avery and Teddy turned their attention to the action on the field. They cheered loudly for the home team, exchanging high fives when the team scored, Avery keenly aware every time their palms touched and savoring the sting of his hand slapping hers.

She felt heaviness in her chest as the game clock wound down. Fake or not, it was one of the best dates she'd ever been on, not that she had a ton of dates to compare it to.

As soon as the final whistle blew, AC Milan security met them at their seats to escort them onto the field. Despite the burly Italian security guard clearing the path in front of them, Avery's scalp prickled at the thought of making her way through the crowd. She rubbed the back of her neck, and pulled her curls over one side of her shoulder, her other fist clenched by her side.

Teddy must have sensed her unease; he gently offered his hand out to her. She unfurled her fingers just enough to accept his. His large hand enveloped her own, and she relaxed into it. He took a step in front of her, hanging on to her hand, firmly leading her down the stairs toward the pitch below. Despite her desire to take care of herself, she let him. Her heart beat steadied. His hand felt warm and solid in her palm. *Feels right.*

Once they arrived on the field, the announcer introduced Teddy in Italian. Avery stood off to the side with the other AC Milan and Silver Racing staff, including James, while Teddy strode confidently to centerfield where the spotlight was shining. He waved to the crowd and shook hands with one of the AC Milan players, who took the microphone from the announcer, gave a short speech, and then promptly took the sweaty jersey off his back and gave it to Teddy.

Avery gasped.

James looked at her and chuckled, "Soccer players your type?"

"No," Avery shook her head. *There's only one man on that field I'd like to see with his shirt off, and he doesn't play soccer.* "Teddy doesn't have anything with him to swap for the jersey," she whispered. The last thing they needed was for the press about their date to be overshadowed by Teddy embarrassing himself by showing up ended-handed.

"Not much we can do about it at this point," James shrugged, seemingly unconcerned.

Teddy didn't seem phased either. He graciously accepted the jersey and addressed the crowd.

"Grazie, Tomas! This is a huge honor. I came tonight as a fan, so I don't have a jersey to give back to you my friend," he pointed to his shirt, a simple, yet high-end black Tom Ford polo. "But, I will send you my helmet after the Italian Grand Prix on Sunday, if you agree?"

Tomas raised his arms in a cheer.

Avery looked up. *Thank you heavens. Thank you Teddy.* He had handled the hiccup like a pro.

The two men shook hands and posed for pictures. She couldn't take her eyes off Teddy as he ran his hands through his floppy hair between photos. She was seriously impressed by how he was able to think quickly and act so gracefully. Whereas she almost had a heart attack when Tomas went off-script. The fact that nothing seemed to ruffle his feathers was probably also what made him a great race car driver. That serious, cool-as-a-cucumber vibe was a serious asset while driving two hundred miles per hour on a narrow, twisting track. No wonder her dad had wanted Teddy on the team. *Lucky for me, as it turns out.*

Teddy gave one more wave to the crowd, before joining her on the sidelines again as the remaining fans emptied out of the stadium. His hand found hers once again and squeezed. She squeezed back. Moments later, security ushered them again, this time off the field and through a tunnel on field level toward the exit.

James, who had walked off the field right behind them, caught up.

"Hey, you two. You know you don't have to do that back here—show's over and you're off the clock for the night," he grinned, pointing to their fingers still firmly intertwined.

Avery felt the tips of her ears grow hot and pulled her hand away from Teddy's grasp as if his hand were the handle of a boiling pot. She took a step away from him, too embarrassed and too nervous to make eye contact with him and find out if he had held onto her intentionally. Instead, she turned her eyes to the side and feigned interest in the trophies, banners, and old photos hanging on the walls.

"Right. Yes. So, James," she said, hoping neither Teddy nor James had noticed the heat she felt in her cheeks. "What's next on Teddy and Zack's publicity agenda this week?"

"Media day tomorrow. But you two could squeeze in another photo-op date mid-afternoon. Try to make it more romantic this time than a futball game, if you want to keep up the ruse," he wiggled his eyebrows at them.

Teddy looked over at her, tilting his head to the side, "What do you say, Avery, would you like to pretend to go on a date with me tomorrow?"

Avery felt a flutter in her belly at the prospect. "Sure, what should we pretend to do?"

"How about we go out for gelato?" Teddy suggested, "I know we are in Milan, but as the saying goes – 'When in Rome...'"

"Perfect. I can't spend a whole week in Italy without going for a scoop of stracciatella," she said. The heat she felt in her ears and cheeks spread throughout her body at the thought of more one-on-one time with Teddy.

ten

MILAN, ITALY

The next afternoon, Avery was sitting outdoors at a charming cafe savoring a perfectly hot cappuccino (another must while in Italy) with an array of gossip rags fanned out on the table in front of her. The photos from the AC Milan game were *everywhere*. At least one photographer had managed to catch the exact moment that she and Teddy had leaned into each other to try to have a conversation over the noise. In the photos, it looked like Avery was nuzzling Teddy, his eyes completely locked on her. It looked so real.

She felt a tightness in her chest when she looked at the accompanying headlines. The tabloid writers were having a field day: "Silver Heiress and Scottish Speedster Caught Canoodling" and "Daddy's New Driver Becomes Daughter's New Boy Toy" were two of the more benign of what she had seen so far.

She was pleased that they were succeeding in looking like a real couple, but being in the spotlight for her relationship with a man made her feel twitchy. She'd only ever been known as Michael Silver's daughter, and now she was going to be known publicly as Teddy's rich girlfriend. She wanted to make news for her contributions to the community, for knocking the gala out of the park. If she screwed it up, she'd not only let herself and the charities down, but she'd be proving her mother, and the gossip columnists, right—that she was most valuable as an accessory for a notable man.

She inhaled a long breath. *Time to get to work.* She folded the papers back up in a neat stack on the empty chair across from her and opened her laptop to turn her attention to the gala. She still had several sponsorship opportunities to fill if there was any chance of raising double last year's total, and now it was go-time on all of the other event details—seating charts, the evening program, decor, and menus. It was enough to make her head spin. Adding to the stress was the fact that she'd convinced her parents to try a new venue as part of her strategy to bring in a new crowd. She'd proposed that they hold it downtown at a sleek, new hotel that hadn't opened yet; the gala would be the first major event there.

She got so lost in thought composing emails that hit exactly the right tone and updating her spreadsheets, that she hadn't even looked up to enjoy the splendid view of the Duomo or the art nouveau tiling on the patio below her feet by the time she had to meet Teddy.

She took a final sip of her cappuccino, which was now cold, licking the last of the foam, before patting her lips dry with a napkin and reapplying her lipstick. *Not that I'm trying to impress Teddy or anything*. A little color always looked better in photos. She gathered her belongings and walked across the plaza on Milan's signature pavé streets to meet Teddy at one of the city's most famous gelato shops, carefully placing each foot on one cobblestone and then another.

Brand new boots were not a practical choice. But the camel-colored pair made with local Italian leather had been too perfect not to wear immediately after purchasing them the day before. She'd paired them with cropped bootcut jeans, a white tee, and an oversized blazer. The put-together ensemble left her feeling very Euro-chic for her date with Teddy.

When she got there, Teddy was waiting for her, bouncing on his toes while he waited in a long line that went out the shop's front doors, his chocolate-brown hair falling into his eyes. He had also dressed as if he were on a real date: jeans and a black t-shirt with a leather jacket, instead of the branded apparel he must have worn to his interviews earlier. She was suddenly aware of her own heartbeat.

"Hello, Avery," he said. His tone was neutral, but his eyes lit up as she approached. He took his hands out his pockets, stretching them out for a hug.

"Hello to you, too," Avery eagerly stepped into his arms, and wrapped hers around his back, her nose searching for the cologne from the night before underneath the strong scent of leather.

She reluctantly let go after what felt like an appropriate amount of time for a friendly hug, ignoring the draw to stay in his arms indefinitely. She'd have an excuse to if there were an audience, but so far no one had recognized them.

"How's media day going?" she asked.

"Nothing too exciting, fortunately. Routine questions from the reporters," he answered. "What have you been up to?"

"Just working on the gala." Her work was boring in comparison to his. He couldn't possibly care about her spreadsheets, pitch emails, or the stress she was feeling about having the gala somewhere new.

But his attention was squarely on her, his head tilted in interest. "Tell me more about what goes into planning an event of that scale. I mean, I'm a part of a large-scale sporting event every weekend. But I never really know what's going on behind the scenes."

"You really want to know?" He'd made it very clear that he didn't have the bandwidth for a real relationship, and unloading her worries and work minutiae on him seemed exactly like the type of thing he didn't want to be burdened with.

"I do. Everyone tries to shield the drivers from thinking about anything other than the race itself, but I am interested in the business side of things. And I'm interested in learning more about you."

She flushed. Even a polite interest in her work made her lose her cool when it came to him.

They stepped forward as the line moved.

"Well, today, I worked on the timeline of events for the evening and I sent reminder emails to everyone who had purchased a table last year but hasn't yet this year. I need to raise double last year's total, so I'll need them to return, and also find new donors. And, I'm stressing about the venue." She filled him in on the whole story as the line crawled forward.

His eyes, and his attention never wandered. *A driver who can listen to me talk about work for more than thirty seconds is not at all what I was expecting. Not even my own family seems capable of that lately.*

Teddy held open the glass doors for her as they entered the shop. The sweet scent of the freshly baked cones and the decadent aroma of dark chocolate stopped her in her tracks as she finally paused her monologue.

She inhaled. "Yum."

Teddy's eyes softened from their focused intensity as he watched her nearly drool at the scent. He licked his lips. *The heady aroma must be making his mouth water too.*

"Moving such a time-honored event is certainly bold. Was it hard to get your dad on board?" Teddy asked after their sense of smell adjusted.

She nodded her head slowly. "I almost forgot he's your boss too. You know what it's like to work with my family."

"Not the whole family. I haven't met your mum, or your brother. Is he involved with Silver Racing too?"

"Not really," Avery answered. "He's a stay-at-home parent in LA. But, my dad listens to him more than me. I'm afraid my dad will always see me as his little girl, and never as a capable businesswoman."

"Ah, I see." Teddy was quiet for a moment, deep in thought. "I don't know what it's like to work in the family business, but I do know what it's like to feel like you have to prove your worth. My mom and brother gave up so much for me to pursue F1 and I'm still proving it was worth it."

She reached out and leaned her head against his shoulder, the leather buttery soft against her cheek, as they read the menu. They were on a fake date after all, a fan could spot them and her head on his shoulder would seem perfectly natural. It didn't matter that she really did it because her heart lurched thinking of the weight he had to carry each time he got in his race car.

"What are you going to get?" he asked, without flinching, as if her leaning on him was the most natural thing in the world.

Avery ordered two scoops of stracciatella in a cone; Teddy a single scoop of berry sorbet.

"Why don't we take these outside and enjoy being in Italy for a few minutes?" Teddy offered.

"This is almost too beautiful to eat," Avery said looking admiringly at her picture-perfect cone. The shop had even topped her double scoop with a cute mini macaron and a chocolate drizzle.

They walked outside and she held up her gelato with one hand, while using her other hand to take a picture of it before she took her first lick.

"Sadly, mine is not quite as photogenic," Teddy said with a laugh, examining his relatively plain cup.

"I wasn't going to say anything, but that is a sad-looking gelato," Avery agreed, chuckling.

"Watching what I eat is a small price to pay for one of those twenty seats," Teddy explained. Like all athletes at his level of competition, Teddy carefully monitored his nutrition for top performance. In addition, drivers have to maintain their weight at the right level because extra weight could make a car slower, and conversely, not enough weight could affect the driver's safety.

Avery slowly took another big lick of her ice cream, savoring the creamy vanilla treat as it cooled her mouth.

"You are missing out," she taunted him, trying on a more flirtatious tone, "Sure you don't want a bit of mine?"

"I really shouldn't," he sighed, looking longingly as she plucked the macaron off the top and popped it in her mouth.

"Tell you what," she answered. "Someday, after you've retired from F1, you and I will come back here and I'll buy you a double scoop with as many toppings as you want."

"It's a date," Teddy said, lifting his cup to toast with her cone. "Hopefully not for many, many, years."

"Hopefully, your future wife doesn't mind when I whisk you off to Italy for gelato," Avery teased.

Teddy froze, his spoon left suspended in mid-air between his cup and his mouth.

Willing to talk about professional future, but not personal. Noted.

"Did you tag me in your gelato picture, or do we need to take a selfie in front of that neon ice cream cone to prove we are in a relationship?" Teddy asked, regaining his wits. He pointed to the photo-op wall on the side of the building.

"Let's do both. I guess there is no point in being subtle," she said. "The gossip rags are already having a field day. Did you see the coverage we got last night?"

"No, I haven't. I try to avoid anything media-related and let it all go through James. Too—"

Avery cut him off. "Too distracting. Of course, I should know that much about you by now," she added, offering him a small smile of understanding.

"I can guess what the rags will say about us tomorrow, though," Teddy volunteered, "Teddy Bear sweetens the deal for A-list Avery?"

Avery groaned. "That's so lame it might work. Or how about, 'The Latest Scoop on F1's It Couple?'"

"Is Teddy too Vanilla for Avery's Rich Taste Buds?" he offered.

She chuckled, feeling a genuine lightness she hadn't felt in weeks.

The sun was setting, bathing the beautiful old buildings in a golden hour glow, the perfect light for a photo session, reminding Avery that they still had to document their time together.

"Come on, let's take that selfie," Avery paused their silly game and pointed to a mural that was clearly painted with Instagram tourists in mind.

Teddy nodded in agreement and followed her to the side of the shop.

"One, two, three, gelato!" Avery said cheerfully, maneuvering the angle of her phone trying to get the artwork and both their faces in the frame.

"Here, I'm taller, let me do it." Teddy took his phone out of his pocket and held it above them to get the shot. Avery's internal temperature rose a degree seeing his toned bicep as his arm lightly flexed right in front of her face holding up the camera.

"Has Avery Silver melted Teddy's heart?" she picked up their game right where that left off as soon as Teddy's phone was back in his pocket.

Teddy and Avery continued to one-up each other with more ridiculous headlines until their gelatos started to melt. Avery dabbed at the tears in the corners of her eyes. She couldn't remember the last time someone had made her laugh so hard she cried.

"Are you sure you don't want a bite of this before I toss it?" she asked.

"I'm sure," Teddy said as the gold in his eyes shimmered. He cocked his head, "But I have thoroughly enjoyed watching you devour it."

A shiver that was both hot and cold raced up Avery's spine. She smirked back at him, leaning into the moment, as she walked to the nearby garbage can.

What now? Sure, he'd flirted even when it wasn't strictly necessary. But now that they'd gotten their requisite photos done and finished their gelatos, would he bounce? She knew he had a tight schedule.

"Let's go sit on that bench?" Teddy suggested.

She exhaled the breath she didn't realize she'd been holding and found seats on the bench in the center of the piazza.

"I haven't laughed that hard in a long time," he smiled ear to ear.

Avery's breath caught. *Ohh, so that's his real smile.* It was the first time she'd seen it—it was different than his practiced one—it reached all the way to his eyes, where the corners crinkled.

"I was just thinking the same thing," Avery returned his genuine smile with her own grin stretched across her face.

"Let's do this again sometime?" he asked, gently biting his lower lip, as if he was uncertain what her response would be, but hopeful it would be a yes.

She felt her core heat another degree, but she turned her lips into a wry smile, trying to keep the conversation light, to linger in the laughter they shared, "Yes, I think that we will have to do something like this again, since the whole world thinks we are in a hot-and-heavy romantic relationship."

"Right, of course," Teddy rubbed the back of his neck, "What I meant to say was, this was fun. I don't know what I was expecting exactly from our fake dates, but I definitely was not expecting to laugh so hard."

"Hey!" Avery put her hands on her hips. "I'm offended. Hanging out with me is always a good time! Ask Stacey." She nodded, "But I get it, I know you were just doing this for the optics. I hope it didn't ruin you for the race with all this fun and sugar."

As soon as the words were out of her mouth, Avery wished she had leaned into their moment of sincerity instead of making light of it with self-deprecating jokes. She was worth his time, she knew that logically, but she needed her heart to believe it.

"Quite the contrary. I didn't realize how much I needed to clear my head and take a break, even for an hour or two. I think it might help me focus more this weekend." Teddy said earnestly, looking straight at her.

She felt a heaviness in her chest as she realized that Teddy's playful side was so quick to disappear.

She looked up to meet his gaze, searching for the funny guy who had made her laugh until she cried. But he had been tucked away for the day it seemed.

"I'm glad I could help. And I had a good time too," she said.

He looked at his watch. "I could sit here with you all day, but I have to go record a podcast. Skynews waits for no one." Teddy looked at her apologetically.

"No need to apologize. I'm here to help you get the job done, remember. But I wouldn't hate it if the gala happens to come up in conversation during the episode." *No harm in putting it out there.*

"I'll see what I can do," he said with a wink that accentuated his long, dark lashes. "I'll see you soon?" he asked, shifting his weight from one foot to the other.

Was it her imagination or did Avery see a flash of disappointment on Teddy's face? Maybe he was equally bummed to see their conversation return to business and racing so quickly.

"Of course, see you at the track." He gave her a peck on the cheek that left a warm, tingly impression where his lips touched her skin ever so briefly.

Avery watched him go, his steps purposeful and quick as he headed to his engagement – all business. *Bringing the conversation back to our arrangement when he mentioned seeing me again didn't quash our burgeoning friendship, dare I say flirtation, did it? I certainly hope not.*

Her wildly disparate feelings tumbled around in her chest, eventually settling in her belly as she stood in the piazza, leaving her a bit queasy. She was having real doubts about this arrangement. Given the physical attraction blossoming between them, the transactional nature of their relationship was starting to leave a sour taste in her mouth, quickly replacing the afternoon's sweetness.

* * *

As soon as Avery got back to her hotel room, she kicked off her boots, flopped down on her bed and leaned back on the fluffy white hotel pillows. Her cheek still tingled where his lips had touched.

She replayed the time she'd just spent with Teddy in her head, over-analyzing everything he'd said.

It's a date.

I haven't laughed that hard in a long time.

Let's do this again sometime?

. . .

Would he have asked me out on a real date if I hadn't reminded him of our agreement to spend time together right as we were wrapping up?

She needed to get a second opinion, and luckily one of her best friends happened to be right down the hall. She stood back up and walked to Stacey's room.

Stacey answered the door after one knock. "What did Teddy order during your ice cream date?" she asked Avery without asking how *she* was.

"Hello to you too. I'm doing well, thanks for asking," Avery deadpanned as she gave Stacey a pointed look, eyebrows raised.

"Sorry, sorry. I'm in the middle of planning Teddy's meals for the weekend, so I need to know what he ate." Stacey sat back down in front of her computer at the small hotel room desk, poised to enter whatever data Avery was about to give her.

"Your job is weird," Avery commented, entering the room and resuming her bed flop position, this time on top of Stacey's covers. "But, one scoop of sorbet in a cup. Are you free to talk about him in a non-work way, or should I come back later, once you've calculated how many glasses of water vs Gatorade he needs to have tomorrow?"

"Gatorade?! What year is this, 1995?"

"What concoction should I be drinking then?"

"Here," Stacey pulled a small packet from a caddy on the desk next to her laptop and tossed it to Avery. "Much lower sugar content but has electrolytes and added magnesium. Not enough calories for a driver during the race, but probably good for your needs."

Avery turned it over, reading the ingredient list. "Got it, thanks."

"So, I'm assuming you didn't knock on my door for nutritional supplements," Stacey raised her eyebrows, revealing lines across her forehead that were not always visible. "What's up? How did the dates go last night and today?"

Avery paused. *Where to start? There's so much to unpack.* "Well, I certainly enjoyed seeing him do his thing at the game, and we had such a good laugh at the gelateria today. Better than any of my recent real dates, in fact." Her cheeks burned as she said it.

Stacey's eyes went wide in surprise. "Okay. This sounds like a conversation that requires my full attention." She got up from her desk and joined her friend, perching on the edge of the bed by Avery's feet. "Do you wish they were real dates?"

Avery grabbed a pillow and covered her face. *Not sure I'm ready to admit this to Stacey, or to myself.*

She lowered the pillow, but held it against her chest like it was a little kid's comfort item. "Maybe? I mean, have I noticed his gorgeous green-brown eyes, and perfectly sculpted torso, the way he looks effortlessly cool in a race suit? Sure, I have. But doesn't everyone else?"

"Nope. There's a difference between recognizing his general good looks and swooning. *I* have never noticed the color of his eyes before," she grinned at Avery.

"I thought that these dates would be all business-friendly hello, staged photos, and then back to work for both of us. But it feels so natural and comfortable when we are together. And then today I saw a whole new side of him." Avery paused.

"Go on," Stacey said, eyebrows raised.

She clutched her emotional support pillow tighter. "He was playful and flirty. We made up this silly game and we couldn't stop laughing. It was fun."

"Well, it sounds like you wouldn't hate it if these were real dates."

Avery returned the pillow to its face-covering position. "Why universe? Why of all people, did I have to develop a massive crush on an F1 driver? I wish I knew how he was feeling, though. Just because we are having fun getting to know each other, it doesn't mean he has changed his mind about dating anyone during the racing season."

"I'll tell you this much, Teddy laughing and being silly is not nothing, Aves." Stacey gave her a pointed look, "I've only worked with him for a few months, but I do see him nearly every day, and he's never let his guard down with me like that. I know plenty of drivers rely on their trainers to be quasi-therapists, but Teddy is always a professional."

Avery felt a flutter in her belly. *He's different with me.*

Stacey continued, "Why don't you tell him how you feel? Or make a move?"

"No, definitely not. It would be way, way too awkward if he turned me down! I need to have a working relationship."

"Suit yourself. I'll happily watch from the sidelines as you moon over him until you can't take it anymore. And you are welcome to hide behind that pillow for as long as you like, but I do need to get back to work, now that we've established you are officially crushing on Teddy Ross," Stacey teased, patting Avery on the knee before standing back up.

Avery sat up and threw the pillow at Stacey. "I'm glad my ridiculous life is entertaining you. I need to get back to work too." She stood up from the bed and hugged her friend, "Thanks for listening."

"Of course, what are friends for?" Stacey hugged back. "I'm

here anytime you need to talk. We'll get these feelings sorted out."

Avery closed the door behind her and put her head in her hands. *How am I supposed to focus on the gala, now? I can't stop thinking about Teddy's real smile and how being on the receiving end of it made me feel like the sun was shining on me.* All she knew was that she'd do almost anything to coax it out of hiding when she saw him next.

eleven

AMSTERDAM, NETHERLANDS

Avery brushed her fingers on the brassy teak wood of the boat's railing, the waxy polish leaving a sticky residue on her fingers. She wiped them on her cream-colored linen trousers. The century-old canal boat practically glistened in the soft light emanating from the vintage Tiffany lamp hanging from the ceiling. She shook her head. *Iconic.* The scenery, and the moment, felt ripe for something momentous to happen. Their tall, blonde, stereotypically Dutch Captain, Hendrick, had just announced that Queen Elizabeth and Winston Churchill had toured Amsterdam in this very boat. And now Avery and Teddy had it to themselves for a 90-minute private cruise, after not seeing each other for nearly two weeks.

James had booked it for them while they were in town for the Dutch Grand Prix in nearby Zandvoort, knowing that a ride on the charming refurbished 20th-century vessel would be an excellent chance to create more Avery and Teddy content. The fans had been eating it up. The team's and the foundation's reach were definitely benefitting. And today, James had instructed them to make lots of videos, and whatever they did, they had to ask the captain to take a picture of them with the iconic bridges and bicycles of Holland in the background.

"In a moment we will pass through the first of the Seven Bridges, where at the right angle seven bridges line up for a simply stunning photograph."

That's our cue. "Hendrik, would you mind?" Avery asked, holding out her phone.

"Of course, but first may I offer you some champagne?" he asked, walking into the narrow galley and pulling out a bottle of Veuve Clicquot.

"I don't see why I couldn't have just a little glass?" Teddy grinned.

"Teddy, care to do the honors?" Hendrick asked, passing him the sweating bottle.

Teddy cleared his throat. "Sure. Let's see if I can manage this without taking out someone's eye."

Teddy grimaced and turned his head away from the cork as he tried to work it loose.

Avery raised her hand to her mouth and stifled a giggle. He cut an absolutely dashing figure on the boat, wearing those rolled-up jeans with a few centimeters of ankle showing above his navy loafers, looking like he'd stepped out of the pages of Yachting Weekly Magazine. And yet, he was afraid of a flying cork. *This is intimate, learning the little idiosyncrasies that make him a person, not just a ruthless driver in a helmet.*

"Here, hand it over to the expert," she smirked.

"By all means," Teddy said, bending over into a little bow of deference.

Avery shook her shoulders out and stretched her arms. She'd known how to do this since she was eleven. She'd done it so many times that the only sound was a faint hiss as she removed the cork. "The trick is..." she said, handing the cork to Teddy, "... to keep your thumb steady on the cork on the top and just twist the bottom back and forth."

"Well, color me impressed," he said, grinning. The way his hazel eyes shined when he looked at her made her insides fizz as much as the champagne he was pouring.

"And now you are ready for your photo with the seven bridges," Hendrick announced, ushering them to the back deck of the boat.

They held their glasses up in a mock toast and smiled as Hendrick captured the moment.

The captain handed Avery back her phone. "And now I'll get out of your hair and back to the captain's chair up front. Please let me know if you need anything at all."

He retreated, leaving Avery truly alone with Teddy for the first time since they'd originally hatched their plan in London. No fan was going to interrupt them, there was no one to put on a show for. The line between fake and real was muddier than ever.

The fact that they had never set any ground rules for their fake dating relationship had been gnawing at her since Italy. She couldn't deny her attraction to him, or the fact that she was beginning to care for him. *And now we're alone. With champagne. For ninety minutes.* You'd have to have a heart of stone not to enjoy being on a romantic boat ride with an insanely attractive man, no matter how weird the circumstances were.

She took a sip and admired the historic townhomes as the

boat slowly glided down the canal, a light breeze off the water mussing her hair.

"Lovely," Teddy said quietly right behind her.

"This city is so charming," Avery said in agreement, warmth spreading through her chest.

"Sure, I was talking about the city," he said, taking a few of her curls that had flown in her face and tucking them back behind her ear.

A pleasant shiver ran down Avery's spine.

"Have you ever been here before? Wait, that's a dumb question, of course you've been here for the race before," Avery bit her lip, suddenly feeling shy in his presence.

"Right, I've been to the track, but I've never had the opportunity to tour like this. We didn't have much growing up. My dad left my mom to raise me and my brother on her own. We never got a penny from him."

Avery burned at the injustice. What kind of man did that to his family?

"You told me your family had made sacrifices for you, and you'd never mentioned your dad, but I didn't know any details." She gently touched his forearm. "I'm sorry you had to go through that. Your dad leaving, I mean."

"It was a long time ago, but thank you." He looked her deep in the eyes before he cleared his throat. "Now, tell me where you learned how to pop a bottle like that," he said, changing the subject. "I've never managed it without everyone in a 5k radius having to duck and cover."

"Well, when I was little, my parents threw tons of cocktail parties at our house. I would always sneak downstairs after bedtime and hang out in the kitchen with the staff. By the time I was eleven, I convinced a bartender to teach me." Her chest glowed with pride at the memory. "And then I walked into the living room in my pajamas, grabbed a bottle from the wet bar, and offered my parents' guests champagne."

"Cheeky," he chuckled. "Were your parents mad?"

"Nah. Once they saw how delighted their guests were by my performance, they didn't care. Plus, my mom was probably two sheets to the wind by that point in the night. It wasn't long after that she had to go take a little break from life for ninety days, if you get my drift."

Teddy pursed his lips.

Avery's hand flew to her mouth. *Shit.* She'd never told anyone about her mom's drinking problem, or her stint in rehab. Not Stacey, not Caroline, not Josh. It was a well-guarded family secret, one that her mother was deeply ashamed of. Somehow, telling Teddy felt safe, maybe because they were already in on a big secret together, or maybe because he was becoming Teddy to her. Not young gun Silver driver or partner in crime, but her Teddy.

"I had assumed every family with as much money as yours has at least one family member with a drinking or drug problem. I'm glad you didn't tell me you were a secret sex addict. Now that would send me running for the hills. Or not," Teddy raised his eyebrows.

Suddenly, every nerve ending in her body was on guard.

"Seriously. Don't sweat it," he added. "It doesn't change my opinion of you, or of her. I'm glad you feel comfortable enough with me to be vulnerable. Most people don't."

That had been the perfect response. She tilted her head to look at him as her lips turned up in a small smile.

He put his arm around her. An arm around her shoulder could be a friendly gesture meant to comfort her after what she had just confided. But the way he was tenderly rubbing her arm; it didn't feel like the sort of thing a buddy would do, not after making a sex joke.

She put her head on his shoulder, and her hand naturally slipped around to his back. She could feel the dip in his back between mounds of smooth muscle on either side. She wanted to slide her hand under his shirt and run it up along his spine through that divot. To see if she could give him the same tingling nerves she always felt being this close to him. But that would be crossing the unspoken, invisible line they were skating on.

twelve

ZANDVOORT, NETHERLANDS

The yellow flag indicating danger or debris on the track waved high from the official's booth above the starting line. Avery's breath hitched. What had happened? From her vantage point above pit lane, Avery hadn't seen an incident at the Dutch Grand Prix's famous hairpin turn at the end of the starting line straight. It must have happened elsewhere on the track. She held her breath and crossed her fingers until the replay was shown on the big screen.

One of the Griffin Point cars had spun out at another corner.

Phew. It wasn't a Silver. It wasn't Teddy.

No one was hurt, which was the most important thing, so she didn't feel any remorse immediately focusing on how it would affect her guys. The team desperately wanted to end the first half of the season in the top five of ten teams competing for the Constructors' championship, the season-long battle for the team with the most total points.

Currently, they were neck and neck with Griffin Point, and today's outcome would determine who was fifth and who was sixth going into the summer break. Silver was probably too far back from the leading constructor, Archer, to win the championship at the end of the season. But moving into the top five before the mandated fourteen-day summer shut down would allow everyone from the factory technicians to the drivers to enjoy the time off and re-energize before gearing up for the final ten races.

She watched as the marshals struggled to remove the car from the track, and bit her lip as the safety car was deployed from pit lane. The drivers would have to slow down significantly and stay behind the safety car, no passing allowed. It was plain bad luck for Zack, who had managed to take the lead and had built a nice gap between himself and the Archer behind him in second place, who would now get to catch up to Zack as the cars bunched up behind the safety car.

Her dad shook his head in frustration. "There goes that five second lead," he said, his voice bitter.

"I know. Sucks. But he can still pull it out," Avery said, trying to sound positive. "At least it's good for Teddy?"

She knew that securing the win for Zack was the team's top priority, but Teddy was currently in third, keeping the pressure on the Archer from behind. When the yellow flag ended and the safety car went back in the pit, the Archer would not only have to try and overtake Zack in front, but would also have to play defense. Teddy was right behind him aiming for a one-two finish for Silver Racing, or at least both drivers on the podium.

Avery picked at her nail polish, not caring that she was

ruining her manicure, while the cars zig-zagged like a long snake behind the safety car, trying to keep their tires warm until the yellow flag turned green. As soon as the safety car was out of the way, the cars returned to full speed. Avery heard the sounds of shaky laughter and big exhales all around her as Zack held onto his lead, rebuilding the distance between himself and the Archer.

It was in no small part thanks to Teddy, who was pushing flat out, making the Archer look behind him at every turn to keep Teddy in third. Avery wasn't sure that Teddy's tires would last the way he was driving. She clenched her fists at the thought that the team might be sacrificing Teddy's spot on the podium for a Zack win. Someone with more data and more power than she had gotten to make that call. And it wasn't necessarily the wrong one. They had to execute whatever strategy was likely to get the team the most overall points.

She grimaced as Teddy started to fall back from the Archer by fractions of a second each lap. His tires were cooked. But he'd bought enough time for Zack to regain a safe lead over the Archer.

Her ribs quivered as the fourth place car got closer and closer to Teddy until Teddy was less than one second ahead. He didn't even fight for his spot when they got to the hairpin, almost allowing the fourth place car to overtake him, knowing his pace just wasn't there. Not worth taking the risk of crashing and ending up with no points. But Avery's heart sank, here went Teddy's chance at his first podium finish.

The car in fifth was way too far behind Teddy to catch him on his spent tires, and the rest of the race was fairly uneventful. A win for Zack and a fourth place finish for Teddy was a really strong result for the team, clinching that fifth place standing ahead of Griffin Point. But it still left a sour taste in her mouth on Teddy's behalf.

Avery went through the motions of celebrating Zack's win, joining the exuberant team doling out congratulatory hugs and cheering at the podium ceremony. But her mind was squarely on the guy who had come in fourth, narrowly missing the limelight on the podium. He had quietly and politely disappeared.

As soon as the champagne had been sprayed, Avery followed, walking up the stairs to the driver's private rooms.

She knocked on the door, hoping she'd find Teddy there.

"Who is it?" his voice sounded tired, the Scottish brogue more audible than she'd heard before.

"It's Avery," she said, softly.

She heard him get up and unlock the door. "Come in."

"Amazing drive, Teddy. And what you did for the team was invaluable," Avery said, wanting to make him feel appreciated and special.

"Thanks, still stings though. Following team orders when my first podium was so close I could taste it," he shook his head.

"I know. I wish I had something profound to say, but it just sucks. And I just wanted to say I'm in your corner. Team Teddy," she gave him a half smile. It was the most she could muster through the thick fog of disappointment and longing that permeated the room.

He reached out and took one of her curls between his fingers and tugged it straight.

Avery's breath caught in her throat as he gently let go, allowing it to bounce back into its natural state. The dressing room suddenly felt small, like it couldn't contain both of them and the heat that was building between them.

"That officially makes two of us on Team Teddy, today anyway," he paused. "Thank you."

"What are you doing over the summer break?" she asked. "I suppose the fans are going to expect pictures of us on a yacht off the coast of Ibiza or something." Avery blushed at Teddy's bemused smile. "I'm heading back to LA. No shut down for the foundation."

"Well, the fans are going to be disappointed. No yacht. No photos of a gorgeous girlfriend in a bikini," he said, a smile finally forming on his lips, his eyes skating up and down her body.

Avery suddenly felt feverish.

"But I am going to spend a few days recharging on the French Riviera with some of the guys, which will be nice."

"You deserve it," she managed to whisper.

He nodded as if he were trying to convince himself of the words he was hearing.

"I'll see you in three weeks in Austin, then," Avery said. Her heart felt heavy at the thought of going so long without seeing him.

Avery watched as Teddy swallowed. "I suppose so," he agreed.

Avery had to repress her desire to throw herself into his body and bury her face into his chiseled chest. Instead, she stepped closer to him slowly but confidently, wrapping her arms around his broad shoulders. A hug left room for interpretation, a chance to de-escalate into faux-girlfriend/friend territory or to go somewhere else entirely.

He put his arms around her waist in return. Avery felt the heat dancing back and forth between them where his forearms rested on her hips, as his strong arms encircled her petite frame.

She drank in the feel of his thumbs pressed into the small of her back and tucked her nose into his neck, trying to memorize his scent in anticipation of being apart for several weeks. In just a few months, he'd become such a consuming part of her life, and the weeks ahead felt bleak without the thrill of their dates to break up her otherwise anxiety-filled days.

thirteen

LOS ANGELES, CA

The sound of dozens of basketballs bouncing against the gym floors filled Avery's ears as she and Caroline, her friend and her father's assistant, entered the Southside Youth Sports Complex, overpowering the faint rhythm of uplifting pop music being played from someone's cell phone in the corner. *Going to need to add a blue-tooth speaker system to the remodel budget.* Coach Tony, the after-school program director, was leading a group of kids through a series of dribbling exercises up and down the court. The gym looked even more scuffed and dull than she remembered, the blue paint lines cracked and faded.

Coach Tony saw them and waved, blowing three short blasts on his whistle. "Boys and girls, that's all the time we have for today. The big kids need their turn," he said to a chorus of moans and groans. "I know, I know, but thanks to these ladies over here..." he pointed to Avery and Caroline, "...next year we will have a brand new gym for you guys with double the space *and* tennis courts, how does that sound?"

A bunch of five-to-seven-year-olds jumped up and down and hollered, tugging at Avery's heartstrings. One led a little booty shake in response. *These kids deserve so much more than thirty minutes of playing time on a beat-up court. I have to raise the money. No matter what.*

"You are all dismissed back to the community room," Coach Tony announced, blowing his whistle one more time, before he greeted Avery and Caroline with an appreciative grin. "Ladies, what can I do for you today?"

"I'm hoping we can get some photos and videos of the facilities to use at the gala. I think if our donors can see where their money is going, it will be more impactful," Avery said. "Maybe we could interview you on camera to talk about how much this place means to the community?"

"I like where you're going with this," the coach nodded in agreement. "But I can do you one better." He blew his whistle again, "Claudia, Walker, come here please."

"Yes, coach?" an adorable little boy grinned, looking halfway nervous. Avery knew that feeling, could tell the boy was wondering if he'd somehow gotten himself in trouble. A girl with her dark hair twisted in neat rows of braids trailed behind him.

"I'd like you to meet Ms. Silver and Ms. O'Brien. If it's okay with you, they are going to ask you a few questions about the new courts and why you are so excited about them?"

The kids nodded enthusiastically.

Avery crouched down and gave them a warm smile, trying her best to put the two youngsters at ease. "You can call me

Avery. And that is my friend Caroline. We could really use your help."

Walker stood up a little straighter and Claudia tilted her head, intrigued. Avery had to hide a smile as she caught Caroline's eye, who was setting up her camera on a tripod. This was going to work out perfectly.

Caroline nodded, ready to roll.

"I'm going to ask you a few questions, and you can take your time to answer, there's no rush. And you can ignore the camera behind me, we're just having a conversation," Avery said.

"What do you like about coming to the Southside Youth Sports Complex after school?"

"It's so much more fun than going to my neighbor's house after school while my dad is still at work," Walker said. "We get to learn basketball and other sports, and there's also someone who can help me with my homework and reading. Now that I'm in first grade, I need to fill in my reading log every night."

"And what about you, Claudia?" Avery asked. "What's your favorite part of coming here after school?"

"The snacks. They have such good snacks here, like any kind of fruit you want and they always have the good kinds of cereal."

Avery nodded seriously at the kids. *Gold. This was pure gold.* Exactly what they needed for their video.

"Why are you excited to have more space here next year?"

"I want to keep playing basketball! More basketball, and I want my sister to be able to play with Coach Tony and the other coaches," Claudia said, bouncing up and down on her toes.

"A little sister? Will she be old enough to come next year?"

"No, my big sister. She's in sixth grade and she wants to be on a real team. But there aren't enough courts for the girls' team and the boys' team to both have practice after school."

Avery's stomach lurched. *What the... That's a completely unacceptable state of affairs.*

She made eye contact with Caroline over the camera, who mouthed "WTF?" back at her. She gripped the hem of her shirt, her palms sweaty, as a wave of nausea passed over her. It would be her fault if they didn't have enough space for the girls to practice next year. She could try and cover some of it with her trust fund, but she only had access to $50,000 per year until she turned thirty.

She took a deep breath and turned her attention to Walker, the little boy.

"What do you want people to know about the Sports Complex?"

"I love it so much. Oh, and the Sports Complex needs some new, *real*, jerseys for our games. The old ones are gross and smelly."

Jerseys? Now that was an easy fix. She could take care of that tomorrow with a few phone calls, so long as Coach Tony didn't mind the back of the jerseys having a Silver Racing logo.

* * *

"Earth to Avery? What's so interesting on that phone of yours?" Caroline teased. "Do you think I should get off and take Sepulveda?" She quickly glanced sideways from the driver's seat. They were stuck in traffic driving back to the Santa Monica office from the Sports Complex.

"Just texting," Avery replied, trying her best to sound nonchalant.

"With Teddy?" Caroline guessed.

"Maybe..." *Busted.* She was in fact texting with Teddy. They'd been in daily communication since they'd parted ways in Amsterdam ten days ago, mostly by text, chatting about everything and nothing. The boring, mundane everyday stuff that only a close confidant would care to know. It had allowed her to get to know him on a deeper level even from a distance. He liked oatmeal for breakfast and preferred coffee over tea, despite being a Brit. She'd FaceTimed one night from the balcony of her apartment to show him the sun setting over the Pacific Ocean and the palm trees swaying in the wind.

"I can't wait to see it in person with you someday," he'd said, his lips parted in a way that she'd be tempted to kiss if he weren't halfway around the world.

"That would be fun," she'd said, her heart nearly aching for him. *I miss you. What if you fly here right now and spend the rest of the break with me?*

A new message from him popped up on her screen, breaking her daydream:

> Teddy—How did it go at the Sports Complex today?

> Avery—It was GREAT. I'm more fired up than ever - we have got to deliver for these kids. Did you see any good apartments yesterday?

She typed quickly, trying to shield her phone from Caroline's prying eyes.

After a few days at the beach, Teddy had spent the rest of his time in Monaco, where he was considering moving at the end of the year. The majority of F1 drivers had their home bases in the city-state for its tax and privacy laws.

> Teddy—Yes. What do you think of
> this one?

Photos of a sleek, modern black-and-white space popped up on her phone. It was nice, chic, and matched Teddy's public image to a tee. Exactly what a real estate agent would think he'd want to see. But it lacked a certain warmth that she'd come to associate with him.

> Avery—It's really nice. But I'm not sure
> it's homey enough for you.

His reply came quickly.

> It is a bit cold, isn't it? The location is
> great, so I said maybe. You're right, it's
> not for me. Back to the drawing board.
> What would I do without you?

A blush crept up her neck. *If we dated for real, you'd never have to know.*

"What are you grinning about over there?" Caroline teased. "That's a lot of smiling for a fake-boyfriend/co-conspirator?"

Avery shrugged. Guilty as charged.

"You two need to hook up already. Pretending you don't want to jump each other is getting silly."

"Well, I wouldn't kick him out of bed," Avery laughed. "But he must be into me too. For sure. Once we cross that line, I don't know how I'll be able to tell fact from fiction."

Avery sighed, "It's already so messy. The whole point of this for both of us was to focus on our careers and not get distracted by romance this season."

Caroline smirked. "That ship has sailed my friend. Consider yourself distracted."

Avery put her head in her hands and groaned. Caroline was right. There was no business reason for their texting all break. Despite how busy she'd been, the summer break from racing had been inching by at a snail's pace. There was still a week to go until she'd see Teddy again in Austin, and they didn't have any dates, fake or otherwise, on the calendar there.

Should I reach out to James and see if we can squeeze in a trip to a local BBQ joint? No, the schedule is already jam-packed with promotional events at the team pop-up shop. She stared at the window as the traffic lightened up and Caroline's focus returned to the road. *If only we didn't need a reason, an excuse, to spend time together.*

She tried to distract herself by checking out the vehicles on either side, which makes and models drove past, what colors seemed to be most popular. Cars. It always came back to cars.

fourteen

LOS ANGELES, CA

Avery's shoes click-clacked against the linoleum flooring of the team's factory headquarters, east of LA, making sure no one in the small group she was leading got left behind. She'd worn flats, knowing she'd be doing a lot of walking today, but the loafers still made a ton of noise with each step. The summer shutdown was over, and it was all hands on deck at the factory as the team geared up for the second half of the season, which would kick off that weekend in Austin, TX. Today she and Caroline were taking a small group of donors on a behind-the-scenes factory tour, which would end with a not-so-subtle pitch for a gala sponsorship. Not that she minded, any excuse to be in the thick of the racing world was a good one.

"And through these doors is our state-of-the-art simulator where our drivers and engineers map out the best plan for each and every turn on the track," she explained, stopping in front of a set of frosted double glass doors.

"Oh, can we take a looksie?" Susan, a woman representing one of the city's prominent family foundations, asked with a conspiratorial wink.

Avery hesitated for a moment. She didn't want to interrupt any prep for that weekend's race. But making a potential donor happy was also important. A little VIP treatment would go a long way in securing a donation, heck, maybe the group would buy a whole table. "That's not usually part of the tour, but let me see what I can do," Avery winked back, laying it on a bit thick.

Avery knocked gently on the glass door, and when no one answered immediately, she opened it a crack and looked into the dimly lit space. A trio of engineers sat with their backs to her, facing their computer monitors, clearly reviewing some data. Beyond their bay, another set of doors lead to the actual simulator set-up: a stationary replica of the team's current car parked in front of movie-theater-sized screens that could project a realistic view of the track from the driver's perspective.

"Hello?" she asked, her voice going up an octave.

The guy closest to the door pulled off his headphones and turned around, "Hi there, Avery. Teddy's on his lunch break," he looked at his watch, "But he should be back here for the afternoon in a few minutes."

Teddy? Here? She tried to simultaneously mask her surprise and shove away the butterflies that fluttered their wings in her belly at the mere mention of his proximity. Of course, the staff assumed she'd stop by to see her "boyfriend" at work, if he was in town.

She tried to keep her expression neutral. "Oh, of course. Actually, I have a favor to ask?" she pointed beyond the glass. "I have a small group of foundation donors on a tour, can I bring them in and show them what you do here in sim?" She felt a bit guilty as she asked, knowing how much pressure the engineers were under.

"Sure, no problem at all," Alan replied, pushing up his glasses. "Come on in," he stood up and helped open the doors, as the group of donors shuffled in.

"Please allow me to introduce Alan, our lead engineer for simulation, who was kind enough to take a moment away from his work on the next race to show us around," Avery said to the group.

"Yes, as Avery mentioned, what we do here in the simulator is help plan exactly what setting the driver should use at each segment of the lap..."

Avery tuned him out as soon as she could see that he had her tour's attention. Her whole body was on high alert knowing Teddy was in the building. *How did I not know he was here?* Her body positively lit up at the news he was nearby. *But my heart feels more than a twinge of disappointment that he didn't let me know he was going to be here.* He was under no obligation to, of course, it wasn't like their deal made it so that he had to report his whereabouts to her. She knew that. It was just that she'd thought things had changed between them in Amsterdam. And they'd been in contact nearly every day. It would have been so easy for him to tell her he was going to be in LA. Did he not want to see her? Had she misread the situation entirely?

"Great question, we work with several test drivers each week, not only our track drivers," Alan explained to the group. "If there are no other questions, it was a pleasure meeting all of you. I do hope I'll see you at our gala?" Alan turned to Avery and she smiled back appreciatively.

"Alan, thank you so much for your time," Avery said

emphatically. She ushered the group out of the room, a few of whom were clearly trying to linger in hopes of catching a glimpse of Teddy. She couldn't blame them.

Avery felt her own eyes darting around, looking for Teddy as much as her tour group was, as they filed back out into the hallway.

"Avery, are you sticking around? Teddy should be here any minute," Alan asked nonchalantly before she closed the doors behind her.

She looked at the group of donors, then back longingly at the sim set-up. "Well, I need to wrap up this tour and show our guests out..."

"I've got this, I can take them," Caroline offered.

"Really? You sure?" Avery asked, not used to handing off her responsibilities to anyone. "I'm sure," Caroline confirmed, tapping her low-heeled boot on the floor. "Who do you think gives these tours when you're out of town?"

"Good point. Okay, I'll hang out for a minute," she said, instinctively grabbing for one of her curls.

Avery watched as the group marched down the hallway, gazing at the back of Caroline's shoulder-length blonde hair, before turning her thoughts back to Teddy. *Will he be happy to see me here?* She didn't want to be a nuisance to him—or any of the engineers for that matter—with the next race days away.

"Don't let me keep you," she told Alan.

"No worries," he said. "Come check out this setup we are working on. I know you know what you're looking at," Alan gestured over to the screen.

Avery beamed. *This, the feeling of really being a part of the work, lights me up inside.* Avery hovered over Alan's shoulder as he explained the microchanges he was making to the car's balance and steering to see if they could get the car to improve a couple of tenths of seconds each lap based on Teddy's feedback earlier in the day.

"And what about that number there, what –" Avery was interrupted mid-question when Teddy and an engineer came barreling through the doors, deep in conversation.

She knew he would be walking in any second, and yet his commanding presence still surprised her. The way that everyone in the room straightened their shoulders a bit, and stopped what they were doing when he entered. Was it because he was the driver who could make or break all their hard work when he was out on the track in real life?

Or, because he was the face of the team, the guy who got paid the big bucks?

Or was it just his essence, his "it-factor"?

Probably all of the above.

Teddy's eyes went wide with surprise seeing her shoulder-to-shoulder with Alan, but his mouth quickly turned into a smile. The big smile Avery had thought about every day since she'd last coaxed it out of him. Had it really only been three weeks since they'd seen each other? He'd let his facial hair grow out since she'd seen him; the days-old scruff she was used to seeing him rock had grown into the beginning of a goatee. She didn't hate it.

"Avery, hi. I didn't know you were going to be here today," Teddy said as their eyes locked. She could have sworn she saw the golden-brown flecks dance.

"I didn't know *you* were in town at all," she cocked her head.

He ran his hands through his hair and broke their eye contact, as if embarrassed to have been caught once she pointed it out.

Crap. She hadn't meant to put him on the spot in front of the engineers. Had she crossed some kind of line in their relationship? "Not that you have to give me your schedule..." she winced.

Alan drifted away, giving them as much room as was possible in the enclosed space.

"Yes, since Austin is relatively close to LA, I decided it would be nice to pop into the factory for the day, and do my sim work here," he paused. "As soon as I finish here tonight, I fly straight to Austin," he offered up, "Quick trip, that's why—"

"Totally, I get it," she said, letting him off the hook, even as her heart smarted a bit.

"Stay and watch this next set of laps?" he offered.

Her posture softened a bit. She could do that. "Sure."

There was that smile again, how could she resist that smile?

"Alright, let's get started then," Alan interrupted. "I made the changes we talked about before lunch to the steering, so let's try again option B on the big hill and turns 1 and 2."

Teddy nodded—he'd become serious, Work-Mode Teddy again before her eyes. The smile replaced with a straight face that was all business.

Someone handed him a helmet, and he walked through the second set of doors to the car setup.

"Okay, Teddy. Option B when you're ready," Alan spoke into his headset that would be delivered to Teddy's radio like he'd talk to his race engineer in a real race.

Avery couldn't hear Teddy's responses as Alan continued to give Teddy instructions lap after lap, trying a number of different options as the team engineers recorded every minute difference, looking for correlations between settings and lap times. She stayed where she was, and watched the screen with his helmet cam view lap after lap with genuine interest as Teddy breaked at every corner and then picked up his speed on every straightaway.

"Good. Let's jump out and do a debrief," Alan instructed.

He strode through the double doors, his presence once again filling the room.

"Option B felt best, I think. Little bit of understeer by turn twelve in Option A," Teddy started the conversation.

"The data agrees," Alan answered. Teddy and the engineers all huddled around the screen and looked at lap times, mapping out a final plan for the weekend, while Avery hung back.

"I think we've got it, boys. Good work," Teddy concluded the debrief. "And now I think it's Avery's turn to have a go," Teddy looked at her, daring her to take him up on his offer.

They were the first words he'd said to her, the first time he'd acknowledged her presence since he'd slipped his helmet on an hour earlier.

She looked back at him, considering whether it was a good idea. "I don't want to screw anything up," she hesitated, not wanting to force Alan and his team into it.

"There's nothing you can screw up here," Alan said. "You can't actually crash our million-dollar car into a wall. It's just a sim. Let's have some fun."

"Alright, let's do it," Avery said, her fingers tingling at the thought of gripping the steering wheel.

"Come on, then," Teddy held the doors open for her and guided her to the car, before taking off his helmet and handing it to her.

"You really want me to wear your helmet? Is this your

move? You offer women a turn in your sim and a chance to wear your sweaty helmet and they swoon?" she raised an eyebrow.

"Nope, you're the first, Avery," he said, shaking his head.

Her heart slammed into her throat as she pulled it on. It was too big, slipping down and almost covering her eyes, but it didn't matter, it wasn't like she was going to get in a real crash.

"Okay, so you'll need to jump over the halo, there, to get in the seat," Teddy explained.

"Teddy, it may be the first time you've given a girl your helmet, but it's not my first time in a race car," she winked and hopped in. She wasn't a professional race car driver, but Teddy and the team had no idea how many times her dad had let her do this before when no one was watching, not to mention all the hot laps she'd taken, the go-karts she had raced.

"Avery, when you're ready," she heard Alan address her through the speaker, as he had with Teddy.

"The question is whether you're ready," she cackled. Teddy's confusing behavior aside, this would be fun.

She took hold of the steering wheel and pushed down on the accelerator, the car biting back immediately. She eased up the hill as a lifesize view of the Circuit of the Americas appeared on the screens in front and all around her like a 3D movie theater. She played it safe her first lap, trying hard to keep it clean and avoid any crashes, while Teddy leaned on the door-frame, watching with a sly smile.

"What was my time?" she asked, as she crossed the finish line.

"2:30:22" Alan answered back. "Damn, I didn't know you could drive!"

Avery grinned. "Ehh, not good enough. Let's go again." Teddy's laps had been in the 1:40-1:45 range. She knew she wouldn't get there, or she'd be driving in F1 Academy, the women's series, but she knew she could go faster.

Avery rolled out her wrists, stretched her neck side-to-side. "I'm going for 2:15 this lap," she looked back at Teddy, who nodded at her.

She braced the steering wheel again, nodded to herself as much as to Teddy and focused, pressing the balls of her foot into the pedal, doubly glad that she hadn't worn heels today. Wouldn't have been able to do this, that's for sure. She pushed down on the accelerator even harder, easing up a tad as she rounded turn one. Crunch. The car whipped back. Into the gravel it went.

"Shit," she shook her head, looking back to Teddy to see his reaction.

"It's alright, bella. Happens to the best of us, go again," he nodded.

Bella. He'd called her that in Italy too.

"Try steering into the turn using a wide racing line," Alan coached her through the radio.

"Yes, again," she took a deep breath.

She started up the hill, again. "NOW, steer left now," Alan shouted through the headset. Crunch. Gravel. Again.

"Damn it," she took her fingers off the wheel and exhaled. *Frustrating.*

Teddy had a coy smirk on his face.

"Here, let me show you," Teddy offered from his spot on the wall, striding up to the left side of the fake car setup. "Like this," he leaned over, and put his hands on top of hers.

Avery felt heat rush up her neck at his touch. His hands felt warm and strong, steadying hers which had involuntarily begun to shake.

"Okay, start accelerating," he instructed her.

She pushed down on the petal.

"More," his voice was deep, commanding.

Avery pushed down again, nearly bringing it to full throttle as the car zipped up the hill.

"Okay, now don't let up but put your other foot on the break," he explained. His face was so close to hers she could feel the breath from his words, like a tickle, a very serious tickle. There was no lightness when it came to Teddy Ross and mastering a race corner.

He pressed down harder on her hands, generating an almost electric heat between them. Did he feel it too? That chemistry she felt with his hands splayed out above hers? What would it feel like to have the rest of his capable body pressed up against hers? Her crush, her body, momentarily distracting her from the task at hand, while Teddy took control, firmly, but quickly whipping the wheel to the left, before allowing it to straighten itself back out.

"Ohhh," Avery breathed. "So that's how it feels?"

Teddy smiled satisfactorily, and leaned in closer, his lips almost grazing her earlobe. Avery's pulse quickened. If she turned her head, their lips would be a mere inch apart. She didn't dare, there's no way she'd be able to resist the temptation of leaning in even closer, seeing if he was feeling that same magnetic pull.

"That's how it feels when you don't hold back. When you take control," he whispered into her ear, before letting go of her hands and pulling back, his eyes assessing her as if he had just *really seen her* for the first time.

"Now try it again, by yourself," he nodded, resuming his coaching stance by the wall. Avery remembered that they weren't alone, her cheeks warmed at the thought that Alan and a handful of engineers had witnessed that moment on their cameras, and had probably thought Teddy was whispering something much more risqué in her ear. Not that what Teddy had said, hadn't affected her. *Like a bolt of lightning down my spine.*

Avery shook off the remaining heat from Teddy's hands, tried to free her mind from thoughts of Teddy's lips, his hands, and felt the oxygen return to her lungs as she took a deep steadying breath.

I've got this.

She went pedal to the metal once more, her adrenaline pumping through her as she raced up the hill, applying the break how Teddy had coached her. She gripped the wheel as tightly as her smaller, untrained hands allowed, and whipped the wheel like Teddy's hands had guided her to a moment ago. The muscles in her forearms burned as she clenched her fists, fighting the weight of the car and pulling it away from the barrier. Damn, Teddy had really done the heavy lifting. Avery made a mental note to hit the gym more often. And then she was out of the turn, guiding the car down the track to the next turn. She'd done it. She'd actually freaking done it by herself.

"Wooo!" she yelled out as she did as much of a victory dance as she could without taking her hands off the steering wheel. By the time she slowed to a stop past the finish line, her breath was ragged and her body hot from the exertion. "That was awesome! What was my time?"

"2:25, way to go, kiddo!" Alan's voice crackled through the speaker.

Avery grinned and twisted around to see what Teddy's reaction to her success was, and saw that he was also grinning ear to ear, his eyes crinkling. He gave her a thumbs up and a wink. Avery bit her lip and shrugged her shoulders in response, playing it cool, but inside she was a puddle of satisfaction.

"Want to go again and see if you can get it down to 2:20?" Alan asked.

"No, thanks. I think I'll end on that high note," Avery answered, unbuckling and hopping back out of the car's cockpit.

She pulled the helmet off and shook out her now slightly damp curls. She took a step toward Teddy, fighting the urge to leap into his arms and throw her arms around his neck.

"Must be a lucky helmet," she said, her traitorous cheeks heating at his proximity as she held it out to him.

"It is now," he winked, maintaining his effortless cool eye-contact while he took the helmet back from her.

"That was so fun. Thanks for taking the time," she said, letting out a big exhale as she continued to catch her breath.

"The pleasure was all mine Avery," Teddy cocked his head and gave her a wry smile. He fiddled with the zipper on his racing suit, zipping and unzipping it at his waist, drawing her attention to his perfectly trim torso. "So, when do you get to Austin?" he asked.

"I'm heading out tomorrow mid-day. I'm planning to be at the pop-up most of the day Wednesday," she answered.

Teddy nodded his head several times, "Nice. I'll be there for a bit in the afternoon to sign autographs."

That was it? He wasn't going to ask to see her in Austin outside work?

She wrung her hands, feeling overwhelmed. "I should get going. I guess I'll see you there."

"Of course," he said. "Safe travels, bella," he leaned in again.

Avery's breath caught in her throat. It almost felt like he was going to kiss her. There was no one around. No journalists, James wasn't there to capture any content. If he did kiss her, it would be out of desire, not performance, just like it had been in Amsterdam. *Right?*

She felt his soft lips brush her cheek and then pull away. It was over before it began. Avery's heart somehow sank and soared at the same time. His lips didn't meet hers. He paused long enough to muddle the line between friendship and romance even more, leaving her hot and bothered, and more confused about them than ever.

fifteen

AUSTIN, TX

Avery looked anxiously over her shoulder toward the entrance to the team's pop-up shop. She was in an industrial space in downtown Austin, and her parents were expected to arrive any moment now. Fans were lined up along one wall, waiting for their turn to go up on stage and have Teddy or Zack sign the merch they had purchased from the display at the front. She walked over to the uniformed security guard manning the front doors. "Excuse me, do you have an updated ETA for Michael Silver?" she asked.

He adjusted his holster, taking out his phone to confirm. "They are still expected in the next five minutes or so, but it looks like there's some traffic on I-35."

"Ok, thanks," she answered.

"I'll let you know if I hear anything different," he looked at her sympathetically, sensing her apprehension.

Her dad was scheduled to take part in the fan Q&A that

was starting in half an hour, and her mom had traveled with him to Austin for the United States Grand Prix. Sharon Silver did not attend many races, but given Austin's relative proximity to LA, Avery's mom always made the trip down to Texas each year.

Avery felt sick to her stomach at the thought of introducing her mom to Teddy. Sharon still had no idea they weren't really a couple, and her overwhelming introductions alone could be enough to scare Teddy out of pursuing anything real. One time in high school, Sharon invited Avery's homecoming date on their family vacation when he came to pick her up for the dance. Avery barely knew the guy—he was the friend of a friend. The poor kid was so flustered that he could hardly stand to look at Avery the entire night, which had put a real damper on the whole homecoming experience.

Sharon also had a habit of flaunting her wealth and status quite a bit when meeting someone new. When Avery moved into her college dorm, her mom outfitted the small space with a wall-mounted TV, a pink mini fridge, and two sets of matching linens, all in an effort to impress Avery's new roommate. Avery never saw the girl again after freshman year.

Now that she knew about Teddy's humble beginnings, Avery knew he was unlikely to be impressed by her mom's signature showiness. Would Teddy confuse her mom's attitude toward money with Avery and be turned off?

Avery nervously paced around the space, pretending to check out the various displays showcasing the team's sponsors. Her attention ping-ponged between Teddy signing autographs at the table and the front doors, dreading the inevitable.

The security guard from earlier tapped her on the shoulder and pointed at a black SUV pulling-up outside, before joining other members of the venue's security team, who were wearing plain black attire and headsets, as they got into position to escort her parents through the crowd to the stage area in the back.

Her dad emerged first, wearing a team branded polo shirt, a cashmere sweater tied over his shoulders, and slacks. His dark, but thinning, hair was slicked back, and his natural tan and vivacious demeanor made him look younger than his sixty-five years. Her mom's petite figure followed him out of the car, overdressed for the occasion in a vintage Chanel jacket paired with tailored trousers, her icy blonde hair in a low chignon that showed off large diamond earrings.

Avery took a deep breath, trying to ease the pit of dread that had formed deep in her belly. She was able to move through the crowd unnoticed since she was wearing the staff uniform and her curls were tucked into a messy bun that stuck out the bottom of her baseball cap. She hadn't washed and styled her hair yet because she was hoping to have time to go to a pilates class at a local studio later.

"Hello, darling," her mother leaned in to give Avery a hug and a kiss.

"Hi, Mom. Welcome to Austin," she plastered a fake smile on her face, pretending to be delighted to see her mom too.

"Thanks, sweetheart," Sharon said, pulling out a compact mirror to make sure her lipstick hadn't been smudged while giving her daughter a kiss. "I'm *so* looking forward to meeting Teddy. You haven't brought a date to the gala since you were dating Josh, way back when. So, I know you two must be getting serious." She winked at Avery as if they were girlfriends who shared all their secrets.

At least Avery wouldn't have to work too hard to convince her mom that she and Teddy were dating for real. Her brother and brother-in-law, however, would be much harder to convince. They were due to arrive in a few hours, and she would have to play it just right. Ben and Adam were definitely more skeptical of anyone who tried to penetrate the family's inner circle, and normally Avery was grateful that they were always looking out for her best interest. On the flip side, their presence this time was going to make it even more tricky to walk the line with Teddy. If Avery and Teddy laid it on too thick, they would know something was up. On the other hand, if she didn't at least show some PDA, they wouldn't believe she was actually into him.

"There's my girl!" her dad nearly shouted as he too gave her a big hug. "Good crowd, right? How have the merch sales been? These pop-ups are huge for us this season, just huge."

Before she could answer, their conversation was interrupted when a staff member went on stage and announced the end of the drivers' meet and greet session.

Teddy and Zack approached their family huddle, two of the security guards parting the fans in front of them like the Red Sea. She made eye contact with Teddy and gave him a half smile. She felt butterflies in her stomach. *Who knows what he is thinking after our almost-kiss in the sim?*

Teddy gave her a chaste peck on the cheek, leaving Avery craving more connection with him. She longed to be alone with him, to see his eyes crinkle up in that real smile of his, to hear more stories about growing up with his mom and brother. Her physical reaction to being with him again confirmed what Stacey had figured out weeks ago, she wanted it to be real. *I'm certainly not going to be the one to suggest it first. Putting my feelings out there now could ruin everything we have going for us.*

Avery was grateful on multiple levels that Teddy stuck close to her side, waiting for her to set the tone with her parents. They hung back as Zack paid his respects, shaking hands with Michael and making small talk with her mother before he was quickly whisked away to his next obligation.

Well, here goes nothing. She wasn't sure exactly what label, if any, to give him when introducing Teddy to her mom. There was no way she could get through saying "This is my boyfriend, Teddy." Boyfriend wasn't a word they had used in their pretend romance. And "This is our new driver, Teddy," was too obvious and too impersonal.

"Mom, I'd like you to meet Teddy. Teddy, this is my mom, Sharon," Avery said, finally.

Teddy stuck out his hand for a handshake. "It's so nice to meet you, Mrs. Silver. I'm Teddy Ross."

"Teddy, what a pleasure to finally meet you. And, please, call me Sharon. I mean you're practically part of the family."

Avery cringed. *Part of the family? A few dates and her mother was calling him part of the family? Peak Sharon.*

Teddy froze for a second, his eyes wide, before quickly resuming his rehearsed picture-perfect smile.

Avery was sure that an overbearing would-be mother-in-law was exactly the type of thing Teddy was trying to avoid in a real relationship. Avery clenched her fists by her sides, hoping no one would notice her growing discomfort.

"Well, you have a lovely daughter, and I hope I haven't been keeping her on the road and away from her family obligations in California too much this season," Teddy said, easily slipping into his poised public persona.

"Don't be silly. It's so important for young couples to be together. I just don't understand all these long-distance relationships your generation tries to make work. If you love someone, you make sacrifices to support their career."

Avery could practically feel the steam coming out of her ears in response to her mom's anti-feminist statement. Of course, her mom would think that she should spend her time being a cheerleader for Teddy instead of focusing on her own goals. Giving up her own ambitions to be with Avery's dad and support his career had worked out quite well for Sharon Silver, with the charmed life she led. But Avery wanted more out of her life, wanted to make her own mark.

"Well, Mom, Teddy really has to get going. He's due for his next event," she said.

Teddy winked at her. There was no next event.

"Yes, Mrs. Silver, I mean Sharon, your husband runs a tight ship and I best be off to work. I do hope we will get to see each other again this week," he stuck out his hand for a parting handshake, but to Avery's horror, her mother pulled him in for a hug.

Avery put her manicured hand on Teddy's arm and started physically moving him away from her mother. "Bye, Mom. Love you."

She followed Teddy outside as the security team made a path for him to walk through the crowd. *That certainly could have gone a lot worse. At least it's over.*

A queue of people had formed outside the doors waiting for their turn to come inside. Among them was a little boy who couldn't have been more than seven years old who was holding up a sign that read "Future Silver Driver."

"You're my favorite driver, ever! I hope you get pole position," he yelled to Teddy. Pole position, the first place on the starting grid (the order in which cars line up to start the race), was given to the driver who recorded the fastest lap time in qualifying rounds each week. Starting in front highly increased their chances of winning.

Teddy stopped in his tracks and knelt down to be eye-level with the boy. She couldn't hear what he was saying, but Avery studied the way Teddy focused his complete attention on the boy as he engaged in conversation with the youngster for a full thirty seconds. The boy's whole face lit up, clearly delighted in Teddy's attention.

I know the feeling, kiddo. When Teddy made you the center of his universe, even for a moment, it was as if the rest of the world disappeared. She felt any remaining wariness about Teddy's polished facade melt away, now that she knew he had a warm personality and genuine interest in other people underneath the serious exterior.

When they reached Teddy's car, a bright green Silver R8 on loan from a local dealership, Teddy wrapped his arms around Avery's hips in full view of the fans waiting to go inside for the Q&A. Avery gasped in surprise at the unexpected heat of his fingers pressed tightly into her small of her back. This certainly didn't feel like a staged photo-op.

"I'm sorry, I didn't mean to surprise you. Is this okay? Too much?" Teddy blinked.

"No—I mean yes, it's okay. Really." Avery submitted to the tingling in her hands as she wrapped her hands around his neck, trying to ignore the fans whipping out their phones to take videos of them, wishing she had done her hair. The phones and the busy city street beyond them faded from her view as she basked in the glow of Teddy's warm hands and full attention.

"Avery! Teddy! Can I get a selfie?" she heard a voice yell from the crowd.

"Teddy, over here!" another voice chirped.

"Give me one second, mate," Teddy said to the guy shoving a baseball cap and sharpie in between their faces, bursting their momentary bubble.

He squeezed her tighter for another moment, before untangling himself from her arms, a reluctant look on his face. He held his hand out for the guy who was still standing there with his baseball cap in hand. He accepted the sharpie and signed it, stealing glances at Avery as he did.

Avery marveled at his effortless cool as he handed back the hat, waved and nodded at fans, and walked around to the driver's side of the sporty street legal Silver. He got in, the car door slamming shut behind him. A pair of sunglasses had magically appeared on his face, adding to his movie star good looks. She shook her head. *Where did those come from?* She wished she could hop into the passenger seat next to him and drive off into the proverbial sunset, but duty called and she wistfully walked back into the event space to face her family.

sixteen

CIRCUIT OF THE AMERICAS
Austin, Texas

It was a hot, semi-humid day, not atypical this time of year in Texas. The sun was beating down on the grandstands as Avery, her brother Ben, her brother-in-law Adam, and a couple hundred thousand spectators streamed into the sprawling Circuit of the Americas motorsport complex on the outskirts of town. Avery could see the track's signature observation tower soaring 250 feet above the track. *We must look like ants from up there.*

Silver was poised for a big day, with both drivers in contention to win. Avery's heart was already pounding in her chest with anticipation, and the race hadn't started yet. It was going to be a long day for her nervous system.

"Should we head straight to the garage and wish everyone a good race?" Ben asked innocently enough. But Avery knew that behind his well-coiffed hair (jet-black like her own) and a half smirk, he was really gunning to meet Teddy in person and suss him out.

She really, really did not want to interrupt his race prepara-tion by bringing her brothers around for an introduction. She had sent him a quick text that morning wishing him a great race, and otherwise planned to give him a wide berth. If he didn't like seeing his own family before a race, surely he wouldn't want to see Avery's on the biggest day of his career.

"Um, I think Mom is already in the Paddock Club, so we should probably go help her entertain all the guests," Avery countered.

The Paddock Club, overlooking pit lane, was considered the most desirable place to watch the race from, with a price to match. When Sharon, Avery's mom, came to town she always took advantage of the opportunity to turn the race into a social event, inviting friends and relatives to join them in the club.

"Are you going to go make an appearance and then watch from the garage, now that you're an official girlfriend?" Adam, Ben's husband, asked, wiggling his eyebrows from behind his sunglasses. Both men were wearing v-neck, blue short-sleeve shirts, Ben's a lighter shade, Adam's darker one featuring a subtle Silver logo on the sleeve.

"Haven't decided, but maybe you two should stop in here and get tattoos?" Avery pointed to one of the many merchant stalls, this one run by a local tattoo parlor offering their services on the spot. It wasn't a crazy question—girlfriends often watched the race from the driver's garage, headset and all. *But I'm pretty sure that's crossing a line for a fake relationship.*

"No way, sis, this body is a temple" Ben flexed his biceps, inducing an eye-roll from Avery. Ben and Adam had put in a state-of-the-art gym in the sprawling mansion they'd built in the suburbs, but she doubted he'd stepped foot in it more than twice. Adam on the other hand, could often be found there dancing it out on his spin bike.

"Okay, then we don't need to walk through the Texas fan plaza and sample some BBQ on our way to Mom?" she countered.

"Well, that would just be rude," Ben grinned. "I have to try the local cuisine or I might offend someone. Are you thinking brisket?"

Avery's stomach churned. She was way too nervous about the race to eat. "Um, I'm good for now. Let's go get in the AC at the club."

"Well, you look absolutely perfect," her mom said approvingly, after looking up and down at Avery's floral printed midi-dress with side cutouts at her ribs. She'd accessorized with ankle-height cowboy boots and large hoop earrings, a big departure from her usual low-key race-day look. *Mom will parade me around, no doubt. At least I can dress the part.* She felt more pressure than usual to be the flawless daughter, showing nothing but appreciation for her charmed life.

On top of that, she now had to play the part of the smitten girlfriend. Which, to be honest, wasn't much of a stretch. She was, in fact, halfway to smitten. Mentally, she was with Teddy in the garage, even if she was watching from her seats above pit lane. How was she going to make it through the day serving as assistant hostess to her mom when she felt out-of-sorts?

"Avery, come say hello," her mother instructed, turning to

her older sister, Avery's aunt, who had come in from California for the race.

"Hi, Aunt Mel, how are you?" Avery put on her best hostess smile, and leaned in for a hug and kiss. She tried to wipe her cheek as subtly as she could, hoping her aunt's magenta lipstick hadn't left a smudge on her cheek.

"Well, you know with the twin's senior year it has been busy, busy, busy..." Avery pretended to listen to stories of SAT scores, reach schools and safety schools, but her mind wandered back to Teddy.

Normally, she'd be the first one to remember to ask about her cousins' college applications. But all she could think about was how Teddy was. Was he feeling confident and energized? Nervous or anxious? Was he warming up with Stacey already? Or getting last instructions from Brandon, the team principal? Had the team told him to go for a win or to play a supporting role for Zack?

She "mm hmmd" and nodded as appropriate for what felt like an eternity, until she freed herself from the conversation. She spotted Ben and Adam at the bar. How had they managed to escape the small talk? *Not fair*.

Ben waved her over with a mischievous glint in his eyes.

"Okay," Ben whispered. "Game time. How many people in this room are on Ozempic, if you had to guess?"

"More than half, for sure, but I really can't just stand around figuring out who is taking skinny shots. This race is actually a big deal to me, whether you care or not," Avery sounded harsh to her own ears.

"Woah, okay," Ben put his hands up in a defensive position and took a step back. "I guess there will be no joking with my baby sister today.

She regretted it immediately. Ben didn't know how tired, truly exhausted, she felt from constantly switching modes, and playing all her different roles. When she was with Teddy, she was pretending she wasn't falling for him, which was hard enough. And then when she wasn't with him, she was pretending they were in a completely normal relationship. It was all starting to make her head spin.

"Sorry, it's not your fault I'm on edge. I'm so nervous for the race, and for Teddy. And you know that being around mom doesn't always bring out my best," she admitted. It was a partial truth at least.

"Sounds like you need a mimosa. Come on, my treat," Adam joked, gesturing to the open bar. Ben had come out to his family when he was fifteen and ever since, though no one had said it out loud, Avery thought that her parents had given Ben a pass on conforming to society's expectations. Conversely, the pressure for Avery to assume the traditional life of marriage and kids had ramped up over time. The irony was that Ben and Adam had married young and Ben adored being a stay-at-home dad, while Avery was the one focused on her career and carrying on the family business.

"You are correct, thank you," Avery said. Adam handed her the drink and she took a huge gulp, nearly draining the glass in one sip.

"That bad, huh? I thought you'd be floating around on cloud nine now that you're in love," Adam teased.

Here we go, time to convince Ben and Adam that I'm really dating Teddy. As much as she wanted to be honest with Ben and Adam, she didn't trust Ben not to blab to their mom. They had always been close. *Closer than she and I have ever been.*

"You have no idea. Dating a Formula One driver is like

being under a microscope, and I thought being a Silver was a lot of pressure," Avery explained. "I'm really glad you guys are here. I've missed you." It was true, she had missed them the last few weeks, and also she wanted to move the conversation to safer territory.

Avery's phone buzzed in her pocket. "Who would call me right now?" she asked aloud in disbelief.

Adam and Ben exchanged bewildered looks and shrugged, agreeing that it was a weird time for anyone to reach out to them. Their entire circle knew that they'd be totally immersed in the race today.

She looked down at the caller ID. "It's my contact at the gala venue, I really should take this. Excuse me." She walked out of the suite and slipped into a hallway bathroom to take the call in private. Her heart started beating faster. *This can't be good. Why would the hotel's GM call me on a weekend?*

"Hello. This is Avery," her voice quivered along with her nerves.

"Avery, it's Sofia with The Monarch Downtown LA," her voice sounded serious. "I'm sorry to bother you on a Sunday. I'm afraid I have some bad news for you. I did a walk-through of the property with our builder, and construction is very behind schedule."

Avery's hands were full-on shaking now, she could barely keep the phone held up to her ear, dreading whatever it was she was about to say next.

"I still think we will probably be open in time for your event in December, but I can't guarantee it. I wanted to let you know as soon as possible so you can look at back-up options."

Avery felt her breath catch in her throat. She knew she should be pushy here, take a tough stance, and demand that they speed up the process, but her shock rendered her speechless.

"Of course, if you want to cancel and get your deposit back now, we can do that. Or, we can hold onto it and see how things go the next few weeks."

"I appreciate the call, and your transparency. Please keep me updated on the progress," she said, finally finding her voice. She felt dizzy, unable to take charge and make a decision about the deposit on the spot.

Avery ended the call and stood frozen at the bathroom counter. This was really bad news on multiple fronts. How would she find somewhere available on a Saturday night in the height of holiday party season? It was already September, everything was probably already booked.

There was nothing she could do about it right this second. Right now, she had to go back into the suite, smile and cheer, and pretend some more. She splashed some cold water on her face, patted it dry, and looked in the mirror.

"You can do this, Avery." She assumed her favorite power pose, the Superwoman, placing her hands on her hips and puffing out her chest. "This is supposed to be fun. Be in the present. Focus on being Teddy's girlfriend and a Silver daughter today. Monday you will get to work on finding that venue."

"Where have you been??" her mother scolded her as soon as she re-entered the club.

"I had to take a work call." Avery tried not to let her annoyance show on her face.

"On a Sunday? When we are entertaining? Really, Avery?" Sharon shook her head, giving Avery a look that would be a frown, if she didn't have so much botox immobilizing her face.

"Yes, Mom. Really. It was important." *Obviously. Or I wouldn't have taken the call.*

"Nothing is as important as time with your family. And what about, Teddy? I'm sure he's counting on your support today," Sharon nagged her daughter.

And then it dawned on her. Her mom. She'd be able to help find a back-up venue; Sharon had chaired so many events in LA that she knew every catering manager at every hotel. She was going to have to suck it up and ask her mom to pull some strings and find a back-up venue. All she had wanted was to prove she could handle a project of this magnitude on her own, and now she'd have to go to the last person in the world she wanted helping her.

A tension headache was building at the base of her neck, but there was nothing she could do to relieve it right now with the race about to start. She would have to wait and have that unpleasant conversation with her mom once she'd flown back to LA.

"Yes, well in that case, we should probably go watch the race." Avery kept her cool and gave her mom a sweet smile, but inside she was seething. Yes, she did genuinely want to watch Teddy and cheer for him, but why couldn't her mom understand that her work was also important to her?

seventeen

AUSTIN, TX

Avery and her mom joined her dad, Ben, and Adam standing up against the plexiglass railing at the edge of the balcony. Below them the pit lane, where the drivers would pull in for new tires during the race, was empty.

Avery's heart pounded as all twenty cars made their way around the track, zig-zagging back and forth to heat up their tires during their formation, or warm-up, lap before the lights went out. The start was crucial for the Silver team. Zack was starting in P2, the front row. If he had a faster reaction than the Ferrari driver in P1 when the starting lights went out, he had a shot at getting out in front and taking the lead from the get-go. And Teddy would be right behind him in P4, battling driver Andre Tiago, who was driving for Golden Phoenix, in the second row. It was the best chance their team had had all season at getting two drivers on the podium.

The contest between Teddy and Tiago was especially poignant, as he was the other candidate Michael had considered before hiring Teddy. She looked over at her dad, who was looking nervously down the track through his binoculars and gave him a confident thumbs up. Michael had more at stake than anyone. He'd taken a calculated risk making Teddy the second driver on the team over Tiago, a former world champion at the end of his career. She recalled their conversations about it nearly a year ago.

The old champ would have been the safe choice, but Michael wanted to build for the future. Teddy had shown promise during his rookie season on Alpha Fuerte, but they had one of the slowest cars on the track, so no one had seen what Teddy was truly capable of. Avery had encouraged her dad to go with the seasoned veteran driver at the time, but now she couldn't imagine what this year would have been like if her dad had listened to her.

The crowd stood in excitement as the race started. Zack had an unbelievable reaction time at the start and pulled out ahead of the Ferrari. Avery's family erupted into cheers, her dad pumping his fist in the air. But Avery couldn't take her eyes off Teddy's car. She couldn't quite make out the tartan on his helmet, but she was glued to the bright blue Silver in the second row. He didn't overtake the Golden Phoenix in the run up the steep hill or on the first turn, but he managed to hold off the cars behind him and maintain his fourth-place position. She breathed a short-lived sigh of relief, her headache momentarily releasing its grip on her skull. *Solid start.* Now they would have to settle in and let things unfold. It would be a long race ahead. Anything could happen over the course of fifty-six laps.

Ben leaned over and gave her a high five. "Your boy is doing good," he said, his eyes twinkling.

Avery smiled, but her ribs clenched. She felt like a part of her own body was squeezed into the tiny driver's cockpit with Teddy as his car spun around the track at a nauseating two-hundred miles per hour. There was no way she could relax until the chequered flag waved.

The next ten laps or so went by without incident, her heart and head pounding all the while. A few cars in the middle of the pack battled wheel-to-wheel to break into the top ten, which would earn them points toward the end-of-year championship, but both Silvers maintained their positions.

Eventually, Avery settled into the rhythm of the race. Every sixty seconds or so the crowd would stand up and look right as the cars rounded the corner and came into view, and then ping pong left as they whizzed by, leaving smoke and sparks in their wake. Avery held her breath every single time until Teddy was out of view again, leaving her momentarily dizzy. She had just enough time to recover before the cycle repeated itself over and over again.

Without the excitement of a crash or a ton of passing, the attention of the less committed fans started to waiver. Sharon abandoned her post at the front of the balcony and went back inside for refreshments. But Avery stayed put next to her dad and brother, not daring to move an inch, watching intently for Teddy's bright blue Silver to come into view with each lap.

On lap twenty-two, she saw Teddy's car slow down and pull into the pit lane. Her head whipped over to her dad–had this been the original strategy? *Or is something going on in the garage I don't know about?* Coming in early for a fresh set of tires to try and gain on the third-place car in front of him was a gamble. She wondered who had made the call—hopefully, Teddy thought the undercut was the right one. If only she had been able to hear the radio conversation between Teddy and his race engineer.

Less than three seconds later, the pit crew had completed their task.

"Was that early pit stop Plan A?" she whispered anxiously to her dad.

"I think so. Don't fret. The strategy team knows what they are doing," Michael answered confidently, even though a small frown tugged at the corners of his mouth.

Avery didn't feel nearly as certain as her dad pretended he was. She wished she could send Teddy some sort of signal to let him know she was right there with him, breathing the same air. She sent some good vibes his way through the atmosphere.

With each lap, Teddy got a bit closer to Tiago, who was now only ten seconds in front of him, slowly but surely closing the gap. Would Teddy be able to catch him on fresher tires? Avery could barely contain the butterflies in her stomach, which seemed to be growing restless, ready to take flight and follow the cars out onto the circuit.

The Golden Phoenix team must also have been getting nervous about Teddy gaining as they called their car into the pit for a fresh set of tires in order to keep up with Teddy's fast pace. Would their pit stop be fast enough for the car to exit the pit lane in front of Teddy? Or would Teddy be able to move ahead of him?

Avery was on her feet again, her body positively buzzing.

"Come on Teddy!" her dad hollered, pumping his fists.

Avery grabbed onto her dad's arm and squeezed it hard as

she saw the Golden Phoenix pit crew struggle for a split second with one of the old tires before it came loose. Every tenth of a second mattered. Her heart palpitated. The tiny delay might just be enough to put Teddy in front.

"Go, go, go," she yelled, her heart racing now, digging her nails harder into her dad's arm as the Golden Phoenix raced to the pit lane exit in a last attempt to make up for the lost second.

But it was too little, too late. Teddy had gone all out, pushing his car to the maximum speed. He tore by, the Golden Phoenix car pulling back out on the track behind him.

"Woooo! Yes!" *He did it. The gamble had paid off, Teddy had executed the strategy perfectly!* Adrenaline rushed through her body. She jumped up and down, screaming with abandon.

"Let's go!" Ben leaned over and gave her another high-five.

Her dad nodded and clapped along, the frown from earlier replaced by a cautiously optimistic smile while he rubbed the red mark she'd left on his arm from squeezing him.

The second half of the race felt like both the shortest and longest forty minutes of Avery's life, her pulse racing as she anxiously continued to watch to see if Teddy could maintain his now third place position. She made some small talk and accepted compliments on the maneuver on Teddy's behalf, but it was all a blur as she knew the podium position could be snatched away any second.

What felt like both a lifetime and only seconds later, her mom was elbowing her. "Avery, Teddy is about to get his first podium. Don't you want to be down with the team so you can congratulate him right away?"

Of course, I should have thought of that.

For once, her mom's pushiness was coming in handy. The press and the fans would definitely expect that his girlfriend would be trackside to congratulate him. But the authenticity of their relationship felt irrelevant at the moment. She had to be there to see him cross the finish line, appearances were completely unrelated to her wild, jumping heart.

"Yes. Mom, you're right!" she squealed. She couldn't wait to see Teddy when he got out of the car. His first podium finish! *Incredible.*

Avery flew down the stairs to line up beside the track with the team. The atmosphere was positively electric.

She'd been so wrapped up in Teddy's race that she'd nearly forgotten that Zack was about to win the whole damn thing. She clapped her hands high above her head as Zack crossed the finish line and jumped victoriously onto the hood of his car, waving to the crowd. The crowd and the team roared back, the jubilant sounds deafening.

But Zack was merely a sideshow, a momentary distraction, from the true object of her focus. She only had eyes for the driver who pulled up seconds later in the third-place spot. Teddy's helmet and fireproof balaclava made it impossible for Avery to read his expression, but he pumped his fists and slapped the front wing of his car as he hopped out.

Teddy went to his teammate first and clapped Zack on the back. Zack turned around to embrace him. Avery felt tears well in the corner of her eyes. Many teams in the sport dealt with rivalries between their drivers, but Teddy and Zack had not only avoided conflict so far, they were becoming friends.

Teddy then quickly turned his attention to the line of staff and guests who were still clapping. He made his way down the row, embracing his coworkers and giving high fives, Avery's heart beating wildly as she waited for him to get to her. As soon as he did, he reached over the barrier and embraced her, literally sweeping her off her feet as he lifted her a few inches off the ground. Avery felt weightless in his arms, like she was floating above the ground.

"You did it! Your first podium finish!" Avery beamed at him.

Teddy looked like he was positively glowing, that real, eye-crinkling smile making its appearance on his face. Her heart swelled knowing she was probably one of only a few people who knew the difference between his two smiles.

"Don't go anywhere. I'll be right back," he said quickly as her feet touched the ground again.

She watched adoringly as Teddy and Stacey had their moment and Teddy gave a few more hugs to his crew. Avery loved seeing him triumphant like this, basking in the glory of his success. Finally, he got to the end of the row of handshakes and hugs and as soon as he could, he ripped off his helmet and pulled down his mask covering, revealing his gorgeous face underneath, his hair and eyes shining with sweat and tears.

As soon as he made the rounds, he trotted back to Avery. They made joyful, deep eye contact as he approached, her whole body was shaking with anticipation. She was giddy for him. *Him, Teddy, the real Teddy who had earned this moment through blood, sweat, and tears.*

She gazed up at his face towering over hers and reached her arms up behind his neck. She ran her fingers through the flippy ends of his hair, briefly massaging the back of his neck beneath. His hands came to her waist and he pulled her flush against his chest. She was hyper-aware of every inch where their body touched.

The gold in his eyes danced at her and then his lips were on hers, hot and forceful. She could taste the salt from his skin, feel the heat of his flushed cheeks. *Finally.* The tension she'd felt all day, for weeks, really, melted from her body as she kissed him back. She pressed into his mouth, trying to infuse her lips with all she wanted to say out loud. *I like you for real. Let's not pretend anymore.*

The world around them fell away for a moment. Avery barely registered the clicks and flashes, not caring how many cameras had captured their moment or how she looked. Breathless, she came up for air and Teddy touched his forehead to hers. The energy of the moment and the kiss buzzed back and forth between them, and Avery could feel their connection vibrating through her body.

"I'm so proud of you!" she murmured.

"Thank you," he whispered back.

She brought her finger to his supple bottom lip, tracing the white scar there. She felt him exhale deeply into her hand.

"Ahem, Teddy, mate, sorry to interrupt, but you've got to actually go collect your trophy." James poked Teddy awkwardly on the shoulder.

Teddy shook his head, "Right."

He reached out and cupped her face and pressed his lips to hers one more time, quickly. It took every morsel of self-control in her body not to grab him around the waist and pull him toward her, give in to the way her body was screaming for more, more, more.

"Go," she breathed in his ear. "I'll be here watching."

Avery's heart drummed loudly in her chest as she watched her dad, Zack, and Teddy up on stage. She would never, ever forget this moment: the roar of the crowd as Matthew McConaughey handed trophies to Teddy, then Andre, and finally Zack; the mix of sunscreen, sweat, and rubber filling her nose. She swore she could hear the splash as the drivers doused each other in champagne. She watched Teddy tip his face up toward the sky as Zack drenched him, droplets cascading off his baseball cap and race suit. She followed his gaze, noticing for the first time how bright and blue the sky was today, like a cornflower blue Crayola crayon. Not a cloud in the sky.

eighteen

AUSTIN, TX

Avery leaned back into Teddy's arms, the vibe of his burnt orange Longhorn t-shirt and jeans so different than his usual polished appearance. Bistro lights twinkled overhead, casting a glowy light. She could see the glimmer of Lake Austin beyond the musician playing on a makeshift stage. It hadn't taken much convincing for Avery to join Teddy at a post-race party at the sprawling waterfront home on Lake Austin that Cody, the Archer driver Josh worked with, rented for the week. There were two full weeks until the next race in Mexico City, and most of the drivers were taking advantage of the time off by extending their stays in Austin for a few days.

She looked around the patio, trying to soak up the euphoric atmosphere. They were all young, at the top of their sport, and money was no object. The privilege that came with the moment was not lost on her. She felt like the luckiest girl in the world, cuddled up with Teddy, surrounded by friends.

She nuzzled his neck, taking in a deep breath of his woodsy scent, which had quickly become her favorite smell in the world.

Despite the fact that it was nearly a perfect night; she couldn't entirely escape the nagging thought she hadn't *earned* her place in this crowd, that it had been handed to her on a silver (pun intended) platter. *One day, I'll be at a party like this not as someone's daughter or as someone's date, but because of what I've accomplished too.* It wasn't that she couldn't appreciate her good fortune. She was well aware that most people would kill to be in her position.

She closed her eyes and let the music wash over her, the sound of the cowboy-hat-wearing guitar player serenading them with his deep Texas drawl. *Stay in the present, Avery. Just relax and enjoy the company of your best friends and your... boyfriend?* No, certainly Teddy wasn't her actual boyfriend, but they weren't just friends who were faking it anymore. The sparks she'd felt during their kiss had confirmed that. It felt like all the fake dates, the fun, the flirting, had all led to this inevitable night.

Avery looked over to her side where Stacey was relaxing on a lounge chair and made eye contact. Stacey gave her a knowing look.

The musician finished his song and the small crowd erupted in a round of applause. Cody, who had quickly earned a reputation as the biggest partier among the drivers, joined the musicians on the porch. "Thank y'all for being here tonight, to celebrate my first home race. Driving in F1 is a dream come true, even when you end the weekend out of the points. How about a round of applause for Zack and Teddy for that awesome team performance today?" He paused for another round of applause and a few whistles. "Have fun, stay as late as you like, and I'll see y'all in Mexico City."

"I'm going to grab another beer, do either of you want anything?" Stacey asked.

"I'm good, thanks!" Avery said. She turned her head and asked Teddy. "Want anything?

"Sex." He whispered into her ear, so that no one around them could hear.

Avery's mind went blank as her brain tried to process what it heard. But her body was already there—heat instantly building in her core. She whipped her head around to face him head on, her lips parted, trying to form a response.

"Um, with you, in case that wasn't clear," he grinned mischievously, but his eyes were smoldering. She hadn't been imagining things. The weeks-long flirtation wasn't just for the cameras, the celebration kiss that afternoon wasn't a one-time victory celebration. *Am I ready for this?*

His eyes were fixed on her, waiting on her response, but her breath caught in her throat. Her body craved him and wanted nothing more than to give itself to him, but her mind had not only caught up, it had raced five steps ahead. What would happen after they hooked up? Was it a one-time thing for him while he was riding the high of his successful race? Or would it be the start of something else entirely?

Shh, brain, just stop. The heat that was flooding her body was desperately trying to burn away any rational thought.

"I'm game," Avery dared him back, sounding cool and confident. Inside, however, she was nearly bursting with both desire and apprehension. She wanted Teddy more than she had ever wanted a man before, but what would he think of her in bed? Surely, he had been with tons of women: would she be able to satisfy him with her limited experience to draw from?

Avery looked around self-consciously out of habit to see if anyone was watching (they weren't), and then remembered that everyone here thought they were already dating. Walking out of the party together wouldn't raise any eyebrows.

He pulled her to her feet and put his hand on the small of her back, guiding her back through the house and out front where their town car was waiting. She felt her confidence waning. What underwear was she wearing? How would her undressed body compare to the models and starlets he'd been with?

The ride back to the hotel was one of the most exciting of Avery's life. They sat dangerously close to one another in the back seat, their thighs touching like they had that first night they had talked in the hotel bar. She lifted the pointed toe of her boot and rubbed it up the back of his calf. He shivered and snaked his arm all the way around her waist in response. She scooted even closer to him, putting her arm around his neck and giving him a light shoulder rub. Everything about their bodies touching felt right, and Avery enjoyed the tingling sensation she could feel through her dress where his hand touched her hip.

They were silent, shooting coy glances at each other until their car pulled up at the swanky downtown hotel. Teddy held the door open for her as she stepped out, and grabbed her hand. They walked hand in hand, and Avery couldn't help but giggle as she led him straight to the elevators.

With a surprisingly shy smile, Teddy looked at Avery questioningly as he pushed the button for his floor only. She nodded in agreement. *This is really happening.* They couldn't keep their hands off each other as they rode the elevator up to the eleventh floor. Teddy kneaded her side above her hip bone as she traced her fingers up and down his back. They stole glances that smoldered as they ascended, a visual confirmation to go along with the physical that this was really happening. That neither one was backing out. Once the elevator doors opened, Teddy reached for his key card and buzzed open the door to his suite. The second the door clicked shut, Avery found herself with her back against the wall, Teddy gazing down at her with heat in his eyes.

"A proper kiss, I've wanted to do this for weeks," he said happily. His mouth was on hers, firm and commanding. Avery kissed him back deeply, urging him on.

She playfully bit his lower lip, and pushed him away from her, away from the wall, and toward the bed. Teddy nearly groaned with want and sat back on the bed, pulling her toward him. Avery straddled him, her dress bunching up over her thighs.

She put her arms around his thick neck and kissed him again, hungrily. His hands slid up and down her exposed thighs, higher and higher until he slipped a finger under her lace underwear. She trembled with excitement and want. She'd felt what those fingers could do to a car's steering wheel, and now she'd get to see what they were capable of doing to her body.

nineteen

AUSTIN, TX

The cool satin sheets tickled Avery's bare skin. *What time was it?* She rolled over to look at the clock and saw Teddy's bright red phone case plugged in on the nightstand next to hers. She turned to her other side to make sure her eyes weren't deceiving her in the dim early morning night. Yep, there he was, sleeping peacefully with his shirt off and the sheet draped right over his navel. He was laying on his back with his hands above his head giving her a perfect view of his well-defined pecs and sculpted abs. Her body flushed remembering the way it had felt to rub her palms over those abs.

Sex with Teddy had been different than it had been with Josh, or with the two other guys she'd slept with. Better, sure, but also different, like they'd been in a technicolor dreamland. Maybe it was the high of the race day, podium finish, the relief that flooded her when she realized he wanted her in that way too. But maybe not.

Teddy's hair had become mussed during sleep (and the romp that preceded it), chocolate brown pieces sticking up every which way. The sweet boyishness of it made her nearly weak in the knees. She wanted to run her hands through it, wake him up, and kiss the soft lips that she could see were slightly open and shaped into a partial smile, run her finger over that little scar again. But he looked so incredibly peaceful, so she quietly slipped out of bed.

She got her phone and went to the bathroom where she eased into the fluffy hotel robe. Should she go hang out in the seating area/living space in his suite and wait for him to wake up? Take the walk of shame down the hallway to her own room and brush her teeth and attempt to freshen up? She didn't have much experience to draw from. One-night stands were certainly not her thing, and the last time she had stayed over somewhere unexpectedly after a hook-up was Josh's dorm room in college, when a walk of shame was also a badge of honor.

She glanced at her phone and saw she had three texts from Stacey.

11 p.m.

> Where are you?? Did you and Teddy ghost??

12 a.m.

> You aren't answering. I'm assuming you and Teddy?!?!

7 a.m.

> Let me know you're alive and well when you can?

Maybe she should go in the other room and call Stacey to let her know she was okay? Before she could make up her mind, there was a light knock on the bathroom door.

"Avery?" Teddy's voice sounded a little gravely.

"One second," She quickly typed out a reply to Stacey.

I'm alive. Can't talk. STILL WITH TEDDY.

"Hi," Avery opened the door and took in his tall, toned body. He'd put his boxer shorts back on, but his broad shoulders and smooth, bare chest were hers to ogle. And ogle she did.

"Good morning," he said tenderly. "Checking me out?" He held his arms so that he was holding onto the top of the door frame, his biceps flexing.

Her cheeks heated. "Good morning to you too. Maybe."

She smoothed down her hair and retied the robe's belt tighter around her waist. She found his bed head endearing and his naked torso utterly drool-worthy, but doubted that her crazy, frizzy curls, after the night they'd had, would have the same effect. Would he regret what happened between them in the light of day?

"You weren't planning an escape were you?" he asked, offering her a bemused smile.

"No, I didn't want to wake you," Avery said, giving him a half truth. No need to let him know that she was, in fact, considering fleeing to her own room before he'd woken up.

"Good, because I haven't gotten my fill of you yet," he grinned. "Do you have plans with your family today? I don't leave until tomorrow, so I have the whole day free. And I plan to enjoy Austin like a proper tourist. Want to join me? Breakfast tacos? Paddle boarding? Shopping for the most obnoxious cowboy hats we can find?"

"Seriously, that sounds amazing. I wish I could, but I have so much work to do. And I should probably go do something about this," she said, pointing to her hair as she squinted her eyes shut.

"First of all, I like to see your hair like that. It's sexy. If a woman didn't have a hair out of place after a night with me, I'd consider myself a failed lover...and second of all, I never get a day off like this, and it would be so much more fun with you. Please? Don't make me beg, Avery Silver," he clasped his hands together in front of his chest and gave her puppy dog eyes.

Avery felt her will bending. On one hand, she really did need to put her head down and get the gala back on track. But on the other, she didn't want last night's magic to end, just yet. She sighed audibly.

"Come on, matching cowboy hats make for great couple-y photos. I'll sign one and announce that I'm going to donate custom leather boots along with the signed hat for auction at the gala," Teddy offered.

Avery's heart sank. *We're back to hang outs manufactured for publicity already? After the night we've had?* She tried to hide her disappointment, hoping that her face hadn't fallen as quickly as her heart had. Maybe for Teddy the spell had already been broken, and they were back to their regularly scheduled photo-ops. Maybe for him, it had all been tangled together - the rush of the podium, the banner day, and now the day was behind them. On the other hand, the way he gently bit his lip as he awaited her answer suggested he might genuinely want to spend time with her.

Regardless, she knew he was right, photos of them galli-vanting around town in hats and boots, plus announcing their first auction item was probably exactly what she needed to get the event some much needed buzz.

"I'll go get ready."

* * *

Two hours later, Avery and Teddy were window shopping hand-in-hand on South Congress in the center of Austin, passing the eclectic mix of funky local stores and chic big-name brands. It was another bright sunny day without a cloud in the sky. Even though it was September, there was no fall feeling in the air, the high temp was going to be ninety. After a quick shower and swipe of lipstick, Avery had thrown on jean shorts and a white ribbed tank in an effort to dress for the weather.

"That has to be our first stop," Teddy pointed to a store with a giant cowboy boot in front. The smell of leather overpowered Avery once they walked inside. She took a sniff and sneezed as dust was blown around by a large overhead fan. How long had some of these boots been sitting on the shelves? Rows and rows of them in every color imaginable, some with fringe, others with patterns stitched, seemed to stretch on forever.

"Yes!" said Teddy, pulling down a completely turquoise pair of women's boots. "What size are you?"

"Ha! There's no way I'm getting those. I could never pull them off."

"Suit yourself," Teddy shrugged and put them back on the shelf.

He slid out of his own sneakers and tried on a pair with fringe. "How do I look?"

He stuck his foot out, and shimmied so the fringe moved a bit.

"Ridiculous," Avery teased. *Ridiculously hot, even when you're being silly.* She wanted to admit it out loud to him, to tell him how much she liked spending time with him, how great last night had been for her, but her stomach quivered at the thought.

It is way too soon to have that conversation. It had been twelve hours since their hook-up and any normal guy would run for the hills if a girl tried to define things that quickly. *And, he already flat-out told me he didn't have time for a girlfriend.*

"Well, if the lady doesn't like them on me," Teddy said, making a sad puppy face as he took the goofy boots off and put them back on the shelf.

It took a minute for him to retie his own sneakers. They looked stiff, fresh out of the box. Avery recognized the logo from another driver's collab with a shoe brand. Super nice of him to wear them and show support for his fellow driver's projects off the circuit. *Le sigh, he is too nice. And making it too easy for me to fall for him.*

"Maybe we will have more luck with hats?" Teddy suggested. "Let's go find one for me to sign for the auction."

They walked to the hat section of the store and settled on a classic light-colored Stetson so that Teddy's signature would really pop. Avery watched appreciatively as Teddy paid.

They ambled back out onto the busy street and Avery squinted, the bright sunlight was disorienting after the dim lighting inside the western store. It took a second for both their eyes to adjust.

"Where to next?" Teddy asked eagerly, putting his sunglasses on.

"How about I get some pics of you in that hat in front of the 'I love you so much' mural?" Avery asked, feeling inspired.

Teddy froze, looking like a deer caught in the headlights, "I love you so much mural? What on earth is that?"

Her breath caught as she felt a painful stab in her chest. If merely hearing the word love sent him running for the hills, it was definitely too soon to tell him she was falling for him. Uncertainty wasn't easy for her. Avery always liked to know where things were headed. From the lost expression on his face, his hazel eyes avoiding her gaze, she needed to do some damage control and fast, before he spiraled any further.

"You've never seen a picture of someone posed in front of Austin's famous 'I love you so much mural'?" Avery asked, trying to return to their easy banter. "My friends all seem to think if you don't post a picture in front of that mural, it's like your trip didn't even happen. It's a tourist right-of-passage here."

Teddy looked at her, still confused. "Nope."

"I'll show you. Come on, it's right down the street next to Jo's Coffee." She grabbed his hand and practically dragged him down the block.

"See that line of people waiting for their turn?" She pointed to the line forming down the block. "They are all waiting for their turn to take a photo with it." *See, I'm not a psycho trying to say I love you after we've had sex one time—it's actually a thing.* "I'll post it on the foundation's page announcing the auction item. It'll be perfect."

He nodded, reluctantly. "If it's for the kids."

Ouch. The words stung even if he'd said them with the best intentions.

He followed her down the street where they joined the line for their turn for a photo-op. When they got to the front, Teddy awkwardly stood in front of the green and red mural, trying to get the large cowboy hat, that was slipping down on his fore-head, to stay high up.

"What should I do with my arms?" he asked Avery, once he stopped fidgeting with the hat.

Avery was surprised to see this small amount of discomfort while he posed for her. For once, his effortless cool didn't look quite so effortless.

"Put your hands in your pockets with your elbows out a bit. Classic American cowboy pose," she directed.

Teddy did as he was told and then looked at her expectantly, a slight wrinkle forming between his eyebrows.

"Loving it, loving it." She tilted her head and smiled, trying to put him at ease. "Okay now try pulling it down over your eyes a bit and leaving it there. Perfect, Jesse James vibes," she said, having fun with her director role-play. She saw him suppress a smile as he brooded for the camera. She felt relieved as the awkwardness dissipated. She wasn't sure how much longer she could have stomached any discomfort between them.

"Got what I need. You're free," Avery said, releasing him from his modeling duties.

He winked at her, or maybe it was for the camera, and stopped trying to hide his smile, his eyes crinkling.

They moved away from the mural to let the next group in line get their turn. They stood on the street corner facing Amy's Ice Creams. Teddy looked at her expectantly, head tilted, as if waiting for her to decide what was next.

"So, um, thanks again for the auction item," she said, not wanting to make room for any love mural awkwardness to slip back in.

"Of course," he answered.

He paused again and rubbed the back of his neck. This was

her opening if she was going to tell him how she felt, but she couldn't bring herself to do it. He was blinking a bit more than seemed natural.

She bit the side of her cheek, the discomfort forcing her to let the moment pass. She definitely didn't want to say something she'd regret later.

"So, I was wondering," Teddy broke the silence, as he rocked back on his heels. "If you'd want to come on a semi-vacation with me this week? To Mayakoba? Near Cancun?"

Whoa. She had to make an effort to keep her jaw from dropping to the floor, or her eyes from bugging out of her head. The invitation was completely out of left field.

"Really?" she couldn't quite believe it. *A vacation. With Teddy.*

"Really," he confirmed. "It doesn't make sense for me to fly back and forth to Europe before the Mexico Grand Prix. Stacey and James will be there too, so we can get some work in, but there will also be plenty of R&R baked into the schedule. What do you say?" Teddy raised his eyebrows and looked at her expectantly.

I should say no.

She opened her mouth. Closed it.

I have a ton of work to do, and I don't have a bathing suit with me.

The list of reasons that this was a bad idea was exponentially long - her obligations, the logistics, the uncertainty of their relationship status. But, damn, the thought of Teddy shirtless in a hot tub beckoning her to join him, the sun setting over the ocean behind him was clouding her judgment. She'd always done the responsible thing. She'd never once failed to show-up for a family event, or turned in an assignment late in college.

Maybe just this once she could do the irresponsible, exhilarating thing. Make the choice a socialite could make. *Jet off into the sunset with my race-car driving love interest, consequences be damned.*

"Yes, I'm in. I'd love to join you," she said the words quickly, before she could talk herself out of it.

twenty

MAYAKOBA, MEXICO

Avery's bare thighs stuck to the electric boat's vinyl seat in the humidity. She smelled the salt wafting off the ocean and heard the palm fronds swaying in the light breeze as the boat quietly glided down the emerald lagoon, bringing Avery, Teddy, Stacey, and James to the private villa they would call home for the next week. Teddy's sinewy arm was hooked over the back of the bench behind her. She looked up and saw that his eyes were at half-mast. Good. He deserved the brief respite from the F1 circus. *And so do I.* Avery took a slow, easy breath. *I feel lighter already.*

The boat came to a stop at a polished wooden dock that gleamed in the sunshine.

"Welcome to paradise," a uniformed butler announced as he helped Avery off the boat and onto the dock. Teddy followed behind her, his white linen shirt still looking fresh and unwrinkled despite a two-hour flight.

James, next to disembark, whistled as he lifted his sunglasses on top of his head and looked admiringly at their pristine pool deck. "Not too shabby. This will definitely do for a few days." He held out his fist to give Stacy a fist bump as she hopped off the boat onto the dock with her usual pep, her blonde hair pulled up into a high ponytail.

"If you'll follow me," the butler gestured to the villa looming ahead, past the sparkling pool, row of four lounge chairs outfitted with sumptuous pool towels, and an ice bucket containing topo chicos and cervezas ready to be enjoyed.

All of her family vacations had basically been a variation on this theme: tropical beach, private villa, staff to attend to your every need. But as she looked around at her travel companions, Avery realized that they weren't jaded like her, and were very much impressed by the set-up. She swallowed away the speck of guilt she felt in her throat about how she grew up compared to her travel companions.

The four of them followed the butler into an expansive kitchen and dining area.

"Chef Matteo prepared his signature guacamole along with ceviche. Please enjoy while we bring in the luggage."

Avery wasted no time, helping herself to a healthy serving of ceviche on a fresh tortilla chip. The fresh fish, tangy citrus, and salt tasted like heaven. Like vacation.

"Excuse me, which bags would you like in which bedroom?" the butler asked, re-entering the kitchen with a rolling luggage cart.

Avery coughed in surprise, nearly choking on a chip. She'd been so wrapped up in Teddy, and then in rearranging her travel plans to come on this trip that bedroom arrangements hadn't even crossed her mind.

Stacey knew they'd spent the night together after Cody's party. But, James, on the other hand, was still in the dark.

Sweat pooled at the base of her spine. Would Teddy want James to know they had hooked up?

Does Teddy want to share a room with me?

She kicked herself for not thinking about this earlier.

Avery looked over at Teddy, her eyes wide. It was his call, since he was the one footing the bill for the week.

"I'll take the primary suite downstairs. You can put my black suitcase in there," Teddy said authoritatively. "The blue one can go in the other bedroom down here on this floor and the rest go upstairs."

The "blue one" was hers.

Avery felt her heart shrink two sizes, but tried not to let it show on her face.

So, we won't share a room. Maybe the other night was a one-time thing for him? Or maybe he's worried about what James will think? Or maybe he figured I needed some private space to work in during the week? I did tell him I was going to work remotely while we're here.

Or maybe there isn't much closet space in the primary suite?

Well, that last one is a stretch.

He had put her in the room next to his, a whole flight of stairs away from James' and Stacey's upstairs. *That has to count for something.* Perhaps the proximity was so that they could easily have a discreet late-night rendezvous.

"I'm going upstairs to claim the best room, sorry not sorry James, and change into my swimsuit while you guys stuff your faces like you've never seen an avocado before," Stacey teased.

Avery shrugged. Teddy looked up at his trainer from where

he was hovering over the guacamole bowl, like a school boy who had been caught with his hand in the cookie jar.

He scratched his face. "Guilty as charged."

There was a chip crumb on the corner of Teddy's bottom lip, right next to his scar. She resisted the urge to go over and wipe it away with her thumb, or better yet, wipe it away with her tongue.

"Teddy, only a couple more of those," Stacey wagged her finger at him. "We can go over the work-out and nutrition plan for the week after dinner tonight. Don't worry I've accounted for a couple of cheat meals."

"You got it, coach," he nodded. "Ok, team, you heard the woman. This afternoon is for relaxation. Bathing suits on. I want to check out the beach club."

"Good call. I hear it's insane," James said and he trotted up the stairs after Stacey, leaving Avery alone with Teddy in the kitchen.

She *could* try to have a conversation with Teddy now to get on the same page about how they wanted to play things in front of Stacey and James. She wanted to be honest, but also come off as confident and not too needy. She needed to protect herself so that even if Teddy wasn't interested in a repeat of their night in Austin, they could make it through the rest of the season amicably. The idea of his rejection stung, but it would be better to know now than fall any harder for him. However, before she formed the words in her mouth, Teddy's phone rang.

"This is Teddy," he answered the call. *Brandon*, he mouthed silently to her. "Yes, I have a minute," he walked into his bedroom and closed the door.

I guess I'll go change into my swimsuit too. She headed for her own, solo, bedroom.

* * *

Avery relaxed on the most comfortable daybed she had ever lounged on. Maybe she'd close her eyes and let herself take a little cat-nap in the sunshine. James had snapped the obligatory photo of Avery and Teddy under a neon sign that read "Mañana trabajo, hoy aquí me quedo" or "Tomorrow I work, today I stay here." James had done it as soon they'd walked into the beach club and posted it, fulfilling their fake dating obligations for the day. The constant documenting of their time together was beginning to get on her nerves.

She didn't say yes to this trip because of the opportunity to sell their fake relationship. *I did it for the chance to get to know Teddy, to blow-off some steam. Were the fans entitled to know where and how Teddy spent his week off?* She'd never felt quite this level of interest and fame before. It gave her a whole new appreciation for Travis Kelce. At least with the photo behind them, the whole crew could take advantage of the rest of the afternoon in the sun.

They started with a mezcal tasting at the bar, leaving Avery with the humming of a light buzz. She wasn't drunk, but the alcohol was helping the tension in her shoulders melt away. Though her body was in paradise, her mind was still working, making a mental to-do list for the gala. Even in vacation mode, she wasn't one to totally forget her responsibilities.

"Fresh coconut?" Avery's thoughts were interrupted by a server in an off-white linen uniform offering her a coconut with a straw.

"We'll take two please," Stacey, who was lying next to her on an identical lounge chair, answered for both of them.

"Shot of rum with that, ladies?" the server offered.

"No, gracias," Stacey answered first

"Wait, I will take the rum," Avery interjected. Maybe another drink would push the remaining nagging work thoughts from her brain.

Stacey looked at her. "Good for you, girlfriend. It really doesn't get any better than this," she shrugged, "You do you."

"It certainly doesn't suck," Avery said, lifting her giant coconut up for a toast.

Their coconuts made a satisfying thunk sound as they touched.

"Now that I have you alone-ish, it's time to Spill. The. Beans," Stacey demanded. "You hooked up with Teddy! I need to know EVERYTHING. Just don't get too graphic. I still have to work with him."

Avery thought back to her night with Teddy—the ticklish sensation as he kissed her ever-so-lightly on the inside of her thighs, the way his hair fell forward when he was above her. Want pulsed through her at the memories. *Ya, that's exactly the stuff Stacey doesn't want to know.* She smiled, keeping those wanton scenes to herself was its own kind of secret pleasure.

"Gaaah, it was amazing. Like SO good. The perfect night. And then..." Avery paused, her heart sinking. She looked toward Teddy, who was standing in the water in one of the club's four rectangular pools on the sand facing the ocean while he chatted with James. She yearned for him, but not only physically. She craved to get in his brain too, to know whether his resistance to a real girlfriend was still there. How could she explain that to Stacey, her fun-loving, live-in-the-moment friend?

"And then he invited you to come on a week-long luxury trip to Mexico?" Stacey teased. "How concerning for you."

Avery swatted Stacey on the arm. She didn't quite have the

words to describe how her feelings for Teddy were evolving, her concern that he didn't feel the same way. Stacey wouldn't relate to the fraught internal conversation that Avery had been having with herself for the last two days.

"Joking aside, what are you overthinking?" Stacey's eyes softened.

"You know me too well," Avery admitted. She sat up, ready to dive in and over-analyze the status of her romantic relationship with her main confidante. "I'm confused about where things are going. I thought our night together was damn near perfect, and the start of something real. But the next morning, Teddy immediately brought up promoting the gala, and then he was so sure about us having separate rooms when we got here..." she knew she was talking fast, but couldn't bring herself to slow down. "...at the beach, he took a picture with me for social media and then went off to the pool with James."

"That is a lot. Try to relax. Take another sip of that drink," Stacey directed her.

Avery complied and tried to focus on the milky, sweet taste of the coconut before swallowing it down.

"First of all, why are you letting him call all the shots? If you want him, Aves, go for it. If you want to sleep in his room, tell him. You're not going to get anywhere by being too afraid to ask for what you want," Stacey lectured.

Avery nodded. *Easier said than done.*

"And don't forget, none of us are totally on vacation this week, including Teddy," Stacey added. "We are still mid-season. So maybe he wanted to make sure he didn't have to wake you up if he has to get up early. Maybe he is being considerate."

"That's all logical," Avery admitted. "But I just never imagined this scenario, and I still can't believe I'm here. I've never done anything like this before. I don't quite feel like myself - abandoning my responsibilities as soon as some guy asked me to. I want to know where this is all going."

Avery looked over at Teddy and James again. A bachelorette party had joined them in the pool, the women's voices louder than necessary, clearly trying to get the guys' attention. Avery rolled her eyes. If only those girls knew how much Teddy loathed that type of attention.

As she expected, Teddy quickly removed himself from the situation, stepping out of the pool and wrapping a towel around his waist. She couldn't believe that only two nights ago she'd seen what was beneath that towel.

Avery stared at his bare torso, his pro-athlete perfect physique stirring her body to life.

He's so hot, and he's mine – sort of. She felt her heart swell with something between pride and admiration. Sure, she knew he might just be escaping the admiring gaggle of flirty girls. But also, he hadn't been faking it in bed. So maybe his disinterest in a bunch of bikini-clad women had something to do with her? *Crazier things have happened.*

Teddy walked in her direction, still soaking wet. She scooted over to make room for him and patted the empty space beside her. He winked at her, picking up his pace. But before he sat down, he leaned over her, pool water dripping from his body and kissed her on the lips. A deep, romantic kiss. Avery lifted her chin toward him, opening her mouth for his tongue.

There, that's better. It didn't *feel* like he was putting on a show for admiring fans. Maybe, Stacey was right. She could just lean into the moment and not overthink it.

"Well, hello to you too," she said, smiling at him.

He plopped down next to her where she had made space for

him. She rested her head on his shoulder, letting the sides of their bodies gently touch all the way down to their bare, sandy toes.

"Are you having fun?" Teddy asked her.

"Yes, thank you for inviting me. I haven't felt this relaxed in a very long time. It feels like playing hooky from school. Except a more adult version."

Teddy laughed. "Good, that's what I wanted you to say. I hope Stacey and James are having fun too," he continued, "I've always wanted to be in a position where I could afford to take my team on a trip like this during an off-week. To thank them for their hard work. Normally when we're between races and don't have time to go home, they just hole up at a Marriott."

"You should feel very proud of yourself, Teddy." She pointed at James, who was still in the pool flirting with a blonde from the bachelorette party. She laughed at everything he said and touched his arm. "I think it's safe to say James is having a good time. And look, even Stacey is still for a moment. I think that's her version of relaxed."

Teddy chuckled. "I have to admit, Avery, it feels quite good to be where I am in my career. I'm finally getting somewhere. A win feels within reach if I just give it everything I've got."

She reached out and took his hand. "I think a win *is* possible. And I'm not just saying that because I'm totally biased, which I am, of course. But I've been around this team since I was a little girl, and this year, and this driver," she squeezed his hand, "feel special." *If only I could live in the moment and let go of the nagging desire to define our relationship beyond our agreement.*

twenty-one

MAYAKOBA, MEXICO

Avery knocked on Teddy's door. There was no answer, so she slowly opened it and peaked inside. After spending a glorious afternoon sharing a lounge chair with him, their bodies passing little volts of electricity back and forth, it was time to finally take Stacey's advice to heart and just go get what she wanted. *And it might be the mezcal and rum talking, but what I want right now is Teddy. Alone.*

She knew he had gone to his room when they'd gotten back from the beach club. She didn't see him, but she heard the sound of running water coming from the patio. He must have been using the outdoor shower she'd heard the butler mention when he'd given his property overview. She lifted her hand to her head, smoothing down her wild curls. The sea breeze and salt air had made them even crazier than usual. At least she knew she looked good in her new bikini, she'd glad that she'd done a little last-minute shopping in Austin once she'd said yes to Teddy's invitation. She threw her shoulders back and slid open the glass doors to the patio.

Stepping onto the patio was like walking into a secluded jungle oasis. Lush palm fronds and Monstera leaves created provided total privacy from neighboring rooms and villas. The shower was on the far wall, with Teddy's back to her as he washed his hair, his perfect tight butt on display.

She swallowed.

The scent of the hotel's eucalyptus shampoo and body wash filled the air along with the steam from the piping hot water coming out of the spigot.

Avery had thought that maybe once she'd finally found him alone she'd summon the courage to bring up her growing feelings for him, but seeing Teddy naked in a steamy tropical paradise made her fluttery and hot all over. Any remaining rational thoughts evaporated into the air with the rising steam from the shower.

She stepped toward him instinctually.

"Care for some company in that shower?"

Teddy turned around and looked her up and down, his eyes landing on her bikini top for a second before he met her eyes. "If you are the company, then absolutely," his eyes smoldered.

Avery stepped under the stream, letting the water drench her hair as she enjoyed the strong water pressure. She untied the straps of her teal bathing suit top seductively, letting it fall below her breasts.

She was unfamiliar with this version of herself – this sexy Avery, the Avery who put her desires before her responsibilities. She liked herself like this.

The air hit her nipples, leaving them hypersensitive to each water droplet that landed on her naked skin.

Teddy's mouth parted as he squeezed a few more pumps of the aromatic body wash in his hands and began rubbing it into her shoulders. His hands were strong and steady, yet he seemed completely attuned to her body as he kneaded, noticing exactly when he hit the knot of tension she stored between her shoulder blades. It shouldn't be a surprise really, for someone who noticed when the floor of his car was raised a quarter of an inch. But somehow, it was. Avery had expected him to be all pure masculine strength, but just like during their night together in Austin he was deeply sensitive to her needs.

As he moved his hands from her shoulder to her upper back, she moaned in appreciation. Teddy took her sounds as an invitation to move his hands around to the front of her body, cupping her breasts from behind her. She pressed herself into his hands, her nipples perking up at his firm touch. She felt him grow hard from behind her, as he pressed himself against her back.

"You are so hot. Bella, bella, bellissima. Your body is everything, you are everything," Teddy breathed into her ear. Knowing that her body, her breasts in his hands, had that effect on him made her feel completely in control, powerful even.

"I've never been this turned on by anyone before," she admitted. Feeling emboldened by her newfound sense of power, she put her hand on top of his, and guided it lower and lower down her abs. His hand, slick with soap, barely skimmed her skin, leaving her aching for more. His touch left her tingling in its wake until she placed it right on top of her bikini bottoms, where her desire had pooled between her legs. He slipped one finger under the wet fabric.

"Mmmm," she moaned, not recognizing her own voice.

Another finger followed, pushing the fabric out of the way. He competently found exactly the spot that ached for him, caressing her with just the right amount of pressure to make her shudder in delight. She closed her eyes and completely lost herself in him, the hot water cascading over her as she arched into his strong chest. She tightened around his fingers, calling out his name. Teddy, over and over again.

And for a few blissful moments she truly forgot everything on her mind as she rode wave after wave of her orgasm.

Finally, she came down, and relaxed into his arms, her back melting into his front. She was completely sated, but she still hadn't had enough of him, and she wanted to return the favor.

She removed herself from his embrace and slid down to her knees, taking him into her mouth. She'd never felt the urge to do that before in her life. Oral sex had always been to please the person she'd been with, or foreplay, but for the first time she was totally into it.

She was tentative at first, and took her time tasting him, exploring him. She paused just for a second.

Is this any good for him?

"You're amazing," Teddy nearly growled, as if he'd read her mind. "Don't stop. Please"

So she didn't, sliding her tongue up and down his erection. He pushed into her mouth, filling her with inch after inch until she couldn't take anymore.

He put his hands on her head, steadying her, massaging her scalp until he couldn't hold on.

"Oh, god. I'm going to come," Teddy nearly whimpered as he pulled away from her mouth before he exploded in pleasure onto the shower floor.

"Come here," he said, pulling her up onto her feet and into his arms. They stayed that way for a moment, completely wrapped up in each other. Avery put her head on his bare chest, and could feel his heart still pounding in tandem with her own as he ran his hands through her wet curls.

"I could stand here for the rest of my time on earth and die a happy man." He sighed.

"Me too, except for the man part of course," Avery murmured in agreement.

The sky had turned a dusky pink.

Teddy looked up.

"I suppose we have to get dressed for our dinner reservation. Shame." He kissed the top of her head before unraveling himself from her arms and grabbing a fluffy white towel from a bench.

He unfurled it and held it out for her to step into. Her heart glowed as he wrapped it around her, before grabbing another and wrapping it around his waist.

There was so much she could, should in fact, say to him. But she didn't want to ruin the mood with more talking. He'd just said he could stand there in post-coital bliss for the rest of his life - what kind of person interrupts that with talk of the future? *And I deserve to enjoy the moment too*. She wordlessly followed him back inside to get ready for dinner, trying to relish the after-glow of her orgasm and the setting sun.

twenty-two

MAYAKOBA, MEXICO

Avery could barely see in the pitch-black night as the group walked back to the villa after dinner. The path was too dimly lit, yet the dark amplified her other senses. The waves crashed in the distance underneath the sound of Teddy, Stacey, and James laughing and talking. The sweet smell of blooming bougainvillea filled her nose.

"I wouldn't be surprised if Archer cans Cody at the end of the season. He's got to be more trouble than he's worth," James said.

"He's young, and green. I hope they give him more time than that to develop," Stacey countered. "Who do you think they'd get to replace him?"

Avery felt Teddy reach for her hand and the two of them naturally dropped back behind Stacey and James. Avery listened as her friends continued to talk shop, managing only to contribute an "uhuh" or "yep" here and there. She was too attuned to Teddy's body, the way he kept rubbing his calloused thumb over her palm, sending little bolts of pleasure up her arm.

"Well, here we are, mates," James announced, unlocking the front door of their villa with his key card.

"G'night everyone," Stacey said, making a beeline for her room upstairs.

"I think I'll turn in too, leave you lovebirds to your own devices," James grinned.

Avery's ears felt hot and her cheeks burned. Teddy squeezed her hand, imbuing her with confidence. "I guess holding hands gave it away, tonight," she admitted, turning to catch Teddy's eye.

"Well, that certainly confirmed my suspicions that you two have been mixing business with pleasure," James smirked.

"Just ignore him," Teddy smiled at her. He didn't take his eyes off her as he told James to get lost. Avery felt squirmy under his gaze, not sure what he was expecting of her. Going back to her room alone seemed pointless now that their entire traveling party knew that there was something more going on between them than fake dating and friendship. And she couldn't ignore the magnetic pull drawing them to each other.

But, she was spent, almost sleeping standing up after a day of sun and fun... and sex. Would he be interested in platonic bed-sharing? Or was that too couple-y? Weren't they a real couple by now? It certainly didn't seem like they were still pretending.

I'm not pretending.

"I had a wonderful time today," Avery said, blushing. *Get it together, Avery. He's seen you naked. Twice.*

Even so, her muscles tensed as she spoke. "I'm exhausted and going to crash as soon as my head hits the pillow. But, do you want to spend the night in my room?" She hoped she got her meaning across, that she simply wanted to be near him.

"Yes," he exhaled. "I'm also completely knackered, and Stacey and I start race prep tomorrow," Teddy said. "I'll go get in my pajamas."

Pajamas. Cute. She'd never seen him in PJs. In Austin, they'd fallen asleep after the deed, no pajamas involved. Getting ready for bed and not falling into it represented a whole new level of their relationship, or at least it did for her.

She slipped into her own cream-colored shorts matching set, and went into the bathroom. She closed the door behind her in case Teddy were to walk back in before she'd completed her nightly routine. Pajamas and cuddles were one thing, but flossing their teeth next to each other was another matter entirely.

When she walked out of the bathroom after applying her nightly lotions and potions, Teddy was standing on the edge of her bedroom, rocking back and forth on his feet. His cozy plaid pajama pants hung loosely on his hips, the edges of the fabric worn and nubby from wear. His white v-neck t-shirt looked equally soft. Tortoise shell glasses framed his hazel eyes. The whole effect was so completely different from the guy she'd first met months ago at the beginning of the season. It was almost impossible to reconcile the suave race car driver with the almost nerdy, yet utterly adorable man waiting for her to come to bed.

"I had no idea you wore glasses," she blurted out. "I mean, they suit you, it's a nice look on you."

"Yeah, I wear them for reading most evenings, but, well, I didn't do any reading the other night in Austin..." he coughed.

Avery blushed again at the memory of their night in Austin.

Even if they were to go to bed together a thousand times, would she ever get used to being with Teddy? Doubtful.

"I didn't know what side of the bed you prefer," Teddy said.

Avery felt her heart positively glow. This man who was absolutely ruthless on the track was hesitant to take the wrong side of the bed. It was incredibly endearing, so sweet. It had to be getting as real for him as it was for her. If only she could work up the courage to bring it up in conversation.

"I've been sleeping there,"Avery pointed to the right side of the bed, where a cup of water and a book were lying on the nightstand.

"Should'a guessed," Teddy said. He walked around to the other side of the bed, and pulled back the fluffy white duvet. Avery followed suit on her side, getting under the covers.

She stretched her hands above her head, cat-like. "Come here, you," Teddy said. She scooted over to him and laid her head into that perfectly Avery shaped spot on his shoulder, turning her body slightly toward him.

"This is nice. I like this," she murmured. "Being near you."

"Me too," he kissed her softly, his lips brushing hers.

Best sleepover ever.

"So tell me about your love for all things plaid. Do you always wear pajama pants that match your helmets?" she asked as she gave his arm a little squeeze.

He laughed. "The pajamas, well they're from Harvey Nichols, and they are particularly comfortable, any similarity to a helmet is purely coincidental. But, the tartan helmets, yeah those are meaningful. My mom's family, the Ross's, can trace their Scottish roots all the way back to the time of Braveheart, more or less. And the colorful pattern on my helmet is one of the traditional clan tartans."

"Oh, Ross is your mom's last name? I didn't know that. That's cool."

"It is. When I entered my first karting race at age eight, I used my mom's surname out of spite. I was still so angry at my dad for leaving her, leaving us. And then later on, a few years ago, I changed it legally too, but I won't bore you with the sordid details of that story."

"It won't bore me Teddy, really. You can tell me anything," she said. And she meant it.

"Well, after my dad took off, we didn't hear from him for years. Then when I started having some success, winning the karting championship, and making it to F3, then F2, he was interested in us, well in me. For a while I was excited, just happy to have his attention."

"Mmhmmm," Avery nodded along.

She removed herself from the world's coziest spot nestled in his arm to scooch her pillow over from her side of the bed, and placed her head on it, rolling over to her side so that she could look him in the eyes, give him her full and undivided attention. "And then? Are you in touch now?"

"No - definitely not. He took a deep breath, exhaled loudly. "Do you remember when I made a bloody mess of that F2 championship?" he asked.

"Yes, I remember it," Avery answered. *Of course I do.* He was a promising driver already back then, and it had made waves. Her pulse picked up.

"Right, naturally." He blinked a few times. "Well, I really blew it that Sunday because the night before, I got a call from my dad." He swallowed.

Avery held her breath. Her gut knew it hadn't been good news.

"I thought it was to congratulate me on my performance in the qualifier, to wish me luck in the race." Avery noticed his eyes were wet.

She cupped his chin, "Whatever it is. You can tell me."

"He asked me to throw the race."

Avery's feet went cold, despite being buried under the covers.

"He'd been betting on me. Well, betting against me in that particular case. And everything became crystal clear. The only reason he tried to have a relationship with me again was to make a quick buck." He shook his head in what Avery assumed was a mixture of sadness and disgust. "Of course, I told him to go to hell. That there was no way I'd ever fix a race."

The rest of her body felt cold now too.

"Oh, Teddy, I'm so sorry. You didn't deserve that." *How could anyone do that to their own kid?*

"The worst part is that I lost the race anyway. He had screwed with my head so badly that I didn't get a bit of sleep that night. I could barely see straight by the time I got to the track the next morning. My head wasn't in it all, and so of course I choked and put the car into the wall. And the bastard got what he wanted," he looked down, and shook his head. "I changed my name legally shortly thereafter and haven't spoken a word to him since."

Avery felt a stabbing pain in her chest. She put her hand on his shoulder and squeezed, giving herself a second to choose her next words carefully.

"I *know* you'd never lose a race on purpose. I see how much integrity you have, how hard you work not only for yourself, but for your family, your team," her heart broke for a young Teddy as she said it. "He should never have put you in that position."

Teddy wiped his eyes and pulled her to him, burying his face in her curls. She relaxed her back into his chest, letting him draw her closer, happy to be his little spoon if it would give him some comfort.

"Your dad knows. Brandon knows. I told them when they hired me," Teddy answered the question she hadn't said aloud. "And they still gave me a chance. I swore I'd never let them regret it."

Her heart ached for him.

"And, I knew I'd have to be damn near perfect, both on and off the track," he added, "If that ever gets out, it could be the end of my career. No one would trust my results."

Now, it made sense. "And that's why you got so nervous about a reporter showing up at your mom's doorstep? Why you needed to offer up a distraction?"

"Yes," she could feel him cringe into her neck. "I'm sorry I didn't explain it earlier. I never thought it would go any further than a few photo ops between us. I should have told you sooner, I...there are so few people I trust."

"It's okay, really. My reasons are completely different, and nothing like the trauma you experienced with your dad," she qualified what she was about to say next, wanting to make sure she was in no way equating a mom with a drinking problem to what he'd been through. "But I understand the pressure of needing to seem perfect all the time. My parents have always made it feel like one slip-up on my part would result in the fall of the empire or something like that. I'm sure it all goes back to the drinking and rehab thing. My mom is so ashamed of her behavior in those years, I think she's still projecting that on me."

"Hmmm," Teddy nodded in a non-judgmental way, his arms tight around her.

"I guess what I'm saying is, I understand it's not easy being in the public eye and maintaining an image that's above reproach. It's a lot. There have been times I was tempted to pose for Maxim magazine or do something totally insane to relieve the pressure, ya know?"

"I know what you mean. I've been tempted to go on a wild bender after a particularly hard week at the track, but then I picture the headlines. I just can't," Teddy added.

"Same, I mean following you here this week is honestly one of the most irresponsible things I've ever done."

"Well, I for one, am very grateful you decided to be irresponsible this week," Teddy buried his face even deeper into her hair, kissing the back of her neck tenderly.

"Me too, I'm glad I'm here," Avery exhaled, allowing her heart rate to slow.

"Okay, I'm going to ask you something a reporter has never asked you," she said as solemnly as she could. She'd do anything to make him feel better.

"Alright," Teddy took a breath.

"What's your favorite color?" she asked.

He pinched her hip playfully.

Mission accomplished.

"Navy blue. Classic. Can't go wrong," he answered. "You?"

"Sunshine yellow. Always has been. It's so happy. So cheerful," she answered in return, stifling a yawn.

They volleyed light-hearted getting-to-know-you questions back-and-forth until she asked him his favorite animal and didn't get a response.

His arms had relaxed around her and she felt his chest rise and fall. He was asleep.

It all made sense now, she thought drowsily. The perfectly

polished answers for reporters, the engineered smile, keeping his family away from him, and the reporters that followed him, on race day. And he'd chosen her, trusted her enough, to confide in.

She yawned and slowly lifted up her arm to turn out the light, trying not to disturb sleeping Teddy, and settled back into him. She felt lighter as his heart beat steadily, calmly against her back. A good night of sleep was just the ticket to erase the deep sadness and shame that she'd heard in his voice.

twenty-three

MAYAKOBA, MEXICO

Avery padded out of her room the next morning and into the kitchen in slippered feet, a short and lightweight Turkish cotton bathrobe over her pajama set. Her bed had been empty when she woke up. The kitchen was silent, but she was greeted by the welcoming, earthy scent of freshly brewed coffee. She longed to find out what Teddy's mouth would taste like mixed with a hint of that coffee. She poured a cup and found a platter of fruit and pastries on the counter.

She'd bring her coffee and the platter out to the pool deck. Maybe Teddy was out there enjoying a moment of zen. She hoped they were the only ones up and she'd find him alone. She wanted to throw her arms around him, before it was back to walking the fine line between fake-dating, fake-dating with benefits, and real relationship. It was less of a line, and more of a triangle? She'd never been good at geometry.

But as soon as she opened the sliding doors and stepped out

onto the deck, her heart sank. The kitchen had been empty because she was the *last* one to rise, not one of the first. So much for coffee-tinged kisses.

Stacey had set up a workout station for Teddy on the dock, with a yoga mat, weights, and a large exercise ball. He was sitting, shirtless, a headband keeping his hair out of his eyes, in a crunch position on the top of the exercise ball.

The position he was in mimicked the angle of his driver's seat, his biceps bulging from exertion, a heavy set of weights out in front of him as if it were a steering wheel.

She imagined herself running her hands over them.

His face was scrunched while Stacey was holding onto his legs, trying to throw him off balance by pulling them in different directions, as if he were rounding a corner. James was stationed by them, capturing the workout. He had swapped his phone for a more high-tech camera and was hovering over Stacey's shoulder to get the right angle so he could capture just how hard Teddy was working, the flex of each muscle in his core. The internet would eat it up.

Like I am. She licked her lips.

"Just four more. You've got this," Stacey encouraged, as Teddy focused on his breathing during the sequence, exhaling out each time he righted himself back to center on the ball. "Grab a sip of water."

"Morning, bella," Teddy winked at Avery, as soon as Stacey took the weights from his hands. *So, he had clocked my presence, but managed to stay focused on the workout. Impressive.* Avery doubted she'd be able to do the same if he walked into her place of work.

"Good morning," she smiled at him, as if she was used to

waking up to sweaty, half-naked men calling her "bella." "Good morning, Stace."

"Morning, Avery," Stacey said. "Okay. Teddy, break is over. Ten minutes of neck work and then you're done," she nearly cackled as she waved some neck stretching torture device in front of him.

Avery's neck heated remembering the feel of his hot breath on *her* neck.

Teddy gulped down a sip of water, drawing Avery's eyes to his mouth, as a drop of water escaped his mouth and trickled over the white scar on his bottom lip.

"I'm going to do a cold plunge and a jacuzzi when I finish. Join me?" he asked, staring at her mouth right back.

She nodded and took her plate and mug to the outdoor dining table on the other side of the pool and stared out over the lagoon. If she stood there watching any longer, she'd start drooling, or worse yet, get in their way. She took a big bite of her croissant, savoring each flaky bite. Steaming cup of coffee. Check. Fresh pastries. Check. Hunky shirtless lover in her peripheral vision. Check. *Another day that did not suck.*

* * *

"Hot or cold first?" Teddy asked Avery.

"You should do the jacuzzi, then the cold plunge, then the jacuzzi again for maximal cellular benefit," Stacey interjected while she wiped down the sweaty workout equipment.

"No cellular benefit talk for me, I'm not a professional athlete. I'm on vacation and have no interest in freezing my ass off in an ice-cold plunge pool. I vote for jacuzzi first, then jacuzzi, and finish with jacuzzi."

Teddy shrugged. "Jacuzzi it is."

Avery shimmied out of her robe. Steam wafted up from the tiled jacuzzi warming the air as she dipped a toe in. The water was scorching hot, almost burning her skin. *Just how I like it.* She lowered herself onto the bench on the side of the jacuzzi tub, letting one of the jets massage her back, groaning in contentment.

Teddy hopped in next to her and looked around to make sure Stacey and James were no longer in earshot. "I like that sound coming out of your mouth, but only when I'm the cause of it," he said, turning his head to hers. He lowered his mouth to hers, and she parted her lips for him. He kissed like he drove, determined and in control. Avery was happy to let him take charge, his tongue everywhere in her mouth.

She whimpered, and he pulled away. Teddy leaned back against the side of the tub, arms folded behind his head. "Precisely," he smirked.

She turned around and straddled him, kissing him this time, deeply and quickly, before running her thumb over his bottom lip, smoothing the spot with the scar. "How did you get this?"

"Go-kart injury. I was about seven, just mucking about and knocked my mouth right into the steering wheel. My front tooth went right through my lip."

"Did it deter you from karting at all?"

"Not at all. But it did force my mum to buy me some proper equipment, and get someone to teach me how to drive the darn thing. In fact, I can probably thank this scar for really launching my career."

Huh. Avery turned this new piece of information about Teddy around in her head. She knew he'd have to be a calculated risk taker, have some tolerance for bodily injury to do what he did, but she'd never taken him for someone to be motivated by it.

"You just keep surprising me, Teddy Ross." Avery felt light-headed. "I'm overheating," she announced, lifting herself off his lap and onto the side of the hot tub, her feet dangling in the water.

"Ah, I often have that effect on you," he teased, grabbing her feet.

She kicked her feet up out of his grasp, splashing him, "Yes, it's either you, or the 104 degree water."

He took her foot back and rubbed, sending a shiver of pleasure from the sole all the way up her inseam.

"Ok, cold plunge time for me," he said.

He stepped out of the jacuzzi, dripping on her in his wake.

He jumped in the narrow pool next to the jacuzzi that was kept at a chilly fifty-five degrees without flinching. "Wooo-wee, that's the stuff.

"How can you just dive right in like that?" she asked.

"It's not so bad. Come see for yourself," he answered.

"Ok fine," Avery took a deep breath and before she could chicken out, stepped into the ice-cold water in the adjacent tub.

She gasped as the cold water shocked her nerve endings.

"Well, now you've surprised me today, too," Teddy said. Exactly what she had been going for. She shivered again.

twenty-four

MAYAKOBA, MEXICO

The team was in full race-prep mode now with the Mexico City GP days away, but Avery was headed to the pool book in hand, intending to soak up every last drop of vacation. It had been, hands down, the best five days of her life. She and Teddy had given up any pretense of a fake relationship as soon as James had caught on, and the whole week had been a dream. She'd spent every night in Teddy's bed as they'd gotten to know every curve and line of one another's body. And then each day had been spent working out with Teddy and Stacey, relaxing by the pool with her book, and biking or golf carting down to the beach. Heaven, in a nutshell. *Or, a coconut shell*.

But sooner or later, they'd have to discuss their relationship status. Avery walked by the closed door of Teddy's room, wearing her teal bathing suit under a long button-up, her sunglasses perched on the top of her head. She could hear Teddy's muffled voice and the sound of him pacing around the room during a call with the team. She frowned. She couldn't exactly hear what he was saying, but his tone was serious, intense. The pacing stopped and the decibel level coming from the other side of the door dropped considerably. The meeting must be wrapping up.

Maybe, she could convince Teddy to take a break and hang out with her for a bit. She'd been imagining a long romantic walk on the beach with him, one where they finally openly discussed their feelings. In the movie version in her head, he'd twirl her around in the sand while the sun was setting, and it would be happily ever after.

The door creaked open and Teddy emerged, running his hands through his hair.

"How did your meeting go?" she asked, gently biting her lip.

"It was productive. Not everyone agrees, but I think the upgrades to the car are going to help next weekend," he said, nodding his head, as if trying to convince himself of his own words.

"And you? Teddy asked, "All good with the Silver Charitable Foundation?

"Foundation? What foundation?" she laughed, though the reality hit a little too close to home, she had definitely spent the morning reading in bed, her laptop firmly closed at the bottom of her suitcase. She'd been hiding from reality in more ways than one this week.

Avery took a deep breath, trying to calm the quivery feeling in her muscles. Maybe the time had come to rejoin reality. Sunset was hours away, but the first step of rejoining real life had to be defining their relationship. She'd be forced to admit to him what she wanted—which was nothing short of everything.

"Do you have time to take a walk on the beach with me?" she asked.

He looked at his watch. "As a matter of fact, I do. That's exactly what I need," Teddy said, smiling at her as he grabbed his flip flops and a baseball cap.

He put his baseball cap on backwards, just as it had been the first day they met at the track back in March. His hair flipped out from under the brim, rendering her completely defenseless to his charms. It was literally adorable and hot at the same time. He grinned at her and held open the door.

Her palms were sweaty as they walked and the hot sand burned her toes, so she made a beeline for the surf. Teddy followed her, eyes on the horizon.

Avery's eyes were instinctively drawn down toward the wet clumpy sand, looking for anything shiny or interesting. She spotted something pink and bent down to examine it, partially out of habit; she'd always been a seashell collector. But, she knew she was stalling, delaying the inevitable. She owed it to herself to have this conversation now, she just needed to find the right words.

"What did you find?" Teddy asked.

"Look, a perfect spiral," she opened her palm, revealing her seashell, completely intact from its pointy end all the way to its smooth opening. "I've collected seashells from beaches around the world ever since I was a little girl. I used to come home from vacation with my family with ziplocks full of whatever I'd found. Now just the special ones make it home."

"Sounds like an idyllic childhood," Teddy mused.

"Yes, those were special times for us. I think that's why I still collect shells. It reminds me of the feeling I had on those family vacations, the rare time we had our parents' full attention: no work, no social engagements."

She remembered how the real world would fade into the background for a week as she and her brother frolicked in the sand while their parents doted on them. *The good old days. The golden age of the Silver family.* Before all of the expectations and pressure. Before her mom's drinking had gotten out of control.

"Beach vacations with your family, I can't say I'm not a bit envious. We spent our school breaks at the track of course, not that my mom had the money to take us on a proper holiday, even if I hadn't been busy with karting."

She felt guilty about her privileged childhood whenever Teddy brought up his own. Their backgrounds were so, so different, and yet they'd both ended up here, at the precipice of motorsport.

It really wasn't fair that it had been so easy for her, really, when compared to Teddy and kids like he had been. It was a good reminder of why she did what she did, and why she needed to break the spell of this magical week and get back to work helping kids get opportunities like the ones she had.

She took his hand with one of hers, rubbing her thumb along his calloused palm. She rubbed the shell in her other hand as if it would reveal the right words to convey what she felt in her heart. That despite their different childhoods, she understood him deeply and saw him to his core, that they were each other's person.

"Teddy, that commitment, those sacrifices. They worked. You are one of the twenty best drivers in the world. You've made it."

He stopped walking and looked at her, his lips forming a tight line. "I don't see it that way. I'm only getting started in this sport. All my dreams are now within my reach, and if I'm not careful, they'll slip away. It will all have been for nothing."

She bit the inside of her lip, her heart crashing into her chest in time with the waves breaking onto the shore. This was her opening.

"I wish you could see yourself the way I see you. The last couple months we've spent getting to know each other have been amazing." She exhaled. "I wasn't expecting this, but I've completely fallen for you." She smiled up at him. "I love your real smile, the one that reaches your eyes. I love how you aren't afraid to look goofy in a cowboy hat. I love how you'd do anything to protect your family. I think I'm falling in love with you..."

He looked down, breaking their eye contact, but held onto her hand.

Avery's mouth went dry. Why wasn't he saying anything back?

He exhaled loudly and spoke quietly. "Someday when I retire, I can imagine falling in love. But I can't give you more than this..." he gestured to himself on the beach, "...Right now."

Avery's heart sank. *It's not no, but it isn't what I was hoping to hear, of course.* If only she could convince him he deserved some happiness along his journey to the top.

She let the shell fall from her hand and land with a soft thud in the sand, and used her fingers to clutch his other hand into hers, so they were face to face.

"Teddy" she said with more conviction than she felt, forcing his eyes back up to meet hers. "I know you feel how magical we are together. I know that you think having a girlfriend would distract you from achieving your goals, but you also know I'm not most girlfriends," Avery said. "I understand you. And I understand the sport. We've made an awesome team this season, Teddy. I want to be the person who supports your career, who lifts you up. And I don't want to wait five years to see if we can work. Let's at least give it a shot?"

This can't be the end, we've only just begun.

Teddy grimaced, and shook his head slightly. "I can't. I'm so sorry, Avery. I really didn't mean to lead you on, but I think you misunderstood what I said—it's not going to happen."

Avery's lungs constricted in her chest, making it hard to breathe. *He's breaking up with me.*

He swallowed. "You're a great girl. You're nothing like what I expected when we first met. I had thought you were a beautiful, spoiled, socialite who wanted to use me to increase her following, which aligned with my needs perfectly." She cringed at his initial impression of her. "But you're so much more than that, your reasons are so pure, and it's been great getting to know you. And obviously we are attracted to each other. But we shouldn't, I shouldn't, have acted on that attraction. It was a mistake, and we can't let it happen again."

Avery looked away from his gaze, tilting her head up, trying to keep the tears that were burning her eyes from spilling over. She was one of those people who cried for any number of emotions, including embarrassment, but Teddy didn't know that. She'd look pathetic, crying over a relationship that wasn't even real to him. Her hands shook from the effort of holding it together in front of him. She had to get away from him. Fast.

She nearly stumbled as she backed away, shaking her head at him. If she opened her mouth to speak, she'd either fully burst into tears or say something unbearably cruel, neither of which seemed like a way to save face. So, she just turned around and walked away as fast as she could without breaking into a full blown run.

"Avery, wait... please," she heard Teddy call after her, but she didn't look back. What else could he possibly want to say to her that wouldn't be more mortifying than what he'd already said?

Beautiful, spoiled socialite.

It was a mistake.

...can't let it happen again.

Her embarrassment morphed into a soupy mixture of shame and anger as she walked back down the beach. She'd allowed herself to be vulnerable and it had blown up in her face. She'd been such an idiot, sharing her family's secrets with him and to complicate things further, her dad was his boss. It was so inappropriate for the team's driver to know so much about the team owner's dysfunctional family. The tears she had tried so hard to keep contained were now spilling down her cheeks. She lifted the bottom of her shirt to wipe them away.

As soon as she made it back to the villa, she made a beeline for her bedroom and pulled her suitcase out of the closet. She packed as fast as she could, tearing clothes off hangers and shoving them in her luggage. She had to escape before Teddy made it back from the beach.

She picked up the receiver from the old-school landline phone on the bedside table. "Hi, this is Avery Silver in Villa 231. Could you please send a golf cart to collect me and my luggage as soon as possible? And I'll need a taxi to the airport. Thank you."

I'll figure out a flight when I get there. There are multiple flights out each day, if I have to connect through somewhere else, it'll be fine.

It felt like she'd been punched in the stomach, but mostly she felt like an idiot. He'd been clear from the beginning that he didn't want a girlfriend— had she really convinced herself that a few fun dates and sex would change that? He'd used her.

She went to zip up her suitcase, but the zipper got half away around its track and wouldn't budge. She hadn't bothered to fold her items and return them to their packing cubes, and now nothing fit. She pulled and pulled on the zipper, with one hand, while using her body weight and her other arm to try and force it closed. Still, no. She moaned in frustration and kicked the hard shell of the suitcase. *I don't have time for this*.

Someone knocked on the door.

Avery froze. *Please don't be Teddy*.

"Aves, everything okay in there? It sounds like a WWE match is going down." *Phew, it's Stacey*. Avery took a deep breath and wiped her face with the bottom of her coverup before opening the door, trying to get ahold of herself.

"What's wrong?" Stacey asked, her voice full of concern. Despite her attempt at drying her eyes, without glancing in the mirror she knew she looked red and puffy.

"And why are you taking it out on that poor defenseless suitcase?" Stacey surveyed the room, noticing the suitcase on the floor.

"Teddy. I told him I was in love with him, and he told me he's not interested in anything other than being fuck buddies," she sobbed, sitting down on the floor. "I'm beyond mortified. I'm heading to the airport, there's no way I can face him right now," Avery barely got the words out, choking on a fresh round of tears.

There was another knock on the door. Avery froze, again, her fight or flight reaction on high alert.

"Ma'am, are you ready for me to collect your luggage?" the bellman asked.

Avery looked down at the half-zipped suitcase, a pair of pants spilling out the side. "One second, please."

"You're leaving? Right now? Do you want to talk it out before you decide?" Stacey raised her eyebrows.

"No, my mind is made up. I have to get out of here. No," Avery shook her head. She did not want to relive what just happened with Teddy anytime soon. If she could wipe it from her memory, that would be even better.

"Okay, well at least let me help you with that while you change," Stacey said. "While you get dressed in something more suitable for the plane?"

Avery looked down. She had almost forgotten she was still in a bathing suit and cover-up. If it weren't for Stacey, she probably would have gone straight to the airport in beachwear. She nodded and grabbed a pair of leggings and a t-shirt from the heap in the suitcase.

Stacey took the rest of the heap out, and started folding clothing items neatly before returning them back inside one-by-one. "There you go," she said as she zipped it back up. "Do you want me to ride with you to the airport?"

Avery shook her head no as she sniffled, trying to catch her breath. "No, I really appreciate the offer. But I don't want to take up your time. Go relax or work. I just want to be alone."

"If you say so. Will I see you at the race?"

"I don't know." *Not a chance.* "I'll call you later."

"Okay. Feel better," Stacey opened her arms wide for a hug. "I'm here for you anytime you want to talk, day or night."

Avery opened her arms and let her friend give her a comforting hug. Stacey's tight squeeze and pat on the back really did help calm her nervous system. She wiped her nose with the back of her hand and grabbed the handle of her roller bag. She smiled weakly before she walked out the door.

Her anger had diffused some with Stacey's kindness, but a fresh wave of yuck rolled over her as she handed her luggage over to the bellman. She walked to the front door of the villa and left her keycard on the front table before hopping in the golf cart. She leaned her head back across the sticky nylon headrest. It was going to be a long, miserable trip home indeed, but she deserved it.

I knew better than to get involved with a race driver.

twenty-five

LOS ANGELES, CA

The next morning, Avery dragged herself to work. She was the very first person to arrive at the Silver Foundation office, the sleek wooden reception desk empty and dark. *Like my mood.* She'd finally given up on sleep at five am after a night of tossing and turning. The sound of Teddy's voice calling for her to wait as she tore down the beach played in her head on repeat all night long, leaving her tired and achy.

She flipped on the lights and watched the space come to life. Trophy cases and plaques of recognition were displayed on floor-to-ceiling shelves, partly to impress visitors, partly because her parents had received so many awards and honors over the years, they simply didn't know where else to store them. It was a glaring reminder of the legacy she had to uphold, the institutions that were counting on the financial success of the gala.

At least it was quiet; the only sounds were the buzzing of the fluorescent overhead lighting and the whirring of the

HVAC system gearing up. Though the office was well-designed and modern, it was modestly outfitted. It was still a non-profit after all, and it went against her family's ethos to have lavish offices for an organization that was supposed to be using its resources to help the underserved. You couldn't exactly tell a youth sports complex you didn't have the funds for a new building while sitting in office chairs that cost thousands of dollars each. *I can't imagine telling them I don't have the money, even if I were sitting on a chair with three legs.*

Avery rubbed her temples as her computer booted up. *Over 200 unread emails. Ugh.* She scanned the subject lines, triaging - lots of newsletters, several funding requests from charities, cold asks for meetings with her and her dad, nothing too crazy or urgent, at least. And then her eyes stopped.

Monarch LA RE: You're Invited! Grand Opening - February 1, 2025

Her stomach dropped. February 1, 2025?! The gala was scheduled for December 15th, 2024. *Is it official then? The hotel is really not going to be ready in time? Why didn't they call me before putting it on blast?* They'd warned her, of course, but it hadn't seemed imminent. Shouldn't she have at least gotten a courtesy call?

Fingers shaking, she picked up the phone on her desk to call Sofia, the hotel manager. Between her mental fog and shaky fingers, it took her a few tries to find her contact details in her phone.

"Monarch LA. Sofia Alarcon speaking."

Avery swallowed, trying to get rid of the sour taste in her mouth. "Hi, Sofia. It's Avery Silver. I just saw your grand opening announcement in February. Does that mean you won't be ready for the gala in December?" She cut to the chase, too anxious to make small talk.

"Avery, hi. I'm so glad you called," Sofia said with genuine relief. "I've been trying to reach you for days. I didn't want you to find out through a mass email, but your cell phone kept sending me straight to voicemail and your mailbox was full."

"You did? She looked at her settings. *Seriously, how could I have missed multiple calls?*

Fuck my life. There it was, international cellular data roaming- OFF. Her ears burned with shame. She hadn't gotten a call in nearly a week, and she hadn't noticed. *I've completely missed important news, and for what? To entertain some self-centered jerk?* The sour taste returned to her mouth.

"Oh my god, Sofia. This is totally my fault. I was out of the country. How does this affect the gala?" Avery asked in a near whisper. She squeezed her eyes shut as she waited for a reply from the other end of the receiver.

Sofia let out a whistle-like breath. "I'm afraid that the hotel, including the ballroom, won't be ready until the new year. I'm so sorry for the inconvenience," she said apologetically. "We will happily refund your deposit, and you will have the first choice of all December 2025 event dates without a deposit fee."

Avery had known this news was a distinct possibility. But hearing it was a punch straight to the gut. She'd let her guard down one freaking time. *For once, I crossed my fingers and hoped everything would work out. And it hadn't.*

"Um, okay," Avery squeaked out. "I will have Caroline call you later to work out the refund. Are there any comparable venues around town that you could recommend? Since you're in the business?" The task of finding a back-up venue was going to be gargantuan, and she could use all the help she could get.

"Gosh. I recently moved here myself to help corporate get this new property up-and-running. So, I don't have any suggestions off-hand, but I will certainly ask around, and get back to you," Sofia said.

So much for that lead.

"Yep, thanks, bye," Avery ended the call swiftly. There wasn't anything left to be said at this point.

She put her head down on her desk, a wooden mid-century modern piece she'd found at the Rose Bowl flea market a few years back, letting her vision fill with the blurry grain of the cherry-colored wood.

When she picked her head back up, she could see that the lights down the hall in her dad's office were on. She took it as a sign that she should just bite the bullet and tell him about the venue. *In an alternate universe I'd be coming to him with a plan B ready to put into action.*

She'd be able to say, "I know I wanted to shake things up this year with a new venue. I knew we were cutting it close on timing with the Monarch, and it turns out it won't be ready in time. But, fear not, I have it all worked out and here's what I propose." Her parents would rubber stamp plan B and she'd be off to the races.

But nope. *Instead, I have to say "Hey mom and dad, ya know that plan I had to freshen up the event with a new venue? Well, it totally backfired. And I need your help to fix it." My role as an important person who gets shit done in the Silver family is over before it began.*

She wished she could fast forward to the end of the day, or at least through the next hour. But there was no avoiding it. She smoothed her pants and trudged down the hall, feeling clammy.

Her dad was seated at his desk as she had expected, the day's newspaper splayed out in front of him. He still liked to start his day reading the physical papers, and Caroline always lined them up on his desk each morning, no matter if he was scheduled to be in the office or not. She wouldn't have been surprised if Caroline ironed them like he was a duke in the English countryside. The TV on the wall across from him was muted, a series of headlines scrolling across the bottom of the screen.

"Avery, darling!" *Oh, fantastic.* Her mother. Now *that* was a surprise. She had not expected her mom to be perched on the leather couch in the corner of the room, doing a crossword puzzle on her tablet, her pleated mid-length skirt splayed out tastefully around her.

Well, at least I won't have to repeat my embarrassing, shameful admission again later to my mom. Let's rip that band-aid right off.

"Mom, what are you doing here?" she asked, feeling an internal pang.

"I could say the same to you. We thought you were in Mexico with Teddy? I have lunch in Beverly Hills, so I thought I would drive into the city with Dad," her mom explained as she rose and gave Avery a somewhat reserved hug and a peck on the cheek.

"Avery! Hello my girl," her dad greeted her next, "I didn't know you would be here today." He rose and enveloped her in a big hug. Avery hugged him back tight. She wanted to bury her head in his chest and let his large frame block out the rest of the world for a moment. Her dad had always been her safe place, her refuge after a bad day as a little girl, and now, even at twenty-three years old, she longed to let her guard down and just spill everything to him.

"You look pale. Come, sit," her mom said with concern, gesturing to a spot next to her on the couch. "Why aren't you frolicking on the beach with your handsome race car driver?" While her relationship with her mother could be complicated, at the end of the day Avery knew her mother loved her deeply, and of course, she'd been able to tell right away that something was wrong.

Avery was tempted to lay down on the couch, put her head in her mother's lap, and let it all come pouring out. But, if she wanted to be treated like a respected professional, she had to act like one. She'd save the Teddy drama for later, but fill them in on the gala. She sat down on the edge of the couch, took a breath, and tried to pretend they weren't her parents, but simply business colleagues who she had to update on a less than ideal situation.

"Well, I came home because I need to get to work on the gala." It wasn't a complete lie, even if it wasn't the whole truth. But admitting things were over with Teddy would send her over the edge, and right now she was trying to keep her cool. "There's an issue that I need to update you both on, and I may need your help," she took another deep breath to steady herself. "The Monarch let me know this morning that they aren't going to be open in time for us to have the gala there. So, we need to find a new venue. Quickly."

"Oh is that all that's bothering you?!" Her mom gave a dismissive wave of her hand, "I'll just call over to the Four Seasons and we will move it there. We'll re-use the layout and menu from last year, and it won't put us too far behind."

Avery knew the Four Seasons wasn't available. She'd inquired before she left for Mexico—the one responsible thing she'd done in the last week.

Avery let out a controlled exhale. "I thought of that already, and their ballroom is booked that evening with a massive holiday party. In fact, they are booked solid right up until Christmas," she explained. *See Mom, it's not that easy.*

"Well, they were booked when you asked, but maybe if Daddy calls over they can work something out," Sharon said. She patted Avery on the knee.

"Mom! They can't just make another ballroom appear or kick-out the couples who have weddings planned. It doesn't matter how much money you can offer or who you are, if they are booked, they are booked," Avery huffed.

Why weren't her parents taking this problem seriously? This was a big deal, and while maybe she should be grateful that they were taking it in stride, she was actually looking for them to match her level of concern.

Her dad finally looked up from over his newspaper, which he'd gone back to skimming while half-heartedly listening. "Well, I'm sure your mother has lots of other event contacts in the city, and yes, I'm always happy to make a phone call and work my magic, if you need me to. I know that you will get this sorted by the end of the week, Avery."

"I also have a very exciting gala update," he continued, folding his newspaper. "You remember Ron from Aurelia Strap? We had drinks with him in the hotel lobby after the Bahrain race? He called me yesterday..."

"And?" Avery asked impatiently. She was not in the mood to hear some crazy event idea from a sponsor. They didn't even have a venue, which apparently, was not a problem as far as her parents were concerned.

Her mom shot her a warning glance from the couch and mouthed "be nice" but her dad had either not noticed her snappish comment or had chosen to ignore it.

"They are releasing a special edition watch for the holidays, and they want to officially debut it at the gala. We will get a ton of extra press for the event because of it, and they will give us one to auction off, which should bring in several grand," he said, his eyes sparkling.

Avery forced herself to smile. "That's great, Dad." It was kind of cool, but the auction was the least of her worries right now.

"I haven't told you the best part," he looked over at her mom, who was beaming, clearly having already heard the announcement.

"The best part is they want Teddy to be the face of the campaign. They'll get a bunch of shots of him at the gala to use for the ads. They even want a few shots of the two of you together. They adore what they've been seeing from the two of you online."

Avery saw spots as her vision swam. Her parents looked at her expectantly, waiting for her to be absolutely delighted. *I wish a hole would open up in the floor below and swallow me whole.* She wasn't even sure Teddy would attend the gala at this point. And if he did, it certainly wouldn't be for a loved-up photo shoot with her.

"You're speechless. Don't worry about it, I've always known you were beautiful enough to do some modeling," her dad assured her.

No, it's not my looks I was worried about, but thanks for

giving me something else to keep me up at night, Dad. She couldn't find the words to tell her parents about the breakup with Teddy, that it all had been fake, then real-ish, and now nothing at all. Instead, she said nothing, wondering how long she could go without telling her parents the truth. She would stick to her plan, nail down a new location and then deal with the Teddy Aurelia Strap situation.

"Let's call Teddy and tell him right now," her mom said, her cheeks rosy pink. "Put him on speaker."

"No. I'll have to tell him later. He's flying to Mexico City today, probably mid-air right now." At least that much was true. Whether she'd get up the nerve to call him later to share the news, or whether she'd use Stacey or James as a messenger remained to be seen.

"Well, then. I'm headed to lunch, and I'm sure the ladies will have some venue ideas. Between them, they must have hosted nearly half the charity events and weddings in Los Angeles last year. I'll call you after and let you know what we've come up with. Really, dear, don't stress over it," her mother said as she stood to usher Avery out the door.

And there it was. End of conversation.

Dismissed.

It's like I'm a teenager all over again with my parents not noticing that all I need is their emotional support. Instead, they did what they had always done: tried to make problems disappear by throwing their weight and money around. Her insides went soupy. What would it take for them to realize that she was more than just stressed, that she was on the verge of a nervous breakdown?

Is it not enough that I'm heartbroken, my family doesn't notice I'm at my wits end.

twenty-six

LOS ANGELES, CA

Pathetic. Avery's limbs felt so heavy she could barely drag herself back to sit at her desk. *Guess I'll just wait here like a useless idiot until my parents have solved my venue problem.*

Her whole plan had been to avoid Teddy at all costs, she'd blocked his number and deleted all social media apps from her phone as soon as she'd landed back in LA. How was she supposed to put him out of her mind and focus on work when her Dad orchestrated a photo shoot for them at the gala? *Just my luck.*

She had no idea how she was going to pull off any of it: find a new venue, find a different star to wear the watch, find a date. She was going to let the kids at the sports center down. Let everyone down.

She had made such a mess of things, she wasn't sure where to start. She looked at the cinnamon latte and blueberry muffin she'd left on her desk and her stomach roiled. She hadn't taken a single bite before she'd talked to Sofia and confirmed the bad news, before she realized how deep a hole she'd dug herself.

She needed someone to help her step back from underneath the waterfall of emotions cascading over her at the moment. There was only one person she could confide in who would understand the family dynamics and pressure—why she'd gone ahead with the fake dating scheme in the first place—her brother, Ben.

When they were little, Avery and Ben had been inseparable, but as they had gotten older they'd drifted apart, seeing each other only at holidays and other Silver family events. Ben would descend on the West Coast for a day or two, get dressed up and smile for the photos for an evening only when absolutely necessary, then head back to his more exciting life, leaving Avery to dutifully fulfill the day-to-day Silver family obligations. She didn't resent him for it, *not really*, but she was envious of his separate life. *And I really missed him.*

But when Ben and Adam became parents, they'd decided to move back to the LA area to raise their daughter. Avery adored her niece, and she and Ben found a way back to the closeness they had once shared, building an adult friendship based on their shared history. They began using the term 'sibling summit' to describe their one-on-one time spent venting about their parents and counseling each other. They could complain to each other in a way they couldn't to anyone outside their family. No one wanted to hear the child of a billionaire complain.

She sent him a text.

> I came back early. I need to talk. Any chance you are free tonight?

> Ben—Hang on. Let me check in with
> Adam and make sure he can be home in
> time to do bedtime. Welcome Home!

Great, more waiting around for members of her family to get back to her. She'd wait with her phone in hand until everyone was ready to solve her problems. A fresh wave of shame rolled over her, heating her face.

Fortunately, Ben got back to her right away.

> I'm in. Any chance you can come out our
> way? I don't think Adam can get home in
> time for me to come to you before traffic.

No problem. She could use the drive out to the valley to figure out how much she wanted to tell Ben. No one knew about the breakup, except Stacey, granted it had only been twenty-four hours. Stacey knew, of course, but they hadn't talked about it. It was too painful. Her heart still felt raw. But she'd probably, well definitely, feel better if she came clean to Ben. About everything.

* * *

Avery walked into the dark and old-fashioned bar at her family's country club. The heavy drapery and mahogany furniture was borderline stuffy, but the fire crackling in the fireplace on the opposite side of the room gave it a cozy feel. The best part of the club was that it tended to clear out early. By seven p.m. on a Wednesday night the golfers had finished their socializing and gone home to their families.

Ben was already there, seated at the long bar, his cashmere sweater draped over the back of his leather barstool. They pretty much had the place to themselves. The only other patrons were two older gentlemen chatting quietly and sipping bourbon in front of the fireplace. She closed her eyes and took a deep breath before she approached Ben, trying to calm her nerves. The weight of all she'd been carrying alone inside for the last day lay heavy in her chest, and she wanted, scratch that, *needed* to unload it.

What if Ben thinks of less of me as a result? She didn't want to lose his respect and trust. She couldn't risk creating emotional distance between them again—he was one of a few people she could confide in.

Ben looked up from his seat at the bar and waved her over, grinning. She returned his enthusiasm with a half-smile, the most happiness she could muster at the moment. She gathered her hair at the back of her neck and twirled it into a big chunk over one of her shoulders.

Her brother stood from his chair and gave her a warm embrace before pulling out the seat next to hers and motioning for her to join him. She took her time hanging her purse on the hook underneath the bar, buying herself one last moment before she had to start spilling her guts.

"What's wrong?" Ben's welcoming smile faded into a thin line of concern. "I thought you wouldn't be able to wipe a smile off your face. You were practically glowing after the race in Austin. And now you look like you ate something sour."

"Ben, my entire life is what's wrong," Avery smoothed her skirt underneath her as she sat.

He had already ordered her an Aperol Spritz. Ever since a family trip to the Amalfi coast a few years ago, it had been her drink of choice, no matter the season. She took a gulp of her drink. The bright orange flavor tasted familiar and sunny, and brought Avery right back to the four original Silvers sitting on a porch playing cards before dinners of pizza and gelato. If only she could recapture that closeness with her parents too. *At least I have Ben.*

"Your whole life?" he questioned.

"Well, I managed to screw up the gala and my relationship with Teddy all in one day."

"Sorry. Sounds rough," he said. "Let's start with Teddy. What happened?"

Where to start? She'd have to go back to the beginning for her anguish to make sense. She took a deep breath and let it all come tumbling out... the crush, the stupid fake-dating plan, falling for him for real, Mexico (she left the sex parts out; it was her big brother she was talking to after all), and then being utterly rejected by Teddy. Her brother let her talk, not saying a word, just nodding and murmuring "hmm" and "I see" as she unburdened herself, trying to shake the weight in her chest loose.

She finally came up for air when she got to the part where she fled Mexico.

Ben cleared his throat. "Wow, that is a mess. I never thought you'd get involved with a driver in the first place," he paused, his brow furrowed. "They don't exactly make ideal boyfriends. I guess we both had to learn that lesson the hard way."

The bartender appeared on the other side of the bar, across the polished wood. "I see you are both low on drinks there. Another round?" he offered.

"Yes, definitely," Ben replied. "But I think my sister here is going to need something stronger than an Aperol Spritz," he looked over at Avery and pointed at her glass.

"Yes, I certainly do. Could I please have a vodka tonic with a splash of cranberry? And I just realized I'm starving. I'd also like a burger and fries." She might as well allow herself to indulge in a juicy cheeseburger and a plate full of steaming, salty fries. So what if she felt bloated and gross tomorrow? It would match her mood. *It's not like Teddy, or anyone else, is going to see me naked again anytime soon.*

"Coming right up," the bartender nodded and scooted away discreetly, giving the pair privacy to restart their conversation.

"Wait a second," Avery narrowed her eyes. "How do you know that drivers make terrible boyfriends?" No way she was letting him skate by that admission.

"Let's just say a certain Italian stallion and I may have had our moment a few seasons back," Ben covered his face with his hand.

No way! Avery brought her hand to her mouth to stifle a giggle. "You and Matteo? That guy, seriously?"

Ben shrugged, "What can I say, I like 'em tall, dark, and handsome. But, you called the summit and tonight is about you and Teddy. I'm not surprised, unfortunately, to hear that he assumed you'd follow him around like a stray dog, taking whatever scraps he gave you."

Avery winced.

Ben continued, "Drivers have to put their needs first and not give a fuck about anyone else to succeed. That spills over into their personal lives." Ben looked around to make sure the bartender wasn't in earshot. "I mean, I'm not sure Matteo knew my first name."

"I know, I know. They are the worst, Teddy included," Avery admitted, her chest aching. "But he actually let me see this whole other side to him: this sensitive, silly, vulnerable side.

And I let him make me feel special, different. I feel so stupid for falling for it, ya know? I'm embarrassed, Ben."

"Well, I get why you're blaming yourself, but as your older brother, I don't see it that way," Ben replied earnestly, his protective side coming out. He swiveled his bar stool so he was facing Avery. "To me, he seems like a complete ass. He took advantage of your proximity to get what he wanted, a fling with no strings attached, without any regard for your feelings and completely forgot that you were an actual human, not simply a convenient opportunity."

She took a gulp of her fresh cocktail, the bite of the vodka and the tart cranberry a distinct contrast to the spritz's effervescent bubbles. *Is Ben right? Was Teddy using me the whole time?* She felt cold all over.

Avery looked down. "Maybe it's not *all* my fault," she stirred her drink with her straw, her head swimming with images of her time with Teddy. "Teddy strung me along. A real dick move. I mean you know how it is being Michael Silver's kids. It's so hard to trust that anyone likes you for you, and not for the money, or the notoriety. But I thought since Teddy has his own money and fame, I didn't have to worry about him using me. I guess I was wrong."

"Maybe he thought that getting involved with me was strategic too. Like Dad or Brandon couldn't fire him if he were with me?" There had to have been a reason Teddy led her on like that when their fake-dating arrangement could have been fulfilled easily without complication. "That it somehow would help save his drive even if he didn't perform on track?"

"Damn, I hadn't thought of that, but you are right, Aves. That could be part of it. What a piece of work," her brother was getting animated now. "If he weren't so damn fast, I'd call

Dad right now and tell him to fire that piece of shit," Ben curled his lip into a sneer. "Well, maybe I should anyway. There's a lot of talented drivers out there who deserve a shot, maybe we can find someone who can both win races and keep it professional."

"No," she held up her hand. "I don't want him to get fired, but I wouldn't mind seeing him suffer a bit. I wish I could get back at him personally without hurting the team or bringing bad press to our family right when I am going to need to use our family name to fix the gala." She drained the rest of her glass.

She was feeling more emboldened now, the alcohol starting to fuel an anger that matched Ben's. Why shouldn't Teddy feel the ramifications of messing with her heart? Had he forgotten who she was, who her dad was? While she was usually hesitant to play the "do you know who I am" card, the vodka was starting to make it seem like a reasonable path to take.

"Maybe I can give him a taste of his own medicine, plant an embarrassing story about him in the press?" Avery suggested. "I do know quite a bit about him now. He may have been using me for sex and job security, but he also confided in me. And I could hurt him if I want to."

"Hmm, this could be fun," Ben said conspiratorially, leaning in and wiggling his eyebrows. "So, what do you have? Does he sleep in women's underwear? Eat burritos by taking a bite out of the middle first?"

Avery rolled her eyes and playfully smacked her brother on the arm. She appreciated that he was trying to lighten the mood.

"Well, if I really wanted to get him where it hurts, he told me the real reason he had that on track melt down a few years and lost the F2 championship. His dad called him the night before and asked him to throw the race. He didn't lose on purpose, but it fucked with his head and he lost anyway. Teddy hasn't spoken to him since."

"Whoa," Ben's eyes went wide. "I did not know that. How did that not make the news?"

Shit, I shouldn't have told him that. Too late. She took a deep breath and quickly looked left then right, making sure the bartender wasn't hovering, before she continued. "Well, Teddy had very little to do with his father. He left Teddy's mom when Teddy and his brother were very young, and he wasn't there for them growing up," Avery explained. "When Teddy was a teenager, he started using his mom's maiden name, Ross, and the press never made the connection. Dad helped the whole thing go away."

Ben's brow knit together. "That would be enough to mess with anyone's head, especially a seventeen-year-old kid under intense pressure."

Avery's heart lurched. An image of a young Teddy, hurt in his eyes, appeared in her head, but she quickly pushed it aside and forced herself to picture him on the beach, the exasperation in his eyes when he rejected her.

He doesn't care about you the way you care about him. Telling herself that hurt like a fresh paper cut.

"Here you are, burger and fries." Avery jumped, the bartender jolted her out of her thoughts as he set down a plate in front of her. Avery picked up a handful of the piping hot fries and dunked them in the little white ramekin of ketchup next to her plate before shoving them in her mouth. She washed it down with the last of her vodka soda.

"Do you want half of this?" Avery offered her burger to her brother before she started in.

"Sure."

"And, I haven't told you about what's going on with the gala yet," she groaned. "This was only Part One of Avery's Life is A Dumpster Fire."

"Hit me with Part Two, I can handle it," Ben offered.

"I'm not sure I can without another one of these," she pointed to her empty glass. "Excuse me," she called to the bartender, her voice way louder than necessary, considering he was about two feet away. "Could we get another round?"

"One Aperol Spritz and one vodka martini coming up."

"Actually, just the martini, I'm all set for tonight," Ben corrected.

"Don't make me drink alone! What kind of fun, older brother are you?" Avery pouted.

"The kind who has a preschooler who wakes up at six a.m. and a family history of alcohol addiction. Also, the kind who is not going to let you drive home after a third drink," he pulled out his phone. "I will let Adam know you'll be spending the night in our guest room."

"That is probably wise. Thank you," Avery accepted his offer.

Avery took a big bite out of her half of the burger before she filled her brother in on her other major failure. "We officially have no venue. No Monarch. No Four Seasons," she said between bites, "Mom asked her friends today for ideas, and even they came up empty. We are royally screwed, and it's all my fault."

Ben used his napkin to wipe some ketchup from his face and gave her a small smile, but didn't argue that it wasn't her fault.

"And Dad arranged for Teddy and I to do some Aurelia Strap photos at the gala, *together*. And we really need their sponsorship money."

"I know you want to transform the event and be able to donate to your new causes, but you don't have to put so much pressure on yourself," he gave her a pointed look. "Just let Mom find a suitable alternative and focus on changing the world next year."

Avery looked down at her burger and suddenly couldn't take another bite. Her ravenous hunger and buzzy anger had morphed into a bone-deep weariness. She longed to put her head down on the bar—she could probably fall asleep right there.

She summoned the strength to look back up at Ben. "I sort of already promised the Youth Sports Complex that we'd fund the construction of the new gym. I can't go back on my word. I *have* to make the gala better, more successful than ever."

Ben shook his head. "Bold move, kid. Okay, here's what we are going to do. Adam joined the Automotive History Museum board this year. They have events there all the time. He can call first thing in the morning and check on the date."

"That's not a bad idea," Avery said as the wheels started turning in her head. A fraction of the tension she'd been holding evaporated. Her problem wasn't solved yet, but knowing that her brother was on her side and looking out for her made her feel optimistic for the first time since she'd fled the beach.

"It's a bit on the nose, but we could lean into the theme, I guess. And thank you for helping me out of this mess. For listening too," she said.

"I wish you'd asked me for some advice sooner. I've been on

the foundation board for a decade, and I could have warned you against making promises to charities," he signaled to the bartender for the check. "I'm sorry you had to learn the hard way, but I'm here to help."

twenty-seven

LOS ANGELES, CA

"So, what did you think?" Ben asked, rubbing his hands together. "Food stations and high-topped cocktail tables, could that work?"

Avery wished it could. *If only it were that easy.*

Adam had called the events manager at the Auto History Museum as soon as he'd dropped Sadie off at school. The date was available, and Ben and Avery headed straight there to check out the space after stopping at her apartment to shower and change.

Avery shook her head. "Sadly, I don't think the layout is right. There isn't enough space for a sit-down dinner and we can't hold the crowd's attention during the auction if they aren't all seated formally. It's too risky."

"Yeah, I see what you mean. You really are good at this, Aves, I never would have thought of that."

She felt a weight drop into the pit of her stomach, "I guess it's back to the drawing board."

"I'll keep thinking too, now that I have a better idea of the space requirements - basically an empty square that we can fill with tables and a small stage. I see now why hotels always work out so well."

"Yep," Avery said, popping the p. "It basically has to be a wedding venue. And there's a reason no one gets married during the holiday season."

"We'll figure it out, I promise," Ben gave her a hug before he took off, leaving Avery on the sidewalk, the wheels in her brain turning. A big square room they could put tables and a stage in —there had to be a big blank room somewhere in the city. *Think, Avery, think.*

Avery racked her brain all afternoon for another venue, and was still coming up blank. She was about ready to call it a day when her phone vibrated on her desk. Her heart skipped a beat, her traitorous nervous system held out hope that it would be a certain race car driver, even though she'd blocked him. His golden green eyes, his smile, his broad hands and lean muscular frame—she missed him, the thought of his body, his hands on her body.

But, no. It was Stacey. Avery lifted the phone to her ear.

"I'm calling to check on you after that podcast dropped this morning," Stacey sounded apprehensive. "And I know things are weird between you and Teddy, but you may want to reach out to him."

"What podcast? What's going on?" Avery asked, her skin prickling.

"No one told you yet?" Stacey paused. "I hate to be the bearer of bad news, but I'm going to send it to you right now, so you can hear it yourself. Hang on."

Avery drummed her fingers on her desk impatiently until a link popped up on her screen: "Beyond the Apex Podcast: Breaking News: Teddy Ross's Scandalous Past."

An immediate burst of adrenaline shot through her body. Did this mean news of his dad had gotten out? That was the only Teddy related scandal Avery knew of, and she was quite certain that despite how things ended between them, Teddy hadn't been hiding any other dark secrets from her.

How on earth could this random podcaster dude find out about Teddy's dad? As far as she was aware, only the very top-level executives and the PR team at Silver knew about the situation. *And me. I certainly didn't tell anyone.* Well, except for Ben. But Ben would never, ever in a million years betray her confidence.

"Avery, hello? Are you there? Did you get it?" The sound of Stacey's voice got her out of her head.

"Yes, I'm here. I just got the link—is this about Teddy's dad?" Avery asked.

"Yes, it is. So, you know?" Stacey replied.

"Yeah, he told me in Mexico. Before everything went to hell..."

"I thought he may have told you. We had a 'Team Teddy' crisis management meeting. James and some guy from legal reminded everyone that no one outside Teddy's closest advisors, and his family, of course, knew about his dad betting on races. Legal was there to remind us that we had all signed NDAs and that Teddy would not hesitate to take legal action. And Teddy sheepishly admitted that there was one other person in his life he had told. I assumed it was you."

"It was me," her heart fluttered at the news that she was someone in his "personal life."

"But I haven't told anyone but Ben, and Ben sure as hell wouldn't tell an F1 podcaster..." Avery's voice trailed off. While she wanted to get to the bottom of this, her thoughts drifted to Teddy himself. She could picture him sitting in the meeting, completely stoic, his hazel eyes shimmering with heat, all business-like, but hurting inside, worried about his mom and brother, the impact this would have on them.

"How's Teddy handling all of this? Is he okay?"

"He's holding it together, but I can tell he's upset. He's not going to race this weekend; he's going to fly home to Scotland to be with his family for a couple days," Stacey said.

Avery sagged back into her chair—it was everything he feared coming true. Did Teddy think it was her who tipped off a podcaster in spite? She hoped he knew her better than that.

"I'm going to listen to this thing for myself," Avery sighed. "Before I do, not to sound selfish or anything, but am I mentioned? Did whoever leaked this know about our breakup? I want to prepare myself for what I'm about to hear."

"No, you aren't mentioned at all," Stacey answered. "The podcaster tells the full story of Teddy's dad as if he's a reporter breaking the Watergate scandal and deserves the Pulitzer Prize. It's a bit over-the-top. Well, you'll see. Call me later after you've listened?"

"I will. Thanks for the call Stace, I really appreciate it. Talk to you later," Avery hit the end button and popped in her earbuds to listen.

She felt a dull headache begin to build at the base of her skull, surely a physical reaction to the news. Some fresh air might help. She stood up and grabbed her sweater from the hook on the back of her door and headed outside to stroll along the beach.

The sun was shining brightly and from inside it looked like a beautiful day. But as soon as Avery walked outside the building, a gust of wind came off the water, rattling the palm trees.

She shivered. She thought about turning back, but knew that she wouldn't be able to sit still while she listened, so she ambled on and pressed play.

Blake: Welcome everyone to today's episode of Beyond The Apex: A Formula One Podcast. I'm your host Blake Beckett. And boy, oh boy, is today's episode a juicy one. So buckle up, Silver fans.

Avery groaned and pulled her sweater around her body as she walked further down the beach path. She wasn't entirely sure whether the chill she felt was from the windy ocean air or the dread she felt anticipating what she was about to hear.

Blake: Today we are going to explore the scandalous family history of none other than Silver's golden boy, Teddy Ross. Let's start with this. Did you know that Teddy's real last name is Campbell? So what? You might ask. Celebrities use catchier stage names all the time. Well, I'm about to tell you all about why Teddy Ross wouldn't want to use his given last name, Campbell, right after this break.

Avery fast forwarded through the advertisements.

Blake: And we are back. So who is Teddy Ross, really? Turns out that the notoriously private Teddy was born in Scotland as Teddy Campbell, son of Nigel Campbell and Margaret Ross. And as true Teddy fans already know, his family almost never appears in photos or race coverage. Teddy has maintained that the reason he keeps his family away from the public is to protect their privacy, but maybe it's to protect himself from negative publicity. Because Nigel Campbell, Teddy's estranged father, is a criminal. And Teddy just might be his accomplice.

Avery increased the audio speed to 2x and Blake Beckett raced through the rest of the sordid details of Nigel's sports fixing past. She already knew the facts, and the emotional impact Nigel's crimes had on his family

Blake: Did Teddy lose the F2 championship on purpose? Can his team and fans trust him? Let us know what you think on Facebook, Twitter, or by leaving a voicemail at...

Avery's heart knocked into the walls of her chest. As angry as she still was at Teddy, she knew this was basically his worst nightmare—that fans would lose their faith in him, think that he lost a race on purpose, that it could happen again.

How many people knew Teddy's family secret by now? How many listeners did this guy even have?

She looked down at her phone, and navigated beneath the podcast logo, photo, and description. It wasn't ranked in the top 100 shows or anything, but it had a 4.8 rating and several hundred reviews. Naturally, some of those listeners were F1 reporters, and after other media outlets picked up the story and disseminated it farther, the whole world would know.

The dull headache she'd felt coming on minutes ago was now pounding in her temples.

She turned around and walked back in the direction of her office. She needed to take something before it turned into a full-fledged migraine and rendered her useless the next two days. She also had to get to the bottom of how the secret had gotten to Blake Beckett, not lie in a dark room with ice packs on her head. She knew James and the Silver PR machine would be conducting their own thorough investigation, but her own internet stalking might uncover something useful. It was possible that someone was trying to hurt the Silver family personally by way of hurting Teddy. It wouldn't be the first time someone had sought to bring the seemingly too-fortunate Silver family down a notch or two.

She sat back down at her desk and rummaged through the top drawer until she found her bottle of Excedrin. She poured two of the pills into her hand and swallowed them dry.

Avery's fingers trembled as she typed Blake Beckett into the search bar at the top of her screen, her breath stuck in her throat as her computer loaded the search results. If Blake Beckett was trying to grow a following and audience for his podcast, which presumably he was, it wouldn't be hard to find him. And boom, there he was, the first result on the page was the podcast's website. She clicked on it, a pretty boilerplate site with show notes and links to episodes, but it didn't help her learn anything personal about Blake, except that he was decent at SEO. She'd need to dig a lot deeper—maybe take a deep dive into his social media pages if she was going to be able to deduce how on earth he'd found out about Teddy's dad.

She scrolled further down the search results page and found Blake's Linkedin profile. This might help. Current location -

New York, NY, well that didn't exactly narrow it down. Current job: host of Beyond The Apex pod. Okay, also not that helpful. But his previous job, now here was something: Vice President, Beckett Enterprises in El Segundo, CA. Beckett Enterprises? Like the big construction company in town that had built nearly every new skyscraper in LA County in the past thirty years? Blake's headshot made him look about thirty-ish, so maybe he'd been working for a family member before he decided to launch a F1 podcast.

She started a new search for 'Beckett Enterprises.'

Family business, blah blah blah, started by someone named Samuel Beckett. But then there it was, a picture of Mr. Samuel Beckett, and he looked somehow familiar. She zoomed in to get a better look at his features. Had she met him at a charity event? Maybe the gala last year? And then, it hit her like a bolt of lightning. The gray hair, the bow tie, the cozy fire. Samuel Beckett was one of the older guys she had utterly dismissed at the country club bar. *No, no, no. It couldn't be. Did he overhear us and share the information with his son, who happens to have a Formula One podcast?*

Avery's stomach roiled. She was the source of the leak.

twenty-eight

LOS ANGELES, CA

The acid from the coffee she'd had earlier burned her throat. *This is so bad.* What were the odds? She thought the club's dark bar was the safest possible place for her to vent to Ben, and one of the *two* people in there happened to not only be eavesdropping, but knew who she was talking about and had the means to make it public immediately. That whole time she'd been worried about the bartender hearing them and she'd dismissed the old fogeys by the fireplace.

She grabbed the stainless-steel water bottle she kept on her desk and gulped, trying to keep her coffee down. She'd not only betrayed Teddy, but she'd likely lose her job and whatever remaining confidence her parents and the staff had in her. There's no way they'd let her represent the family or the team in any official capacity after acting so irresponsibly. She started to sweat, feeling the clammy, slick wetness on her palms, behind her knees, under her boobs. She was hot and cold at once, utterly unable to control her body temperature, despite taking several more sips of her water.

I'm going to be sick.

Avery bolted upright out of the chair and ran out of her office, down the hall, and into one of the blue-tiled bathroom stalls and made a beeline for the toilet. Nothing came up, and after a moment, the wave of nausea passed as quickly as it came on, but the pain in her head was worse than ever. She slid down onto the floor next to the toilet and rested her head back onto the stall's door. She wasn't sure she'd ever felt this bad before in her life, physically or mentally. Had Caroline seen her dramatic office hallway sprint from the front desk? The last thing she wanted right now was someone coming in to check on her, she might die of embarrassment on the spot.

How could she have been so stupid, so careless? Teddy had trusted her with his biggest secret, and had shared it with her in bed, completely vulnerable. She'd gone and proved him right, that there was no place in his life for a real relationship.

She let herself slide the rest of the way to the floor, letting the cool blue floor tiles serve as an ice pack of sorts on her cheek as she attempted to regain control over her nervous system. She laid there, breathing in and out, for a few minutes trying to calm herself down, ruminating over how she'd ended up in this precarious position. She knew she had no one but herself to blame for her current state, laying on the grimy office bathroom floor. She'd probably get a stomach bug too. Awesome.

Some minutes later, she summoned the will to stand up and turned the latch on the stall door slowly. She walked to the sink and splashed some cool water on face, then blotted her face using a rough, scratchy, paper towel. She gave herself a good, long look in the mirror. She'd been too stunned to cry, so at least her eyes weren't puffy and red. That would have been a dead giveaway that something was wrong. She smoothed her hair down with shaky hands, pulling it into a tight bun low on her neck. She tried to take a deep breath, but her lungs wouldn't quite cooperate, the air catching in her throat before it could fill her chest.

She made her way back to her desk, stopping by the kitchenette to grab a pack of ice for her head, which still throbbed. She was scooping ice from the freezer into a plastic bag, her back to the doorway, when Caroline walked past her to the coffee maker.

"Oh no, Aves, what's the ice for? Headache again?" Caroline asked, knowing Avery suffered from the occasional migraine.

"Yeah..." Avery slowly dropped a few more cubes in the bag, avoiding turning around and facing Caroline for as long as possible.

When the bag was nearly spilling over, Avery pressed it shut and turned around.

"You really don't look so good," Caroline said, concern in her eyes. "Not just a headache is it? Can I do anything?"

Avery shook her head. "It's not just a headache. I'll fill you in when I can, but I need to wrap my head around it first."

She needed to fess up to what she had done. She knew she could only hang onto whatever self-respect she had remaining if she owned up to her mistake and apologized profusely and genuinely. But she needed to talk to Ben first. He was the only person who could confirm the bizarre sequence of events before she began explaining anything to anyone.

"Okay, you know where to find me," Caroline squeezed

Avery's arm and backed off, making space for Avery to walk out of the narrow kitchenette.

Avery went back to her office and set the ice pack down for a moment, not caring that it would sweat and leave a water ring on her desk, and picked up the phone with her still-trembling hands.

"Hey sis, what's up?" Ben answered on the first ring.

From his light tone, Avery could tell that news of the podcast had not yet reached him.

"I'm going to assume that you haven't heard about this podcast situation since you had to ask," she said, her voice barely a whisper.

"No... what podcast situation?" he asked.

"Well, this morning, a podcast..." Avery filled her brother in, trying to hold back her tears and get the whole story out before she lost it. "And, well, I think... I think it might be our, *my*... fault, it got out," she squeaked.

"Why do you think it's your fault?" Ben asked with concern. "Did you tell anyone besides me?"

"No! There's no one in the world I'd trust, besides you, well maybe Stacey or Caroline, with something that personal. And I wouldn't even have told you if I hadn't had all that liquid courage."

"Well, you know I didn't gossip after you told me. Plus, I would never do anything that would mess with Teddy's head during the middle of the season, that's just bad business."

Avery exhaled, her heart rate slowing a fraction as she pushed the sole of her shoe into the edge of her desk and leaned her head back into the high back of her faux-leather desk chair. The sturdy push back from both pieces of furniture felt supportive.

"Of course. I knew that. I knew you'd never in a million years tell anyone. That's not what I think happened," she took a deep breath, "Do you remember those two older guys sitting by the fireplace at the club when we got there? Did you pay attention to what they looked like or when they left?" Avery asked evenly, not wanting to sway Ben's memory one way or the other.

"Actually, I know one of them and said hello before you arrived. A guy named Howard. He played with dad in the member-member golf tournament last year. He's a studio exec I think. Why?"

"Did he introduce the guy he was with by any chance?" Avery tapped her toes against the firm wood of her desk, waiting for Ben's answer. If this other guy was indeed Samuel Beckett, then it was all over and she'd know for sure what had happened.

"Yes, he introduced him as Sam, his neighbor in Hidden Hills."

Avery's stomach fell. Sam from Hidden Hills had to be Samuel Beckett. There went the last little glimmer of hope that maybe the leak was not her fault. She felt tears welling up behind her eyes, and wasn't sure she was going to be able to get through what she had to explain to Ben without crying.

"I think he was Samuel Beckett, his son Blake, has an F1 gossip podcast," she explained. "He must have eavesdropped once Howard introduced you, and then used what he heard to help his son get a scoop."

One second passed. Two. Three. The tears in her eyes stung with shame.

Avery couldn't take the silence for a single second longer. "Ben?" her voice was barely a whisper as she clutched the phone tight.

"Oh, shit," Ben finally said, processing what he'd heard.

"You're right, I think. What the hell? That's unacceptable." She could hear the agitation and anger in Ben's voice as it grew louder. "That's got to be against official club policy. I'm going to get him kicked out. He can't mess with the Silvers and expect to get away with it."

Avery released her grip on the phone as she let out a long exhale. He was in her corner. *Of course, he's got my back.*

"It's really messed up and as long as it's okay with Dad, go give him the Ben Silver revenge treatment," Avery acquiesced. "But, please, hold off until I give you the ok? I want Dad to hear it from me first. It seems only right." She couldn't bear the thought of a staff member telling him his own daughter was responsible for his team imploding.

"I admire that. Good luck. I'm here for you, and I'm really sorry. It was my fault too, we should both have been more discreet and lowered our voices in there."

"It's not your fault, Ben. I'm the one who shared the secret in a public place," Avery said, her cheeks burning.

"But you're my little sister, and I should have protected you, or stopped you. I trusted those guys, figured they weren't paying any attention to us. It goes to show we can't trust anyone outside our family."

"Stop. Please. I'm a grown woman and I need to start taking responsibility for my life and my actions. I've been acting like life just happens to me for long enough, I do have agency. Weirdly, I'm beginning to think this is my first chance to make that known."

"Wow, I admire that Aves," her brother said with pride in his voice. "Everything will be okay, keep me posted. I love you."

"I will. Love you, bye," she hung up and put her head in her hands on her desk. *Well, fuck.* The long yellow post-it note with the day's to-do list stared back at her as she looked downward. To her right, the ziplock baggie had already started to sag as condensation from the melting ice clung to the clear plastic. Her confession and apologies were going to take all day, resulting in another work day lost to her personal drama.

She put the soggy, yet cool, bag of ice back on the top of her head while she contemplated her next move. She had to reach out to Teddy. The thought filled her with sickly dread. They hadn't spoken once since their dramatic confrontation on the beach in Mexico. She had resisted the urge to drunk-dial or text him after her night out with Ben, which she was, frankly, proud of. And even if he had tried to contact her, she wouldn't have known, since she'd blocked him.

Now she had no choice but to reach out to Teddy. What she had said to Ben had been true, she needed to turn over a new leaf, take responsibility for the mess she'd made. It was the only way she'd ever be seen as a professional, as an adult.

Given her heightened emotional state and her track record with saying horrible things to and about Teddy when triggered, Avery figured email was best, safest. Maybe it was the easy way out, but at least she'd say everything she'd want to with the tone she wanted to say it with. Plus, she knew that he was likely on a plane to Scotland right now, and then she'd have to wait for him to check his voicemails when he landed and call her back, if he even called her back at all. Yeah, email was definitely the best bet.

Dear Teddy, she typed and then erased... *too formal? Too old-fashioned?*

Her mind wandered to the last time she'd fretted about the right tone writing to Teddy. Over a stupid crush. Never in a million years would she have imagined it would have led to all of this.

Teddy, she erased again. *Too straightforward? Too businesslike?*

Hi Teddy, she tried one more time. *There, that seems like the right tone, finally.*

Hi Teddy,

There are so many things I want to say to you. I'm sorry for the way I handled myself on the beach that last day in Mexico and for not hearing you out. We should probably talk about how we are going to move forward at some point... But, the reason that I'm writing today is to let you know that the podcast is my fault. I'd never hurt you on purpose; I hope you know me well enough by now to know that. But, I told Ben about your past. I think Blake Beckett's dad overheard us and told his son. I only figured it out today after I listened to the podcast and was gutted when I made the connection.

I haven't told anyone on the team yet about the Becketts. Not Stacey. Not my dad. I wanted you to hear it from me directly first. I don't expect a reply, but if you could confirm that you've received and read this email, I'd really appreciate it. I won't tell anyone else that I was the leak until I know you've read this. I am so truly sorry. It's your life and it was your family's story to tell, not mine. Again, I'm so sorry.

Take care, Teddy.

Sincerely, Avery

twenty-nine

LOS ANGELES, CA

Avery's fingers itched and inched toward her phone before she used every last fiber of her willpower to pull her hands back into her lap. She felt a compulsion to scroll, scroll, scroll through social media and see every last thing being said about Teddy in the wake of the podcast. But even though she'd felt that twinge, that itch, approximately every thirty seconds for the last several hours, she'd managed to make it this far without giving into temptation. Yet, she jumped a moment later when it rumbled on her desk as she received an incoming message, sending a jolt of adrenaline up her spine. As if her phone knew she was jonesing for it: a reply from Teddy? It had been hours since she sent it, surely he'd read it by now?

She picked her phone up from its face-down position.

AUNT SHARON—Avery, I listened to the podcast. Please send my best to Teddy.

Her heart sank as she rolled her eyes with annoyance. Maybe it was genuine concern and she should have been more appreciative, but it wasn't the first text like that she'd received today. Cousins, friends, Josh, had all reached out with cheery words of support like "Team Teddy. Don't care who his dad is - no reflection on him!" Deep down she suspected a lot of them were coming out of the woodwork in hopes of getting some inside scoop.

She had her boilerplate response memorized, responding to each person who reached out with precisely the right tone, that of a concerned, supportive girlfriend who had no idea how the leak had happened. Her lips were sealed until she'd heard back from Teddy and fessed up to her dad.

And that was just the friends, family and personal contacts. Then there were the reporters. Even with her office door closed, she could hear the front office's phone ringing off the hook, Caroline's chirpy voice giving out the party line that had been sent out in an organization-wide email: "No, the team and the Silver corporation do not have any comment. No, Teddy will not make a statement and respectfully asks for privacy. No, Teddy will not race this weekend."

Avery's ears felt hot each and every time she'd heard Caroline repeat those words. The knowledge that she was the lynchpin in this disaster felt like a thousand bricks on her chest. She badly wanted to confess what she knew to her dad, to James, but she had to give Teddy the opportunity to reply. In the meantime, the only thing kept her from completely losing was knowing that the well-oiled PR machine at Silver was equipped to handle this sort of thing.

She opened her browser again to see if Teddy had replied in the last thirty seconds, but nope. *What if he never replies? What if he hates me so much for this that he never wants to talk to me again? I have to hear from him before I see my parents tomorrow.*

She flipped tabs to her calendar, the pink square for the ribbon-cutting ceremony for the Silver Sports Medicine Center glaring at her. A lump formed in her throat. There was no way she'd be able to look them in the eye and not tell them about the Beckett connection. She wasn't sure she wouldn't lose her composure entirely. How was she supposed to smile and shake hands and pretend everything was normal? No doubt Teddy's drama would be the elephant in the room, and knowing that it was her fault, but not acknowledging it would be simply unbearable.

Hours passed as Avery continued anxiously clicking back and forth between her calendar, her e-mail, and her texts, only occasionally taking breaks to work on a paper-clip chain, until finally that little number one appeared on the envelope icon on her phone. Her heart nearly jumped out of her chest seeing Teddy's name. Fingers shaking, she clicked into the message.

Avery,

Confirming receipt of your email. Thanks for the heads up, and for your honesty. I recognize you thought that your club was a safe space, but I told you personal information in confidence, and I expected you to honor that and keep it to yourself.

I tried calling you, but you didn't answer. I wanted to clear the air between us, and I was going to keep up my end of the bargain and accompany you to the gala despite the way we left things on the beach. However, due to this unforeseen change in circumstances, I will need to lay low for a while. The International Racing Association has opened an investigation into my conduct, just as I feared, and I anticipate that will be taking a good bit of my time. Other than races, I will not be making any public appearances. I know you'll understand.

    Regards,

    Teddy

Avery's heart cracked in two as his words sunk in. He sounded so cold, so formal, so final. He'd tried to call her. It was something, but what more could he have said that wouldn't have made her feel even worse?

A fresh wave of regret about the whole fiasco rolled over as she slumped back in her chair and closed her eyes for a second. If only she could go back in time and undo... *everything*. Avery brought her fingers to her temples, massaging the pressure points there as she tried to shut out the world for a moment, but the ringing phones were so loud they were making her head explode.

It was back to square one. Plan a gala. Find a date. Earn everyone's respect. Only now, she'd dug herself a deep hole she'd have to find a way to get out of.

thirty

LOS ANGELES, CA

Avery arrived at the ribbon-cutting at the last possible moment, right before the photo op was scheduled, purposefully avoiding any small talk or sympathetic comments for Teddy. She had come for one reason: to find a moment with her parents to tell them the honest truth.

"On three, everybody, big smiles," the photographer directed the group. Avery gave a fake cheery smile as she silently practiced the speech she was going to give her parents as soon as she could get them alone. Now that she'd heard from Teddy, time was of the essence. She had to come clean to her parents before anyone else figured out the Beckett connection.

Next to her, her dad was holding a comically large pair of scissors suspended over a blue ribbon while various hospital executives looked on with delight from behind the photographer. The photographer released them once she got the right shot, and the group moved into the hospital foyer for refreshments and tours of the new space.

"Avery, you have to try this cake," someone from the hospital team insisted, shoving a plate of heavily frosted sheet cake into her hands. Avery's stomach churned as the sweet cloying scent of it hit her nose. Her nerves had left her with no appetite at all.

"Oh, um thanks," Avery took the paper plate, not wanting to be rude. The woman looked at her eagerly, waiting for her to take a bite.

"Can I get a second slice? I'm sure my parents will want some too," Avery lied through her teeth. Her mother would never waste calories on a piece of sheet cake, but at least she'd have an excuse to get her parents' attention.

The hospital staffer returned with a second plate and Avery snatched it out of her hands. "Thanks so much," Avery plastered on another fake smile.

My fake smile is getting almost as good as Teddy's.

Teddy. Just his name flashing in her thoughts left her feeling cold and clammy. She looked down at her hands, now both holding servings of cake.

Might as well get this over with.

"Mom, Dad, come eat this cake with me," she said in an unnaturally loud voice.

Her mom, who was standing a few feet away engaged in a polite conversation, looked at her quizzically and reached for the long strand of pearls around her neck. Sharon expertly excused herself from her conversation and corralled her father.

"Avery, are you okay? I know it's been quite a week. But let's not make a scene," Sharon whispered, her eyes narrow.

Avery let out a huff of breath and cocked her head at her

mother. *God forbid a scene. Always appearances first, family second.*

"No, not really. I need to talk to you guys," Avery replied in an equally hushed voice.

"Let's go in here," Avery's dad suggested, smoothing his royal blue necktie down his chest as he pointed toward an empty, bland conference room off the main foyer.

Avery followed her dad into the room and closed the door firmly behind her, double checking that it was shut, and no one could hear them. She'd learned her lesson.

They sat down at one end of the conference table and her parents looked at her expectantly, her mother's hands folded neatly in her lap, her dad's arms crossed. She unceremoniously plopped the cake down on the table, no longer pretending that any of them were going to eat it.

Avery tugged at her silky floral print skirt, the smooth fabric itchy against her skin, and cleared her throat. "Well, I guess I'll start with the podcast, I know how Blake Beckett found out Teddy's secret."

She carefully monitored her parents' reactions as she told them the whole story, expecting them to look disappointed, maybe even angry. But there was no yelling, no head shaking. They silently nodded, and said only "Hmm," and "Go on," their eyes never straying from her face.

Their quiet concern left her head spinning. *Is it because we are still in a semi-public place? Are they keeping it together now, but then I'll have to pay for it with passive aggressive digs for months?*

Her dad shook his head as she relayed the night at the club with her brother. "Unbelievable," he muttered, shaking his head in disgust.

"Daddy, I'm so sorry. I should have known better. You've always taught us that our wealth and success have given us a target on our backs. I let my guard down."

"I'm not upset with you, Avery," his face softened before reverting to a grimace, "I can't believe that Sam Beckett would do that to you. To me. I've referred him all over town. In fact, I put in a good word for him to get the contract to build this very hospital years ago. And this is how he repays me?"

"And they aren't even particularly charitable," her mom added.

With her parents fixated on the social sins committed by the Beckett family, maybe she could take it one step further and slide in the fact that she and Teddy had been faking it all along? They seem to be taking it all in stride and she had their attention.

"There's more," Avery took a deep breath, clenching her hands in her fist. They might not be upset about the leak, but what she was going to say next was even worse. "Teddy and I aren't together anymore, in fact we never were...really."

"What are you talking about?" her mother asked, her eyes bulging.

Avery rolled her eyes at her mom's shock. "Oh come on, Mom, can you really be that surprised? You had been badgering me for so long about meeting someone special."

"Don't blame this on me," her mother scoffed, clearly offended. "I only wanted you... I always want you to be happy."

"I know you care about me, but you've spent years trying to make sure our family has a sterling reputation. I know your interest in who I was dating was important to you because of how it reflected on you, on the family, not only because you care about my happiness."

Avery paused, looking up at the ceiling. *Breathe, Avery. Focus. Remember, this is about coming clean with them, a fresh start with no secrets, taking my place in the world as an adult.*

"And I wanted so badly to raise the money for the projects I proposed to the board," Avery admitted. "I wanted to get you off my back, Mom, but I also wanted to take advantage of Teddy's popularity to raise the money for the sports complex and scholarships, and now I've messed it all up, even our partnership with Aurelia Strap."

Avery's voice quavered, "I just wanted you both to be proud of me. To make our family's legacy even stronger by using the foundation to be a real changemaker. Now I've made it worse. I'm going to break my word to the sports complex, the sponsors, the team, and damage our family's reputation."

"Nonsense," her dad said, leaning over to give her shoulder a squeeze. "I'll tell Aurelia Strap the truth. That Teddy is not making public appearances at the moment. Zack and his wife can fill in," her dad said, alleviating at least one of her worries.

"Really?" Avery asked.

"Really," he confirmed. "Stuff like this happens all the time, especially when dealing with these egomaniac drivers. You have plenty to worry about right now, but don't let that be one of them. You won't let the sports complex and the kids down, I have faith in you Avery."

"Thanks, Dad," she said, tears welling in the corners of her eyes.

"Of course, we are proud of you," her mom added quietly. "You impress me constantly. I've never been so impressed with someone in my life. You don't have to do any of this, you don't have to work a day in your life, but here you are, focused on your career, and on making a difference. I'm in awe of you."

Avery's heart swelled. She couldn't believe her ears. She knew her parents loved her, but this was something else. *Pride. Respect.*

"You mean that? You always act like I'm wasting my time working, like I should be focused on finding a husband and settling down. I didn't think you understood me at all. I didn't do anything to deserve this life. I want to at least do what I can to use my platform for good."

"I might not understand you, but I'm proud of you. And I'm sorry I don't say it enough," her mom pulled a tissue out of her purse and dabbed her eyes.

Avery stood up from her chair and walked over to her mom and put her arms tenderly around her. "I didn't mean to make you cry, Mama. I know you don't want your mascara to run."

"Hey, I'm proud too, nothing makes me happier than having my daughter work with me," her dad joined their embrace, putting his arms around both of them. "Now, what do you say we get out of here?"

Avery nodded in agreement and wedged herself out from her parents' arms.

"Wait!" Her mom grabbed the plastic fork from the cake plate and scooped a huge gob of frosting into her mouth.

Avery gasped. "Mom! You're eating carbs?! It's not even your birthday."

"Well, it would be rude to lie about having tried it," Sharon explained, going for a second bite.

Avery shook her head. "I'm truly shocked."

"It's only cake, not the devil," Sharon said, smiling. "Come on, here have some, it's actually quite good."

Her mom forked another bite and handed it to her.

Avery bit into the moist chocolate cake, letting the icing melt on her tongue. The sugar tasted like relief.

"Dad, it's your turn," Avery laughed, handing her dad the next bite.

Instead of returning to the event to shake hands, Avery stood hovering over the conference table, eating cake with her parents and giggling until every last crumb was gone.

thirty-one

WESTLAKE VILLAGE, CA

Avery did *not* have time for a day of massages and cucumber water. Her jaw clenched every time she thought about the "Location To Be Announced" banner that loomed large on the foundation website. As reassuring as it was to know that everything was out in the open, it didn't lessen the amount of work needed to pull off the gala. But Caroline and Stacey had insisted on a spa day. The three of them weren't often in the same city, and Stacey stopped in LA on her way to the Las Vegas grand prix. *My girlfriends know I could use a post-Teddy pick-me-up.*

The timing had worked out nicely, she'd give them that much. She had issued a solo statement announcing her and Teddy's breakup the day before. It had been time to give up the charade once and for all. The internet would start speculating when she didn't go to the Vegas race, especially since Teddy was returning to the grid after missing a race, having been cleared of any wrongdoing by the International Racing Association.

She had drafted a statement, had Caroline read it once to make sure it wasn't too curt, and then emailed it to Teddy and James moments before posting it:

"Teddy and I have decided to end our romantic relationship. I wish him success as a valued member of team Silver. Thank you so much for your continued support."

Curt, cold. Just like him. A less hurt version of her would have consulted Teddy first, but after his impersonal email, making it very clear he wanted nothing to do with her, she had decided to do things on her own.

She turned off her phone and placed it in her locker, locking the door behind her. Her skin prickled at the thought of being unreachable when she had so much on her plate, but she knew that completely unplugging was her only hope for enjoying the day. She'd be too tempted to read the comments on her breakup announcement. Caroline and Stacey had carved time out of their busy schedules to spend a day cheering her up. Neither of them had time during the season to take a full day off work either, but they'd done it for her. So, she would at least *try* to enjoy it.

"Okay, first on our agenda: the invigorating foot scrub," Caroline announced, once they'd all gathered in the lounge area in their fluffy spa-issued robes and rubber flip-flops.

Avery followed her friends to the salon room and sank down in a lazyboy chair as a woman got to work scrubbing her feet. She let her eyes close gently, and stretched out her jaw.

"This is way better than a pint of Ben & Jerry's and a rom-com on Netflix. You are the best friends, seriously," she said. "I know you both are so busy, how did you manage to get away for the day?"

"I told your dad we needed an off-site gala planning day,"

Caroline said. "So as long as we talk about something related to the event, we can thank the Silver corporation for our team-building massages."

"And I'm free until I have to fly to Vegas. I'm on the same leave as Te..." Stacey answered.

"It's fine you can say his name around me," Avery sighed. She didn't want her friend to feel like she couldn't talk about her life, her work, which inherently revolved around the sun that was Teddy Ross.

"Well, this is your breakup party. I didn't know if it was the weepy kind, or the I-never-want-to-hear-that-bastard's-name-again kind," Stacey admitted, head tilted.

Avery rubbed her temples."I don't know. I mean, all three of us work with him, so he's unavoidable. But yeah, after yesterday's announcement, I guess I can use a day off from talking about him."

"Speaking of Vegas: my roommates and I are hosting a watch party. Pajamas and poker themed," Caroline offered, changing the subject. The Las Vegas race had an unusual midnight start, hence the pajamas. "Avery, you should come, since you aren't traveling to the race. It'll be fun."

No way. Half watch the race while playing poker? She would never. "Thanks for the offer, but I think I'll watch alone, if at all," Avery replied.

Plus, she knew all eyes would be on her when Teddy was shown on screen. She didn't want the pity, the curiosity of acquaintances she barely knew. It would be way more than she could handle.

"I get it. Okay, next up massages," Caroline directed, "I'll meet you both in the relaxation lounge in an hour."

* * *

Avery's massage was divine. The masseuse's warm hands, and the invigorating minty massage oil had brought her back to life. If only her brain had been able to give into the masseuse's hands the way her muscles had. But instead of deep relaxation, her mind had spent the full hour reliving every conversation she'd ever had with Teddy. *Why oh why can't I get this guy out of my head even after an official breakup announcement?* She was supposed to be done with him –no fake dating, no real dating. It was behind her now, if only her thoughts would cooperate.

She took a sip of hot tea and grabbed a handful of almonds from the spa lounge's snack bar. Caroline and Stacey filed in behind her, looking blissed out. Avery's ribs squeezed with envy.

"How were your massages?" she asked her friends.

"Really good, my masseuse had a great knowledge of the musculoskeletal system," Stacey answered.

"So good," Caroline sighed dreamily. "I feel bad Ben missed out on this. I thought since he'd be in the men's lounge it didn't make sense to invite him, but that massage alone would have been worth it for him to come."

"Don't worry about it, he was busy anyway," Avery said. "They are installing turf across the main lawn at their house today. They can't seem to keep grass alive with all the drought-related watering restrictions. So, I'm sure he's there making sure every single blade meets his standards. Which will take hours."

Avery rolled her eyes. Her brother was obsessed with his show-stopper of a house in an exclusive gated community outside LA where the brick homes were more stately than Monticello itself.

Caroline laughed. She'd been to their house enough times to know what Avery meant.

"How *big* is his lawn?" Stacey asked, her eyes wide.

"As big as a football field, and they have this spectacular garden that he obsesses over," Avery answered. "It's gorgeous, if I ever get married, I'm going to have my wedding at their house. There's this one juniper tree the previous owners planted in the garden. It's iconic."

Avery gasped. A wedding. A wedding venue. It struck her like a bolt of lightning, the answer to her problem suddenly crystal clear. She'd been looking for a blank, square space to have the gala in. And her brother's lawn was the perfect venue.

Avery waved her hands in the air.

"I've got it. We can tent the new turf lawn and have the gala at Ben and Adam's house. You guys!"

She was bouncing on her toes, resisting the urge to sprint back to the locker room so she could ask Ben and Adam. She didn't want to waste another minute.

Caroline clapped her hands in glee. "You're a genius. I can't believe we didn't think of that earlier."

"No, you're a genius. An off-site planning massage was exactly what I needed to come up with it."

"That's brilliant," Stacey agreed.

Avery was already picturing the event. There was just one hitch. Ben and Adam would have to agree to it. But hadn't Ben said he'd help her?

"Okay, we've lost you. I can see it in your eyes," Caroline smiled. "Go and get dressed. You're officially excused from spa day."

She bolted toward the lockers to change and call Ben.

thirty-two

BEVERLY HILLS, CA

"How about this one?" Avery pulled a floor-length, navy blue slip dress from the rack and held it up to show her mom.

"You have the right figure for it. Try it on," Sharon said.

"I'll add it to your dressing room," the stylist who was helping them offered.

The past few days had been such a whirlwind. Ben and Adam had agreed to host the gala at their home, and it was go time as soon as she heard the word yes. She'd met and placed an order with an event rental company, set up a tasting with the caterer, and notified all of the guests and sponsors of the new location. When her mom had suggested they go dress shopping, it had seemed like a good respite. Plus, it was a good distraction knowing the rest of their family and most of her friends were in Vegas for this weekend's race.

"Ready to try on?" her mom interrupted her thoughts.

Avery nodded. "I think we found every evening gown in the store."

Avery slipped into the dressing room and stripped down to her neutral colored undies and strapless bra. She'd come prepared: underwear that would work with any neckline, a pair of heels in her bag to get a better feel for how a dress would look on her, once tailored.

She tried on the first contender. *Hard no.* She'd liked the ruffled skirt on the hanger, but the voluminous fabric was swallowing her petite frame in real life.

"Any luck in there?" her mom called from the other side of the curtain.

"Not yet."

Her phone vibrated in her purse. She pulled it out. *Stacey.*

"Hi Stace!" She'd always pick up for her.

"Just killing time and trying to stay awake since the race is so late tonight. So, I thought I'd check in. How is the event planning going?"

"I'm actually in a dressing room, shopping for a dress for it with my mom."

"Put me on Facetime, I want to see!" Stacey said.

"Hang on, I'm naked. Let me put one on and then I'll turn on my video. How's the weekend?"

"Good, really good. Car's pace is excellent so far. Top form. And Teddy's driving with this intense determination I haven't seen on him before," Avery could hear the excitement in her friend's voice. "He seems hell-bent on making up for missing the last race."

Avery felt her ribs squeeze as she pulled the navy slip dress over her head. And it wasn't from the fabric, which draped her smoothly.

"I'm glad to hear the car is looking good," Avery said, purposefully avoiding engaging in conversation about Teddy's current headspace. Would she always feel guilty for causing Teddy to miss a race, especially right after his first podium? "Here I'm going to hand the phone to my mom so you can see my fashion show."

She stepped out of the dressing room, holding the dress up in one hand so it wouldn't drag on the floor. She gave her mom the phone. "It's Stacey, she wants to see the dress options."

"Hello, Mrs. Silver," Stacey chirped.

"Well, hello Stacey. Now how do I turn this thing around?" Sharon pulled the phone away from her face, squinting her eyes.

"Press that circle with the camera icon and the arrows," Stacey patiently instructed.

Patience came easy when Sharon was not your own mother.

"What do you think of this one?" Avery gave a little twirl.

"It's gorgeous," Stacey gushed through the phone. "Stunner."

Her mother cocked her head, and peered at Stacey through her black-framed glasses. "It looks fabulous on you, but you'll be cold. And you don't want to be messing with a shawl all evening. You'll need your hands free."

Her mother was right, of course. But she hesitated, looking longingly at herself in the mirror before returning to the dressing room. The navy silk dress was so sexy, she felt like a goddess in it. If only Teddy could see it on her, then maybe he'd wish she was his girlfriend.

C'est la vie.

"Do you have anything to try that has sleeves?" Sharon asked.

Avery thumbed through the gowns hanging on the rod.

She carefully stepped into a black, velvet dress. It was a completely different silhouette and style than the navy one. It was fitted at the waist before falling into a swingy skirt, and featured long blouson sleeves. Avery swished the skirt around. *Fun.*

She emerged once again, looking to her mom for approval, before glancing in the mirror. While the skirt made it fun, the top half made it a show-stopper—the split neckline held together by three embellished decorative bows, showing the right amount of skin between each one from her collarbone to her waist. The bows' iridescent beads and glistening crystals gave it a festive pop, just right for a holiday season event.

It was perfect for the gala. Not as sexy, but sophisticated without being dowdy, and no jacket or sweater required.

"You look like an angel," Stacey cooed.

She'd get excited about seeing me in a paper bag. Avery looked to her mom, the much harsher critic. Sharon simply nodded at her. "Yep, that's the one. Unless there are any others in there you want to try?"

Avery pictured the rack. "No, nothing is going to beat this one," she smiled at her reflection, imagining herself gracefully greeting their donors and guests. Now, if only she could surgically remove Teddy from those images. Because try as she might, it was still him by her side when she pictured the evening, his hand lightly touching her back in that subtly protective way she missed, as she charmed everyone in attendance.

"Well, then that's settled" her mom said, ever efficient. Sharon turned her attention to Stacey, "Will we get to see you in real life at the gala? There's an open seat at the family table, now that Teddy, well you know..." Sharon gave Avery an apologetic look, bordering on pity-ing.

Avery tilted her head, giving her mom a pointed look. *Really?* She couldn't help getting in one last dig could she? At least she was offering the empty seat to Stacey, and she hadn't so much as mentioned a "special someone" to Avery all day. Maybe it was her mom's own weird way of trying to do better.

"No, I wish I could," Stacey answered, "But I'm going to be in Australia with my family for the holidays."

"Of course, we understand completely," Sharon trilled. "Family first."

That was quite enough of that. Avery took the phone from her mom's outstretched arms, and retreated into the dressing room, smoothing the velvet skirt under her before sitting on the small bench in the corner.

"I can push my flight to Sydney back and come?" Stacey offered. "I feel like a shit friend for not thinking of it sooner, now that your mom mentioned it."

No, she'd never ask Stacey to delay her flight. She only got to see her family once or twice a year. It would be nice to have a friend there, though. Someone who was in her corner with no other agenda for the evening. Plus, there would be tons of press there, and the last thing she wanted was for the non-profits to be overshadowed by stories about poor Avery going stag.

"I appreciate it, but I can't take away from your limited time at home."

"Well, if you change your mind and want me to come too, say the word," Stacey's genuine warmth radiated through the small screen.

"Thank you. You're the best. Now go win that race for us."

"We will try our best. And great dress choice. It's killer," Stacey grinned.

"It is, isn't it?" Avery took the dress off and put her jeans and cream colored knitted sweater back on.

"Any luck?" The saleslady chirped. Avery rolled her eyes. Right on time to earn her commission.

"Yes," Avery handed her the dress. "We'll take this one."

"And this one," her mom handed the navy slip dress to the saleswoman. "You'll find somewhere to wear it," she added, turning to Avery.

"Excellent choice. How would you like to pay?"

"Oh, she'll be taking care of that," Avery pointed to her mother. Sure, she was working hard to build her career and assert her independence. But that didn't mean she was going to offer to pay for her own designer couture.

Sharon didn't bat an eyelash as she pulled her Platinum Card out of her leather wallet and handed it over.

"I'll go run this and wrap up the dresses for you. Here are some treats while you wait," she offered them a plate of petit fours. "Can I offer you some water, champagne?"

"Two sparkling waters would be lovely," Sharon answered. "Avery, sit with me and have one of these divine looking chocolates."

"Cake at the ribbon-cutting and now middle of the day dessert," Avery raised her eyebrows. "Who are you and what did you do with my real mother?"

"I only want to spend a little more time with you. You've been so busy lately."

Avery raised her eyebrows. Was this going to be another conversation about how she should really settle down and find a husband? Because that was going to ruin an otherwise very pleasant afternoon.

Sharon raised her hands around her face in a defensive position, "Don't take it the wrong way. I simply enjoy your company."

"Two glasses of sparkling water and your card, Mrs. Silver," the saleslady presented the items on a small silver tray. "They're steaming the dress in the back. It should be only a few more minutes."

Avery sat down next to her mom on the velvety sofa in the dressing area and took a sip of her drink.

"Is there anything I can do to help with the event?" Sharon asked. "I know you have a lot on your shoulders. I have the time —with Dad traveling with the team so often—and you and your brother doing your own things..."

Was her mom lonely? Was that what this was about? Avery set her water glass down on a coffee table and put her head on her mom's shoulder, snuggling in close.

"I'm great with seating arrangements. We can make ours a table of nine, and then make the company table an eleven. I'm sure there's someone at the factory who would be happy to attend," her mother offered gently.

"Actually, I think I'm going to invite Josh. He helped me out so much with my pitch to Archer, it would be a nice way to say thank you. Plus it would be nice to have a friend there." Avery didn't want to give her mom the wrong impression.

"As long as it's what you want, I think that's a nice idea. No pressure from me. And no more questions about your love life. It's off the table," her mother promised.

Avery sighed. "No, it's not that you can't ask me about my love life. It's just that the way you ask, it always feels like you're putting pressure on me. And I'm only twenty-three, it's not like I'm an old maid or something. I'm not going to settle for someone because he looks good in family photos."

"I never, ever want you to settle for anything less than great. You and your brother, well you've given me purpose in life. My only regret is that I didn't have you sooner, and I don't want you to wake up one day when you're my age and wish you hadn't wasted time," Sharon said quietly, fingering her pearl necklace. Sharon and Michael had waited until Michael's businesses had taken off to have kids, and then faced fertility struggles. Ben hadn't arrived until they were thirty-eight, and Avery three years after that.

"Mom, I had no idea you felt that way," Avery's heart softened. "I thought you were just trying to use me to make our family look perfect, be perfect, after your, our family's, rough patch."

Her mom's face fell. "I screwed up so royally when you were young and wasted even more time not being present for you. And your dad and I are older and we won't be around forever. I want time with my grandkids, and a chance to get it right as a grandmother."

"Oh, Mom," Avery's voice cracked. "I get it. But, it's different now than when you were growing up in the seventies. I mean not everyone gets married. Success and fulfillment can be found outside of marriage and family. Not everyone even wants kids."

"That's true, but I don't care about everyone. I care about you. And I've seen the way you look at your niece, how you light up when she's around and really engage with her. I'm your mother, I can see the envy in your eyes when Adam reaches for

Ben. And you can't get to any of that if you don't go on a date first." Sharon gave her a pointed look.

"I know," Avery nodded. The problem was there was only one person she could imagine having a future with, and they weren't even speaking to each other at the moment. The closest she was getting to spending time with Teddy was watching him on TV.

thirty-three

LOS ANGELES, CA

Watching the Vegas race alone on her couch had been extraordinarily depressing. At least Teddy had continued his second-half of the season hot streak, earning another third-place finish, and Zack had come in second. A double podium again. But, no one swept Avery off her feet for a kiss this time. Heck, no one had even given her a high five.

She refused to let herself wallow and watch all alone again, so two weeks later she'd invited herself over to Ben and Adam's house to watch the following race. Avery settled into the leather camel-colored sofa in their media room as best she could. It was not the most comfortable piece of furniture imaginable. The cushions were a bit overstuffed and there was no give under her, but she was grateful for the company. She didn't want to watch another race alone in her apartment, shouting at the TV in her sweatpants. Well, she was still wearing sweatpants, but at least she wasn't alone.

"Will you turn up the volume, Ben?" Avery asked her brother, passing him a touchscreen remote with approximately 1200 buttons and options. "I still can't figure this thing out. Why can't you guys have a normal TV remote like everyone else?"

"Here, give it to me," he reached over and grabbed it, ticking up the volume. "See, it's not that hard. And can your TV do this?"

Avery rolled her eyes as the custom shades automatically rolled down, blocking out the sun and turning Ben and Adam's multimedia room as dark as a movie theater.

She'd been so busy running from meeting to meeting that it should have been easy to *not* think about racing, about Teddy. She'd been burning the candle at both ends, and she should have been able to fall asleep the second her head hit her pillow at night.

But everywhere she went, there he was. The gold rimmed plates she'd selected for the tables? They were the golden flecks in his eyes when he smiled his real smile at her. The Silver Racing logo on the event website? The baseball cap he'd worn the first time they met at the track. The holiday plaids in store windows? His helmet. His pajama pants.

"Want a drink?" Adam asked. He motioned to the glass fronted fridge on one side of the room that was stocked with several flavors of sparkling waters, sodas, hard seltzers, and beers.

"I would, but I don't want to have to get up and pee during the race," Avery replied. Another reason she couldn't exactly watch the race with friends, none of them would understand the intensity with which she and her family watched a race. There was no side chit-chat, no bathroom breaks, the only talking a

Silver would do during a race would be nuanced strategy analysis or an emphatic cheer or groan.

"Ok, here we go," Ben shushed his husband and sister as the five lights above the track turned red one by one. The mood was tense: Teddy was starting ninth, Zack sixth. Super disappointing after back-to-back double podiums.

Avery bit the inside of her cheek. Teddy sure had his work cut out for him just to stay in the top ten. His old teammate on Alpha Fuerte was lined up next to him in tenth, and Cody was right behind them in the eleventh spot in his Archer. It would take some real defensive driving to keep those two behind him and earn a few points for the team today.

She sat up a little straighter, the leather squeaking underneath her. She could feel adrenaline course through her, like it did at the start of every race. She'd been doing that her whole life. She was grateful that she couldn't see Teddy's face on the screen, it might have sent her over the edge. With his face hidden beneath a helmet, she could *almost* forget that the boy who had broken her heart was the one behind the wheel.

One. Two. Three. Four. Five. The lights turned red one by one, and then it was lights out.

The two cars in the front row: Ferrari and Phoenix, battled for first place, with the second place Ferrari pulling ahead for a strong start. She knew that it would only be a matter of time before the Phoenix took back the lead, but it was still impressive. Now, if only they would show the cars in mid-field, so she could see how Teddy and Zack had done. Had either of them managed to gain a position or two at the first corner?

Finally, the TV camera zoomed out, showing the full grid from above. Avery saw Cody's Archer go straight up the middle of the track, trying to squeeze between Teddy and the Alpha

Fuerte. *Risky? Yes. Ambitious? Also, yes. But if he pulls it off... I'll be impressed, even if it puts Teddy at a disadvantage.* She looked over to Ben, who wrinkled his nose at her in silent agreement.

The track became blurry, multiple plumes of dark gray smoke shooting into the air, making it hard to see what was going on.

Avery sucked in some air through her teeth, her hand flying to her chest. *Yikes.*

Had Cody misjudged the space down the middle and made contact with one of the other cars?

Two cars spun out of the melee in opposite directions, sparks flying, the sound of crunching metal so loud that the TV cameras were able to pick it up and broadcast it. Avery held her breath, Archer orange spinning to the left, and the Alpha Fuerte stopped in the gravel on the right.

Where's Teddy?

Then out of the smoke, another car went careening across the track, wheels up, like a turtle on its back. It kept going across the asphalt on its shell, leaving a trail of white-hot sparks in its wake.

Oh , no, no. Avery gasped.

Please don't let it be Teddy.

"Someone is upside down. This looks bad," a British voice announced through the TV screen.

"I think it's Teddy Ross," the other commentator announced.

Avery jumped up from her seat and heard a shrill, desperate scream from somewhere.

Oh wait, did that scream come from my throat?

Teddy. She could no longer pretend it was simply another driver inside that blue Silver, it was Teddy, *her Teddy*.

She covered her eyes with her hands, but simultaneously wanted to deny that this was really happening, but couldn't look away. As she peaked through her fingers, she saw the upside down Silver skid over the gravel. She shuddered. *Okay, the gravel will slow it down, and then the tire barrier is right there to stop it.*

She tried to relieve the pressure in her chest by breathing, but she could only manage a short inhale before...

No. Oh my god.

The car didn't stop at the barriers, instead it went airborne, cartwheeling in the air before it finally came to a stop on its side, on top of the barrier, wedged up next to a fence, Avery's heart stopping with it.

"No, no, no." *This can't be happening.* Avery's body shook so hard that she wasn't sure her legs would be able to keep holding her up. "Oh my god, is he alive? Is he okay in there?" Suddenly, it no longer mattered that he hadn't wanted a committed relationship; their connection had still been real. Her feelings for him were *so* real. She'd take back *everything* for the chance to see him again.

She looked over to Ben, who looked aghast, his mouth hanging open.

Emergency personnel and race stewards ran at full speed in the direction of the car, and the driver inside, climbing and clambering up the barrier to provide assistance. The announcers were eerily quiet as they too watched in horror from the press box.

"Go! Get him out of there," she shouted at the stewards through the television.

She felt Ben come and put his arm around her shoulder, trying to steady her, and heard Adam's voice on the phone trying to reach her dad or someone in Miami. Avery thought she might be having an out-of-body experience. It all felt a little far away, like she was watching her hands quiver from above. Ben didn't say anything to her, simply gently led her to sit back down on the couch, and rubbed her back. She'd never experienced shock before, was this what it felt like?

Avery sat and stared at the TV screen, the sound of her thumping heart filling her ears. She tried to breathe, tried to focus on the feeling of Ben sitting solidly beside her, his hand on her back. The cameras kept a respectful distance from the crash scene, and Avery couldn't see much except the backs of suits as they worked to free Teddy.

The announcers finally broke their silence, filling the empty air time with platitudes like "You never want to see a crash like that," and "We're waiting for any indication or news, and will share more as soon as we are able," but Avery barely registered what they were saying. Their voices sounded like they were a million miles away.

Finally, one of the race marshals who had rushed over to Teddy's car to give aid turned to the camera and gave a thumbs-up. Avery's lungs finally allowed her to exhale a gasping, audible breath. *Okay, he must be alive, he must be conscious in there.* She felt a primal urge to go to him, to hold him, and tell him it would be okay. She imagined herself sprinting from the Silver team garage to reach him, but obviously she couldn't do that from her utterly useless location on the couch.

Avery regained control of her limbs and breath, but she still felt a massive pit in her stomach. He was alive, but how badly hurt was he? Would he ever be able to race again? Her heart broke all over again, thinking of him having come so close to realizing all of his dreams only to have them wrecked by an idiot American driver who made a boneheaded move on track. She knew that she no longer had any right to be the one to go to him and comfort him; not for real and not even for pretend. She'd shut that door the moment she'd posted her break-up announcement. If she could go back in time and undo that, she would. But that wasn't an option, so she sat on the couch like every other stupid fangirl watching from home, *because that's all I am now.*

The paramedics lifted Teddy out of the destroyed vehicle and loaded him onto a stretcher. She couldn't see any major injuries during the split second he was visible on TV before someone held up a blanket to shield him from the prying eyes of the crowds.

What if he had broken his neck? Or what if he'd suffered a brain injury? A thumbs up didn't give her nearly enough. Being in the dark, like the millions of other people watching on TV was simply unbearable. She looked over at Adam, who was standing up by the window with his phone up to his ear. She didn't dare say a word, in case he was getting even a morsel of information, hoping he could read the desperation in her eyes.

He shook his head. "Got your Dad's voicemail. I'll keep trying."

He's alive. She repeated the words to herself like a meditation as Adam paced back and forth, trying to reach someone, anyone who was there.

She'd just seen one of the most gruesome, scary crashes in F1 history, and while she was still panicked, she also felt gratitude that a number of new safety features had been introduced in the sport over the past several years. *He's alive.* The car's halo, the tubular frame that surrounds the car's cockpit, had only been mandated in 2018, and it had likely protected Teddy's head when the car was upside down. She shuddered, imagining the outcome for a driver had this incident occurred prior. It was a stark reminder that while Formula One was incredibly fun and exciting, it was still terribly dangerous.

He's alive.

Stacey! She should try calling Stacey. Surely, she would be by Teddy's side now? "Where's my phone?" she practically shouted as she quickly checked her pockets and lifted the throw pillows on the couch to see if it had fallen behind.

"Adam's already calling everyone in Miami, it won't help to have all of us calling. I'm sure they are 100% focused on Teddy and will update us as soon they can," Ben tried to reason with her.

"No, no, you don't understand. I can't find *my* phone," Avery stood up from the couch and crouched down by Ben's feet to look underneath the furniture. "I want to call Stacey. She could be calling me, and she's there. With him!" Avery heard herself shouting at her brother. She had to find her phone. Now.

Because deep down in her heart that she knew that if their roles were reversed, if she'd been in an accident, the first person she'd ask to talk to wouldn't be her parents, wouldn't even be Ben. It would be Teddy. And if there was even a sliver of a chance he felt that way about her still, after everything, she had to be reachable.

"Okay, I get it. Take a deep breath and I will help you look," Ben said, pulling her to her feet.

"Take a deep breath?! How am I supposed to take a deep breath when the man I love got carried away in an ambulance and I am watching it from thousands of miles away on TV?"

Avery yelled at her brother. Before the words were even out of her mouth, she realized what she had announced. And she knew in her heart of hearts that she loved him. She didn't only miss him, or want him, she cared deeply about him. The fear that he might be alone and hurt wasn't empathy, it was love.

Adam stopped his pacing by the window and looked up, his mouth hanging open. But Ben looked at her with nothing but concern in his eyes and pulled her into a tight hug. Avery wondered if he was at all surprised by her declaration. She had spent an evening with him getting totally tipsy and cathartically trashing Teddy, but her brother must have sensed her true feelings, even then. He knew.

He released her from his arms and squeezed her shoulder. "Well, then we better find that phone."

Avery, her heart slamming in her chest, frantically upended the room, tossing couch cushions on the floor, while Ben searched methodically, retracing her steps.

"Bingo," said Ben, holding up her phone in its blue case with the Silver Racing logo, like he'd found the crown jewels.

"Thank you! Where was it?"

"In your purse, on the entry table," Ben raised his eyebrows as Avery practically leapt across the room to grab it from his hands.

She stared down at it, hoping to see something from Teddy, Stacey, or even James. She scrolled quickly through thirty-two texts. But they were all from friends and acquaintances who had seen the crash on TV. There was nothing from the people who mattered. Her brother was right, they were probably completely focused on Teddy and managing the situation.

She closed her eyes, picturing James trying to keep the media at bay, or Brandon, the team principal, in communication with the race officials trying to decide if and when to restart the race, and her dad trying to keep everyone calm. She hoped Stacey had ridden in the ambulance with Teddy, so that he wasn't alone. Had someone notified his mom back in the UK and were made arrangements for her to travel to Miami?

Her thoughts were interrupted by Adam's voice. He'd finally gotten someone to answer.

"Who is it?" she mouthed, moving a step closer to him. He held up his hand, and stepped back, as if it was hard to hear the person on the other end of the line.

"Mm hmm, okay..." was all she could hear. Avery went entirely still, her eyes trained on Adam's face trying to gain any insight from his facial expressions. He looked serious, concerned, but not devastated.

"I can ask her. Thanks for calling," Adam said quietly. She inched closer to him as she waited for him to hang up and fill her in.

"So," she asked. "Who was that? What's going on?"

He took a deep breath, put his hand on her shoulder. "It was your dad. Teddy is ok. He's talking and there are no obviously catastrophic injuries. They are taking him to the University of Miami Hospital for observation and tests, but he's going to be okay. Your dad and Stacey are in a car following the ambulance to the hospital and..."

Avery felt all the hot air inside her slowly but steadily drain out, like she was a helium balloon with a small hole. *He's alive. He's okay.* She tried to get her nervous system to process the news faster.

"And what?" her voice wobbled.

"And he's asking for you. He asked the safety marshalls and the EMTs if you were at the race," Adam said softly.

Avery's heart stopped in her chest.

Teddy had a whole team of professionals looking out for him. There were advanced protocols in place.

And he'd asked for her.

Of course, she'd go. None of them knew him like she did, the warm-hearted, sweet guy underneath the all-business, self-centered exterior. Were any of them thinking of him as a person? Or was he just an asset, no more, no less valuable to the team than the million-dollar car he'd been driving? He needed someone by his side who cared about him, only him, not the team, not how fast he could get back on the track, as he recovered. Even if his family was on the way, she could get there so much faster.

"I need to go," she said out loud to no one in particular, even though both Adam and Ben were in earshot.

"Avery, do you really think that is a good idea?" Ben asked. She could see him go into protective big brother mode. "He is getting the best possible care. And once he is settled in at the hospital, Dad or Stacey can get you on the phone with him, maybe even FaceTime?"

She wasn't sure how to explain the physical tug she felt to go to Teddy. "It's probably *not* a good idea, but I feel a very strong need to be there. I'm not sure whether Teddy will even want to see me in person once the adrenaline wears off, but my gut is telling me to go."

Ben nodded.

"Your gut is one thing. What does your heart say?" Adam asked.

Avery didn't even have to think about the answer.

"My heart says *go!*"she answered.

"Then let's get you to Miami."

thirty-four

MIAMI, FL

Avery unbuckled her seat belt as soon as the large gray hospital building came into view. Once the car stopped, she jumped out and nearly ran inside, only to be stalled at the front desk while a very unhurried receptionist spoke softly into a phone.

"I'm Avery Silver. I'm here to see Teddy Ross," she said as soon as the receiver was back in its cradle.

"ID please," the receptionist said.

She found her wallet inside of her green leather tote bag and pulled out her license. It was all the luggage she'd had with her: she'd gone straight from Ben and Adam's house to the airport, not bothering to stop at home to pack a suitcase. She'd chartered a flight, carbon footprint be damned, and had made it to Miami in record time. Teddy was worth the guilt about the expense and emissions from chartering a jet. For once she felt incredibly grateful that her wealth made it possible. Money couldn't buy happiness but it could get you somewhere faster in an emergency, and she was appreciative.

The receptionist picked up the phone on his desk. "I have Avery Silver here for patient Ross. Can I let her through?"

There was a long pause. She clenched her fists by her side. She was going to explode on this guy if he didn't hurry up.

He finally turned to Avery. "Thanks for your patience. We've had a few reporters and fans try to get in here, so I needed to confirm you were on the approved visitors list.

Avery's dad was waiting when she exited the elevator, and she fell into his outstretched arms. Ever since she had come clean about the podcast and Teddy to her parents, she'd felt closer to them than she had in her adult life. Her family had really shown up for her the last few weeks, and had come together to pull off the gala, which was now in great shape. She was 85% of the way to the funds she needed to cover her parents' commitments and her own vision. They'd offered support and suggestions without bulldozing her, letting her make the decisions and take the lead. For the first time, Avery was feeling like she was working *with* her family, not for or against her family.

Her dad smiled at her. "Sweetheart, he's okay. Everything's going to be okay. You didn't need to fly all this way, but now that you are here, I'm sure glad to see you."

"I'm happy to see you too, Dad," she admitted, letting his familiar scent, cigar smoke and newspapers, comfort her. "I just felt like I had to be here. Thanks for the plane, by the way."

She took a breath and released herself from the comfort of her dad's hug. "How's Teddy? Is he expecting me? Can I see him?" she asked him, the impulsivity of what she'd just done, the lack of information she had about the situation finally hitting her.

"I saw him about thirty minutes ago. Everything looks good so far. Passed every head and spine injury test with flying colors. They took him for some x-rays, but once they have him back in his room, I'm sure you can go in and see him. He'll be happy to see you, who wouldn't be happy to see your beautiful face?"

Avery rolled her eyes, but let go of the strand of hair she hadn't realized she'd been tugging, pulling it straight one last time before it sprang back into place. "I don't know about that, Dad, but I appreciate it."

"Let's sit down while we wait."

Avery followed him down a hallway, past security to a small drab waiting area semi-hidden behind a curtain, nodding to two security guards who stood right in front of the flimsy curtain.

"She's with me guys. In-and-out privileges," her dad informed them.

She had expected a beehive of activity, the full team there waiting with baited breath on any news about Teddy. Instead, the room was nearly empty. James was in one corner quietly talking on his phone, presumably managing all press inquiries. He waved when she walked in, but then got back to his calls. Overhead, a TV was turned to a sports channel that was broadcasting highlights from the race.

Avery shook her head. Right. The race. It must have restarted after the crash debris was cleared. For the first time in her life, she had completely forgotten about a Formula One race.

She took an internal inventory. *Nope,* she wasn't even curious about the results. Her butterflies had nothing to do with race cars, everything to do with seeing a particular guy, who just happened to be a race car driver.

She took a seat on one of the industrial white plastic chairs next to her dad. "Where is everyone?" Avery asked him. "Where's Stacey?"

"Stacey was here for a while, but I sent her back to the hotel to start looking into various rehab scenarios and plans for Teddy. I offered to bring in a specialist, but Teddy didn't want, or trust, anyone else," he cleared his throat. "He's more press shy than ever these days, given the uh, well ya know, podcast disaster," he almost didn't meet Avery's eyes.

Avery looked down at her feet.

"So, you and Mom both found dresses?" her dad asked, unable to sit in silence.

"Yep." She was not in the mood to make small talk.

"Did Sadie show you how she can somersault now?" Her dad tried again.

"Yes. Very cute."

He raised his eyebrows at her, but took the hint and stopped asking questions. The only sounds were the various hospital codes and pages they could hear through the overhead speaker system. Avery tapped her foot on the linoleum floor and looked at her watch every five seconds while they waited.

Finally, a kindly-looking doctor in green scrubs opened the curtain and walked in. Avery and Michael stood. She sucked in as much air as she could, bracing herself for whatever she was about to hear.

"Hey, I've got to go," James told whoever he was talking to, and joined them.

"Hey, cheer up everyone, you already know he's going to be okay," the doctor said. "No head or spine injuries. A broken rib, a couple sprains, and he's going to have some nasty bruises. I want to keep him overnight for observation, but he should be able to get out of here in the morning."

Good. This is all good news. Her dad, brothers, and a number of other people had told her he was going to be okay, but hearing from a medical professional hit differently.

"Can we see him?" she asked.

"Sure," the doctor replied. "If he's up for it, it's fine by me. One visitor at a time, please."

"You go first," her dad gestured toward the door to the hospital room.

Her heart beat wildly. Teddy was right on the other side of that door.

Her hands flew to her hair, trying to smooth down some of the frizz she knew must be there. She wished she had a hair brush with her or maybe something else, *anything else*, to wear other than what basically was pajamas. He probably didn't look his best right now either. But she knew he'd be devastatingly handsome to her, even if he was bruised head-to-toe.

She knocked on the door, holding her breath. Even though she'd had hours to think about what she would say to Teddy, not a single word formed in her mouth. What if he'd been concussed and didn't remember asking for her?

She hadn't seen him in real life since Mexico. *Will I still feel a magnetic pull toward him?* Or would some illusion she had in her head all these weeks shatter once she had to face him in real life?

"Come in."

Hearing the roughness of Teddy's Scottish brogue nearly took her breath away.

She opened the door slowly and took the teeniest, tiniest

step into the room. "Hi," she said, scanning his face, and what she could see of his body from underneath a scratchy looking hospital sheet, for any obvious sign of injury.

She saw a red welt on one cheek, but otherwise he looked okay. There was an IV sticking out of one hand, delivering what she assumed were fluids or pain meds. She felt her shoulders drop away from her ears. He was still him. The Teddy she felt so drawn to and couldn't stay away from forever.

"Avery, hello. Thank you for coming," he replied evenly, without betraying whatever emotions he was feeling at the sight of her.

Did he mean it? It was possible that he was merely being polite. She stared at him, searching for any hint of some emotion. Delight or joy, ideally. But she'd settle for surprise. As long as he didn't look at her with contempt.

He stared back at her and she let herself drown in the green and gold of his eyes. She'd pictured them so many nights while they'd been apart. She hung back in the doorway, completely tongue-tied, but her gut told her this was right, that coming to see Teddy had been the right thing to do.

"You can come in, I don't bite," Teddy finally cracked a smile, the one she couldn't resist, breaking the intensity of the moment and the tension between them.

She smiled back involuntarily, *like a dork*.

"Okay," Avery slowly took a few more steps into the room, and closed the door behind her.

There was a chair, presumably for visitors, that was settled a few feet away from the bed. It felt too presumptuous to sit there, so she stayed on her feet, and tugged at the hem of her oversized t-shirt.

"I heard you asked about me? And I really wanted to make

sure you were okay. I know your family is far away, and I didn't know how quickly they'd be able to be here. I didn't want you to be alone in the hospital. I mean, I knew you wouldn't be *alone* alone, you have a whole team of course, but you know what I mean..."

"Avery..." Teddy's eyes softened, his voice losing any of its earlier roughness. "I did. I asked for you. And you came. It means everything, more than you know. I don't..." Teddy's shoulders dropped, "I don't have many people who would do that for me. People who aren't on my payroll."

Her heart swelled at his admission. She'd been right. She could hear it in his voice, see that his eyes were a bit glassy. He needed someone in his corner. And she could do that. She owed him her friendship and loyalty at the very least.

"Would you sit down, please?" he gestured to the chair. Then he smiled again, his eyes twinkling. "You're making me nervous with all that..." he waved his hand, "...fidgeting."

Teasing. That had to be a good sign. She took him up on his offer.

"Of course, I came. I'd do almost anything for you, Teddy. And again, I'm so sorry about the podcast. I know I said it in my email, but I would never, ever do something to purposefully hurt you, no matter how embarrassed I'd been, or how hurt I felt."

Avery's heart sank as his gorgeous, playful smile faded into a straight line. She looked down, ready to absorb his anger. She deserved it.

"Wait, *you* were embarrassed? When? Why?" Teddy asked. He sounded pained, surprised, but she didn't hear any anger or disdain behind the questions.

She looked back up at him and he straightened up as much as possible within the confines of the hospital bed, his eyes pleading with her for an answer.

Wasn't it obvious? "In Mexico... When you flat out *rejected* me. When I fled. I was really hurt, but also completely mortified," she admitted. "I thought we were beginning a real relationship, and I couldn't have been more wrong. I was imagining a future, and then you basically told me I was no one to you, just another heart-eyed fan happy to be in your orbit, to be able to post a picture with you to my social media."

Are we actually having this conversation?

She couldn't believe how quickly they'd cut to the chase. But there was something about the scenario, Teddy near horizontal, the ambient noise of hospital machines beeping, the slow dripping sounds of fluids hanging in the pouches on his IV pole. She'd been so close to losing him forever today, it seemed pointless to skirt around her feelings. Plus, she'd been on a streak lately. First her parents, now Teddy. Radical candor had kind of been working for her.

Avery felt him looking at her anew, as if maybe he were replaying the scene from the beach in his head. She raised her eyebrows at him and pursed her lips. The ball was in his court. It was his turn to share.

He sighed. "That's definitely *not* how I felt then and it's not how I feel now. You're not *no one* to me, not by any stretch of the imagination. You mean a great deal to me. And I'm the one who should be sorry, if I failed to make you feel important. When we were together."

Were we ever together, though? "It didn't feel like I was important to you at the end. It felt like you were using me. I know we had an arrangement, but when we hooked-up in Austin and then spent all week together in Mexico," Avery felt her cheeks turn pink, and other parts of her start to come to life at the memory. "I didn't think that it happened because of sheer convenience. I thought we had something real, and then I felt really dumb being so wrong."

"It wasn't like that. I promise. I have real feelings for you too. Come on, you were there, you felt it. I felt it."

Have? Teddy used the word have, as in present tense. She couldn't, wouldn't get her hopes up, it would hurt too much to go down that path again.

He ran his hand through his hair. "I know I'm immature, and said all the wrong things on the beach that day. But, you didn't really think I'm such an ass that I was using you for sex, did you?"

Yes. No. "I don't know?" Avery shrugged her shoulders. "I thought I was getting to know the real you, this warm, kind, and generous Teddy. That you don't let anyone see: the you who would always, always do right by the people he loves."

She swallowed the lump in her throat and whispered, "I wanted to think you were an ass because I was hurt when it became clear that you didn't count me among the people you truly—" the word *love* sat on the tip of her tongue, "—care about."

Teddy looked crestfallen. "Come here," he sat up straighter in his bed, and held out his hand.

She leaned forward and looked at her hand, as if it had the answer to whether she should take his. Would touching reignite something she wouldn't be able to control?

But rationality couldn't stop her overeager body, which got up from her chair and made it to Teddy's bedside in two steps.

She grabbed his outstretched hand, and gave it a warm squeeze, hoping it would feel like a burst of electricity between them, the way their inadvertent touch all those months ago at the hotel bar had.

"Avery, bella, you're squeezing the IV, that rather hurts," Teddy said sheepishly.

"Sorry," she said, dropping it as quickly as she had grabbed it. He offered his other hand, the one free from any medical stuff, and she took it, cautiously this time. She sat on the edge of the bed, one leg tucked under her, the other dangling over the side. She wanted to rub her thumb over his palm so badly, reacquaint herself with this small piece of his all-too familiar body, but she refrained.

Instead, she looked down at where their fingers were intertwined. What does this all mean to him? She knew that she genuinely loved him, the crash had proved that the mere *thought* of losing him was unbearable. And yet, before today, she'd *finally* felt like she was really getting somewhere on her own, and was perhaps starting to get over him.

"There. That's better," Teddy gave her a squeeze this time, and her breath caught in her throat. "I was, and still am, immature. I didn't know how to handle what I was feeling for you, and I certainly didn't use the right words on the beach that day. I was scared. I can't afford to let anything distract me, or at least that's how I felt before the crash," Teddy's voice caught. "The intensity of my feelings for you is something I've never experienced before, and I didn't know what to do with those feelings. But today I saw my life flash before my eyes. And all day as I sat here being poked and prodded, I realized how quickly my whole racing career could come to an end, or even worse, my life."

Avery felt dizzy, like she was the one who had been flipped

upside down on the racetrack. She had never seen him like this, even in their most vulnerable conversations. Teddy was always the picture of strength, of stoicism, but she could see that, like her, he'd experienced a light-bulb moment when his car went careening into that wall. And now he was here, voice trembling, opening up to her.

He continued, "And I realized I want more. I want love and adventure and travel for pleasure, the whole kit and caboodle. And I have you to thank for that. You showed me that a life outside of Formula One is possible for me. That someone could love me for the person I am underneath, not only because I'm a race car driver."

Avery was floored. She looked up at the drab tiled gray ceiling, keeping the tears that had welled-up in her eyes to match his from spilling before she spoke. "You deserve it all, Teddy, and I'm so glad you are starting to see that. But you don't need to thank me, I'd do it all again," she whispered.

She had thought Teddy hated her, but instead, he'd admitted that she'd helped him see the type of full life he could have. She hadn't realized that their time together had meant so much to him. It was a relief. *Not like in the I'm going to lean in and kiss him right now type of relief, although part of me certainly still wants that.* It was more the relief that she hadn't been delusional, that she hadn't imagined their connection, that it hadn't only been special for her. And the way he was looking at her, his lips parted, it looked like he might also want to lean over and kiss her.

But he hadn't actually suggested anything about the future. Sure, he had admitted he had feelings for her, but that didn't mean he wanted to act on it.

"I'm not saying it to be nice, Avery. I mean it. You changed me, my life, even if it took a near-death experience for me to realize it. What do you say, should we give it another shot? Pick up where we left off, keep it casual and then someday see if it becomes more?"

He rubbed his thumb over her palm, but she barely registered the touch. His words were like ice water dousing the heat that her body always felt next to his.

Casual? After everything he just admitted? Everything we've been through and he wants to keep it casual?!

"I can't make any promises about the future, but I forgive you for the whole podcast thing. And I think in time I can learn to trust you again," he nodded.

Whoa, this is like emotional whiplash. I changed his life, but he wants to casually date and maybe learn to trust me? Are you kidding me?

Avery gave him a long, pointed look, and shifted off her perch on the hospital bed, creating physical distance between Teddy and herself. Over the last couple of months, she had proved to herself that she was, in fact, a capable adult and worthy of deep love. She'd solved every gala related crisis that had been thrown at her and still had managed to bring in record-breaking sponsorship dollars.

And she'd done it with the support of people who really, truly believed in her and loved her for exactly who she was. She didn't *need* Teddy anymore. She might decide she wanted him, but she didn't need him to feel important and she *certainly* didn't need his fame and clout to make the gala a success. She had so much else going for her: she was finally feeling capable and confident in her career, she'd never felt closer to her parents, and had a team of real friends and family behind her. She was no longer interested in being Teddy's groupy, following him race-to-race, if he wasn't going to commit to supporting her in the same way.

"You *think* you forgive me and will be able to trust me?" Avery asked, shaking her head, her heart breaking all over again. "I'm sorry, but that's not good enough for me. I'm not going to hang around and be your pseudo-girlfriend until you make up your mind about our future."

She started to walk toward the door, but stopped. She turned back around; she didn't want to run away from him, like she'd done the last time.

This was her chance to write a different story.

She took a deep breath. "I'm truly glad you're okay. I was so worried when I saw the crash. I thought the worst was happening, and I would never forgive myself if we didn't clear the air. I really wasn't expecting all of this," she waved her hand in front of her face. "I want to say yes..." *So do it*, her body screamed at her, "...But, I deserve more. I need a partner who is all in."

Teddy hung his head over his slumped shoulders. "I understand, bella. You deserve someone who can be fully committed to you, who would drop everything at a moment's notice and hop on a plane to make sure *you're* okay. I wish I could be that for you, and maybe someday I can, but I don't expect you to wait for me."

"Teddy..." Why was standing up for herself so damn sad? She should feel triumphant, proud, but mostly she just felt heavy.

"Can we at least be friends?" he asked, his voice breaking.

Avery turned his offer over in her mind, shifting her weight back and forth as she considered. Friends? They'd gone from acquaintances to fake lovers to lovers to ex-lovers so fast that they'd never really seen what it was like to be friends.

"Yes, I think I can be your friend. We really did have fun together, didn't we?"

"We did. We really did," Teddy affirmed.

So, now what?... A new friend didn't nurse you back to health. "So what's next? I know you are getting out of here tomorrow..." her voice trailed off.

"Honestly, I'll probably head straight to Brazil. I can't possibly miss another race, especially the last of the season. You don't need to stick around, I'll be okay, I promise."

"Well, I do have a lot to do back in LA," she added, exhaustion hitting her like a ton of bricks. It had been a long day. A long season. And the plane was still sitting on the tarmac. If she left now, they could make it home in time for her to crash for a few hours before she had to be back at the office.

"Go on, of course you do. Please, don't let me keep you from it, but I'm sure glad you came."

"Yeah, me too," she agreed. "So, we're good?"

"Yes, Avery, we are good." He sounded sincere and gave her half a smile. But his eyes looked dull. There was no sign of his usual golden-green sparkle.

She walked over to his bedside to give him a whisper of a peck on the cheek, right above an angry red mark that would soon turn to purple, reminding herself, and hopefully reminding him too, why she had come in the first place. She let her lips lie on his face a moment longer than the typical friend would, enjoying the prickle of his rough stubble. One last nuzzle, one last time to breathe in his scent.

Friends. It was worth a shot, but she had to go, before she changed her mind and slid her mouth over to his soft lips the way her body was begging her to. She stood up straight and made her way to the door for the second time. This time she could walk out with her head held high. She wasn't running away, she wasn't begging for forgiveness. She was leaving on good terms, on her terms. *So why does my chest feel so tight?*

thirty-five

LOS ANGELES, CA

"So, there aren't enough fresh pears in the entire state of California to make pear and gorgonzola salad for 300 people?" Avery asked, narrowing her eyes at Caroline, who sat across from her fiddling with the buttons on her cardigan, while they listened to a very apologetic caterer on speakerphone.

"My suggestion is that we use canned pears instead. I doubt your guests will be able to tell the difference, but it's your call of course," the caterer said. *Serve canned pears? This man had clearly never catered an event for Sharon Silver and her crowd before.*

"Let's go with the arugula and burrata salad instead. Thanks." Avery instructed the caterer. She took a deep, full breath, confident she'd made the right call.

She turned to Caroline once they'd hung up. "I'm sorry, I know you will have to re-design and re-print the menus now."

"That's what I get for trying to work ahead," Caroline

shrugged as she tucked her shoulder-length blonde hair behind her ears. "Okay, I'm going to knock that out now. Anything else you need taken care of today?"

"No, enjoy your weekend. I appreciate all your help this week, seriously," Avery said. She meant it—Caroline had been such a huge help pulling the event together.

Avery rolled her shoulders back and stretched her arms over her head. What time was it? Time had lost all meaning over the last week. She'd spent more hours than she could count holed up with Caroline putting out minor fires. She'd practically been glued to her desk chair—she wouldn't be surprised if there was a permanent imprint of her butt cheeks on the seat cushion. But it was all worth it. She'd been flying through her gala to-do list, and things were coming together, minor produce-related emergencies aside.

She looked down at her watch. Three p.m. Perfect timing, the practice session in Brazil would start in just a few minutes. She could do some busy work uploading photos and descriptions of auction items while she watched.

Her skin prickled as she opened ESPN on her second, smaller monitor. In her pre-gala, pre-Teddy life, she would have been in Sao Paulo or at least watching without multitasking. She was no longer purposefully avoiding Teddy. In fact, she had checked in with him by text more than a few times in the days since he'd gotten out of the hospital. And he'd initiated too, asking her about the gala and how she was doing. *Like any friend would do, right?* Totally a normal friend thing to do: reading each one of his replies a hundred times.

But taking a ten-hour flight to South America when she had so much to do wasn't practical. Heck, her dad hadn't even flown down there this weekend. She didn't want to send mixed signals to him, or to herself. Never again was she going to shirk her responsibilities at home to follow a guy. No sir.

The livestream hadn't started yet, so the cars must still be in the garages. No harm in sending him a friendly good luck text. It was his first time back in the car after the crash, after all, and the kick-off for the last race weekend of the season.

> AVERY—Good luck this weekend!

She wasn't expecting a reply—he was probably in full work-mode. He wasn't close to being in the running for the driver's championship, but the team was in a tight battle for third place in the team standings, and the number of points he scored Sunday would determine whether Silver Racing ended up third, fourth, or fifth in the standings. It was a big deal, not only for the team's pride (and Teddy's), but also because millions of dollars of prize and sponsorship money were at stake for Silver. And every position mattered.

> TEDDY— Thx. You watching FP1?

She felt a little jolt. He cared if she was watching practice.

> AVERY— I am. I'll look for you and Zack
> and cheer you all on!

See, perfectly friendly reply.

Where was I? Right, two floor seats to a Lakers game and a locker room tour, donated by the team's GM. Those should go for at least $7,500. It would be enough to build one of the six courts they were hoping to fund at the community center. And one court was a start. She found a stock image of the purple and gold logo and uploaded it.

The familiar sound of a race car screaming down a track

made her head whip to the other screen. She looked over in time to see both Silvers pull out on the track. Instead of wearing one of his signature Scottish plaid helmets, Teddy was wearing a cheery, sunshine-yellow lid. *Her* favorite color.

What is that all about?

She zoomed in on her screen to take a closer look. She couldn't make it out precisely, but it looked like there were metallic-colored drawings on top of the yellow.

She knew how she could find out, but her stomach flip-flopped at the thought of logging into Instagram. She'd resisted every urge to download the app on her phone since she'd posted the break-up announcement nearly two months earlier. But it would be the fastest way to get the scoop on Teddy's helmet. She'd quickly look at Teddy's recent posts and then delete it again. No harm, no foul.

Teddy (or James more likely) had, in fact, posted about the sunny new helmet. She clicked on the photo of it, the silver and gold drawings appeared to be a child's drawing of sports equipment. She could make out a not-quite circular basketball and a stick figure person holding a baseball bat. And then underneath Teddy's race number 17, was the Silver Charitable Fund logo. Her eyes moved on to the caption below which read, "Proud to support the Silver Family Southside Youth Sports Complex. This special edition helmet will be auctioned off at the upcoming Silver Foundation gala. Link to bid in bio."

Avery gasped out loud even though there was no one in the room to hear her. *How had he pulled this off without her knowing?* She swiped to the next photo, which turned out to be a video of Teddy visiting the Sports Complex. He was shaking hands and giving high fives to kids, and then it cut to him shooting hoops with a few of the kids on the worn, outdoor basketball court and buckled and cracked tennis courts that the foundation's funds would help fix. Avery felt her face stretch into a huge smile. Court number two, check.

She shook her head in wonder. *When had he been in LA? And why?* Maybe her dad had some answers? She bolted out of her chair and ran down the hall, thundering past Caroline's desk.

"Check out Teddy's Instagram post," Avery called to her as she sprinted through the office.

She didn't stop until she was at the other end of the hallway. She found her dad sprawled out on the leather couch in his office watching the practice session on the wall-mounted TV.

She handed him her phone, "Did you know about this? When did Teddy go to the Sports Complex?" She put her hands on her thighs, gulping air between questions. *Need to do more cardio, apparently.*

He picked up the remote and muted the screen before he grinned at her. "Pretty cool, isn't it? I thought you'd like that. It was all Teddy's idea, though. I can't take any credit for it."

"When did he visit the Sports Complex? I had no idea..."

He unbuttoned the sleeves of his dress shirt and pushed them up his forearms, "When he was here before Austin doing some sim work."

The day she had seen him. He hadn't said a word.

She felt a flutter in her belly. Teddy had gone to the Sports Complex before they'd hooked-up. The possibility that he'd planned to surprise her all that time stirred up every sprinkle of regret that still lived in her body. The-could-have-beens left her with a lump in throat.

"So, he's been holding on to this helmet since then?" Avery asked.

Her dad scratched his head. "No, I don't think so. Teddy reached out to me personally on Monday and asked for Coach Tony's number. He had the idea in Miami and needed some help pulling it off on such short notice. We had to have the kids do the drawings and send them directly to the helmet manufacturer. In fact, I didn't know they'd pulled it off in time until you showed me that photo."

Huh. Teddy had executed the whole thing and even enlisted favors to get it done since they'd seen each other in Miami. Her skin tingled at the thought, as her brain struggled to process it all. Was it a romantic gesture, or was it proof of friendship and no ill-will? The possibilities left her lightheaded.

She would reach out to him to say thank you later after the practice session, of course. Given how tentative their friendship seemed at the moment, perhaps she should leave it at that. Thank him for the thoughtful gesture and move on. No questions; accept the generosity with grace. Like her mom would do.

In the meantime, well, if she was going to accept living with that uncertainty, she might as well take a moment with her dad and watch the practice.

"Mind if I join you?" She could finish uploading the gala items later.

"I'd like nothing more," her dad leaned over and tossed her a pillow. She plopped down next to him, and he leaned into her, giving her a sideways hug.

"You've been working so hard on this gala, kiddo. I'm proud of you. I realize I don't say it enough, but I'm impressed with what you've done this year. I think it's going to be a big year for the foundation," he said with a gleam in his eyes.

Avery beamed internally, but squirmed in her seat. This praise for her work was something she was unaccustomed to from her parents. It felt good, but strange, and she didn't know quite how to respond.

"Thanks, I *have been* working hard."

He turned the volume back up on the TV and their conversation veered back into more comfortable territory as her dad pointed out how the cars were handling various turns, which teams seemed to have upgraded their cars since the last race, their usual shared language and passion for motorsport replacing the awkwardness that their newfound closeness brought with it.

The session ended and her dad turned off the TV.

"You're still smiling about that helmet, aren't you?" he asked, bordering on teasing her. "You haven't wiped that grin off your face since you walked in here."

Avery blushed. Her dad was calling her out for still harboring some feelings for Teddy. She was incredibly touched by Teddy's gesture, of course, but maybe if she was being honest with herself, the tingling and the butterflies were a little more than those of a delightfully surprised and thankful friend and colleague.

"I still can't believe it," she said, warmth expanding through her chest. "Millions of people are going to see that helmet on TV during the actual race Sunday. It was so kind of Teddy, and everyone who helped make it happen."

"He's a real team player, that's for sure," her dad said, winking.

Oh great, even her dad could see right through her and her mounting failure at being no more than friends with Teddy.

He stood up and started collecting his things. "I'm going to go join your mother for dinner at Baltaire. Care to join us?"

"Thanks for the invitation, but I really need to finish

entering the auction items and then I'll probably just crash," Avery declined. *I really need some time to sort through my feelings about this helmet situation and my body's over-eager reaction to it.*

She headed back to her desk, immediately texting Stacey. She needed to talk about the helmet with someone in the know, someone female, someone who was NOT her dad.

> AVERY— The helmet! Wow! Did you know about it?
>
> STACEY— No, not until today when I saw it. What do you think?
>
> AVERY— I'm so touched.

Avery took a deep breath. Stacey was her closest friend and she also happened to be the one person who had more insight into Teddy. If there was anyone she could ask this... *Well, here goes nothing.*

> AVERY—Did he do it for me? Was it some grand romantic gesture? Eeek.
>
> STACEY— Honestly, I don't know. It seemed like things were going so well for you two being friends. Do you still want more?
>
> AVERY— You're right. The friendship thing has been working out well for us.

Avery got up from her desk and walked to the window, looking down enviously at the sea of Friday afternoon commuters funneling out of offices and into the street.

STACEY— Well, since you are such good friends with him now, maybe you can ask him? Instead of trying to read his mind?

AVERY— Haha. Ask him - that would be too easy. I need to thank him anyway, so maybe I'll just see what he says.

STACEY— Well, he's out of the car and back in his dressing room, so I know he's available to talk to you as your friend, that is ;)

AVERY— Oh, stop. We are friends now, and I don't have time for drama.

STACEY— You really don't. Ok, ttyl!

AVERY— Ttyl.

Avery sat back down at her desk. She was nervous to call him and say thanks for doing a kind thing. She didn't want to sound too into him either, to come off as if she had assumed it was for her if it wasn't. She took a deep breath and hit the dial button.

Her fingers drummed the desk as the phone rang a couple of times.

"Hello, Avery," Teddy finally answered. Could she hear a satisfied smile in his voice?

He must know why she was calling.

"Teddy, hi!!" She couldn't contain her excitement. Who was she kidding? She wasn't prepared to sound like a robot; she was too pleased with the helmet itself, the good it would do for the kids. "Thank you - the helmet! Thank you."

I need to settle down. Vibe check—genuine, but not swoony.

She took a breath.

"Truly, Teddy, it is going to make such a difference getting last-minute sponsors and selling the remaining tickets. The awareness is priceless. On behalf of the whole Silver Charitable Foundation and the Silver family, a huge thank you," she said, regaining her composure. There, the official thank you was officially completed.

Avery awaited his reply with bated breath.

"I'm so glad that the *entire family and charitable organization* appreciates the gesture," he said playfully. "But..." his voice deepened, "...I am more interested in what the head of the Silver Charitable Foundation thinks."

He sounded almost flirty? They'd always had this fun banter, since the beginning, those first outings in London and Italy. Was this his way of trying to bring their relationship back to its friendly roots—before they'd hooked up and it had gotten messy and complicated?

"The Director of the Charitable Foundation has so many questions for you," she played along with his third-person game. "How did you even come up with the idea? And then pull it off?"

"I mean, I know first and foremost, I'm here to drive the car fast, but I also came to Silver because I believe in the team and the culture of giving back, so I liked the idea of doing a charity helmet for a while. And then your passion for the kids, well, it was contagious."

At least he really is a good guy, even if he didn't do it for me, per se.

Avery stood up from her desk, she needed some air. She peaked out of her office. Empty. Caroline must have taken off already, and most everyone else worked remotely on Fridays. She propped open the door to her shoe-box-sized office.

Teddy continued, "And, well, I was feeling really bad about backing out of the gala. It was the right choice. I can't go." He cleared his throat, "I was, still am, feeling so burned by the spotlight, and the truth about my dad coming out put me in a bad headspace. I thought if I hid from the world for a while, it would all blow over and I could get back to being judged for my performance, and my performance alone. But then the crash happened, and you and I were on good terms again, and I wanted to make it up to you."

"Teddy..." she sighed. She tugged at her curls, twisting them into one spiral over her shoulder.

Her head was spinning. Okay, so the helmet was a very nice gesture, but most likely not a grand romantic one. Just Teddy being the warm, generous, thoughtful guy that she knew he was. She felt both the glow of his kind words and big heart, but also a little twinge of something else that sat a little bit less easy in her body.

"I'm touched, Teddy, really. You didn't have to make it up to me. It was all my fault, that you found yourself in that situation..." her voice trailed off, quieting to a near whisper.

"Stop. You've apologized enough. Really. I was angry at the time, as you know, but I've learned and grown so much as a person this season. The scandal, then the crash, it all forced me to face some hard truths. After you left the hospital, when my mom and brother got there, we finally had some tough conversations that we needed to have for a long time."

Avery wanted to ask follow-up questions: What hard truths? What conclusions had Teddy come to with his family? *I can't go there.* She'd forfeited the right to Teddy's most personal information, certainly when it came to his family.

"It means a lot to me to hear you say that, about the apology.

And it sounds like really positive stuff with your family. I'm happy for you. You sound great, peaceful even."

She was truly happy for him, she wanted him to be at peace with his family's painful past, regardless of how the conversations had been forced upon him. So, she'd be grateful for the extra publicity for the gala and for the thousands of dollars the helmet would bring in.

"Good luck this weekend Teddy. You know I'll be cheering for you," she said, trying to wrap up the conversation.

"Thanks, Avery. Talk to you soon," he replied.

They both sat silently on the phone for a beat, waiting to see if the other hung up first. It wasn't one of those cutesy eye-roll inducing 'no you hang up first' pauses, but rather it felt a bit heavy, as if both of them perhaps felt that there was more to say to each other, but couldn't quite find the words, or if they had the words, was still nervous about how they'd be perceived on the other end of the phone. In the end, it was safer for her to end this conversation right there. To allow those words to remain unsaid.

thirty-six

LOS ANGELES, CA

Avery looked down in horror. Her perfect black velvet dress was a complete disaster. The gala was in two days, and she was picking it up from a last-minute, super simple alteration. It had needed to be hemmed a couple of inches so that it hit her mid-calf instead of hitting her legs at the ankles, since she was approximately a foot shorter than whatever six-foot model it had been designed for.

She stepped out of the dressing room and onto the little platform in front of the tri-paneled mirror. Somehow the front of the dress had been shortened to above her knees and the back was no shorter than when she'd had it pinned the week before. She cringed as all three mirrors confirmed it. Yep, it was the mullet of dresses. Just perfect.

The weather forecast was iffy, so the blue silk one in her closet wasn't an option, and she certainly didn't have time to go shopping.

"Patty, this is not right," Avery said to the tailor, trying to sound assertive rather than shaken. "See how it's too short in the front, and too long in the back?"

Patty knelt and tugged at the fabric of the dress. "You're right, Avery, this is not how we pinned it last week. Let me see if I can fix it." She walked back to the reception desk and pulled up what Avery hoped were her notes and measurements from when they'd pinned it.

Please, let this be fixable. Avery felt her eyes prickle with hot tears.

"Good news. We left enough of the hem in the front and I'll have scraps from the back once we hem that. I should be able to make it work," Patty said.

Oh, thank goodness. For weeks, when she'd pictured the gala in her head, it was in this dress. While she was confident she could find something in her closet that would be fine, she didn't want to have to settle for fine. She could already envision how gorgeous it would photograph, and a small part of her hoped that a picture would make its way to Teddy. Well, more than a small part. She'd imagined his reaction when he saw her in it the moment she'd first tried it on.

Despite how busy she'd been, Teddy still occasionally—more than occasionally, if she was being honest with herself—occupied her thoughts. No matter how dead tired she was after a long work day, when she got in bed at night, her mind couldn't stop replaying all of the fun they had earlier in the season, their most recent conversation after the helmet moment, the shower in Mexico... Most nights she still fell asleep with the image of his dazzling golden green eyes and perfect hair flip in her brain. She wanted him to feel regret, to feel a longing for her, when and if he saw photos from the gala.

It had to be *this* dress that he saw her wearing in photos.

There was one more obstacle, however.

"I need it ready by this time tomorrow," Avery grimaced. She knew she was asking Patty to pull an all-nighter.

Patty let out an exhale. "I can do that for you. Your mother has been such a good customer all these years, and it was our fault."

"Thank you, thank you. I really appreciate it," Avery squealed. She could hug the woman.

Avery dashed out of the shop. She was due at Ben and Adam's house, well, now. The rental furniture was being delivered today.

As soon as the house came into view, Avery felt adrenaline rush through her veins. The massive white event tents were up. And the rental furniture delivery trucks had already arrived. She couldn't believe her vision was finally coming to life after all the hard work and planning. By the end of the day, thousands of twinkly white and green lights would hang from the ceiling of each tent, creating a cozy, festive winter wonderland effect. At least everything *here* was going according to plan.

"Hey. Where do you want these high-top cocktail tables to go?" Caroline was waiting for her, ready to pounce the moment Avery turned off the engine. It was go time.

"Don't you have the layout diagram?" Avery asked, a bit annoyed that Caroline couldn't refer back to the detailed instructions and event binder she'd spent hours putting together for exactly this sort of question. The dress situation had put her on edge. She knew she was the main person in charge of the event, but still, Caroline or anyone else on the team should be able to direct tables to the right spot without her, especially since it had all been carefully planned.

"I do, but the diagram shows seven high-tops on the pool deck, and these guys unloaded ten. Do you have somewhere you want three more to go? Or did they deliver too many?"

Avery's phone buzzed. It was Josh. "Caroline, one second," Avery said, her voice clipped. *Why can't she figure it out?*

She stepped into the home's cavernous entryway where it was quieter to take the call.

"Hi, Josh! How was your flight?" Avery asked, grateful for the momentary break from the chaos outside.

"Flight was fine," Josh answered. "I made it out of LAX alive, and I'm all checked in at the hotel. But I was calling to say thank you. You did not have to send a car service to pick me up. And you had him pick up In-N-Out on the way? You're too good to me."

"You are welcome, and I wanted to," Avery said. "You can't come to LA and not get In-N-Out. Consider it a token of my appreciation for coming to the event all the way from London."

"Avery, seriously, I wouldn't miss it," Josh said earnestly. "And, I'll get to swing by Detroit to see my parents after, so it's a win-win."

Avery nodded. *Good, I'm glad he didn't make a trip overseas just to be my sidekick and purse-holder at an event.*

"Avery," Caroline peeked her head in through the front door. "The guys can't unload all the heat lamps from the truck until we know where the tables go."

Oh for heaven's sake, can no one make a decision without me?

"I have to go. See you tomorrow night!" Avery hung up.

She walked back outside, firing at all cylinders, ready to take charge and get shit done.

"Caroline, you have my attention." She turned to her second

in command. "Let me see that diagram. Did you check the original order? How many high-tops were we supposed to get?"

Avery pulled her clipboard out of her bag and flipped through until she found what she was looking for. "See, you were right, seven by the pool deck, but we need one up on stage to display the watch and helmets, and the last two go..."

"Are you Avery Silver?" a male voice asked.

She turned around. "Yes, I am."

"Hi, I'm Kevin, the A/V guy. I've got the video screens all set up in the tent. We're going to run through the video presentation and slides now, can you come approve?" he asked, "Or will someone else queue the slides during the presentation?"

"Kevin, nice to meet you. Um, I'll be seated at a table with guests by then, so someone else will have to do it..." she replied hastily.

"Avery, and the last two high-tops? Do you want me to have them take them back, or what?" Caroline asked again, a note of frustration in her voice.

The front door opened again, and Ben casually walked over in joggers and a fitted tee to join their huddle.

"We've thrown a lot of parties on this lawn," Ben said, "but I've never seen it quite like this before. This is a real production."

"Ben, you're right on time. This is Kevin, our A/V guy. Ben is going to be your guy."

"Yes, captain," Ben saluted his little sister and ambled off with Kevin. *Ok, that's taken care of. What's next?* She needed Caroline to start making some executive decisions. She couldn't be everywhere at once.

"Caroline," It killed her to talk so sternly to a friend, but it couldn't be helped. "I know you work for my family, and your job as my dad's assistant usually means that you defer to him on all decisions. But this is different. I need you to step up and take control of things around here. I'll be here the rest of the afternoon, but tomorrow I have a full day of beauty and press. The behind-the-scenes logistics are going to be on you."

"Ok, boss. I'll do my best. But can you at least text tomorrow during your hair and makeup appointments?" Caroline asked, a nervous smile scrunching her cheeks.

"You can. But I might not be able to answer right away. You're going to have to get comfortable with making some decisions, and fast," Avery answered. There was no time for handholding, not even for a coworker who also happened to be a dear friend. The guests were going to arrive tomorrow at 6 p.m. whether they were ready or not.

thirty-seven

LOS ANGELES, CA

Avery looked in the full-length mirror one last time, giving herself a once over. The dress looked as good as new, the black velvet brushing her calves at just the right spot. Her dark hair fell over her right shoulder in soft, shiny waves. She smoothed her hand over it, not a single flyaway. She parted her cherry-red lips and smiled. All good, no lipstick on her teeth. She looked over her shoulder and realized in horror, that her mother was doing the exact same thing in the bathroom mirror with her own, more subdued berry-colored lipstick. *Like mother, like daughter.* Avery shook her head. *It's like her mannerisms are hard-wired in my DNA.*

"It's showtime," her mother said in a singsong voice, doing a little shimmy, the light catching on the floral sequins in her long, emerald green dress. Her mom always rose to the occasion for these big nights, effortlessly slipping into the role of hostess and fashionista. Many things about her mother annoyed her, but

Avery couldn't help but admire her mom's ability to be so 'on' when she needed to be. *Why couldn't I have gotten a little more of that DNA?*

"Here we go," Avery said, placing her hand over her heart to try and slow it down. *Am I about to walk into a disaster?* She had been tied up with glam for hours and hadn't peeked in the tent to make sure it was ready. Her mom reached over and gave her other hand an encouraging squeeze. The feeling of the cool, smooth stones of her mother's signature diamond tennis bracelet bumping against her wrist felt comfortingly familiar, even if their newfound emotional closeness would take some getting used to.

"We've got this. Not to worry, darling," her mom added, before dropping Avery's hand and confidently walking out of the main house and into the tents on the lawn, not a single hair out of place in her graceful bun.

Avery took one last deep breath and followed. She had expected the event tent to be buzzing with pre-showtime energy, but it was almost serenely calm. Everything was ready to go: the tables were set, the auction items beautifully displayed, and the heating lamps lit. Avery's hands felt empty without the fat event binder she'd gotten so accustomed to carrying around with her the last few weeks. The only noise was the clinking of champagne bottles being placed in ice buckets behind the bar.

Avery's heart swelled with pride. She'd done it. She'd pulled this whole thing off at Ben's house. Now all there was to do was wait for the guests to arrive. And for them to start drinking all that champagne so that they would feel uninhibited enough to bid big on the auction items.

It's out of my control now.

Her heart lurched imagining two distinct futures. Six months from now she could be in her athletic wear, laughing and shooting hoops with kids when she visited the new sports complex. Or, she'd be meeting with community leaders, apologizing for not being able to deliver what they needed. It could truly go either way—it all came down to how successful the event was tonight.

Avery observed her mom from behind as the older woman sashayed through the space, the long duster coat she wore over her dress trailing behind her like a cape. They'd gone all in on the winter holiday theme. Small bud vases with winter white roses were bunched together on the cocktail-height tables. Table runners made of festive green garland adorned the long rectangular dinner tables. Her mom adjusted a few leaves here and there as she made her way across the room toward Avery.

Of course, she had to touch and fix the tables—truly incapable of letting it be. The old Avery would have rolled her eyes, maybe even made a smart-aleck comment. But the new Avery observed her mom jooj the tables without acting on it. So that was something. Someday, in the not-too-distant future, she'd be able to admire her mom's attention to detail, or laugh off her inability to leave things be. Not tonight, but someday. *Tonight, I'd like some credit for pulling this whole thing off.*

"Well, ladies, you've outdone yourselves this time," her dad said by way of hello as he barreled into the room. His hair looked as coiffed as her own.

"Thanks, Dad," she beamed, the compliment she'd been waiting for filling her with warmth, "Nice tux."

While the event wasn't black tie, her dad, like her mom, used his wardrobe to make an impression. Tonight was their personal runway.

"So, what do we do now?" he asked, checking this watch. Avery knew she got her nervous energy from her dad, who didn't always keep his game face on as well as her mom did. *We have that in common, but wearing your heart on your sleeve isn't always a bad thing, is it?*

"Well, can we get some photos out of the way?" Avery summoned the photographer, and the core Silver family posed for a few staged photographs that would likely accompany the post-event news release the next day.

Avery plastered on her best event smile, channeling Teddy's masterful, practiced grin. He was never far from the surface of her thoughts.

"Okay, looking good folks. Mr. Silver, can you slide that way?" The photographer directed them as Ben and Adam joined them, looking dapper in coordinating, but not matching, dark blue suits. Ben paired his shiny royal blue one with a black bow tie, like their dad. *Like father, like son.* She smiled to herself.

Ben gave her a thumbs up before they slid into their places.

"How about we move to the entrance, and get a shot in front of the big Silver logo?" the photographer suggested.

Josh arrived during photos. As soon as the photographer got what they needed, she went to him while lightly tapping her jaw, afraid to rub off any makeup. She needed to loosen it up after ten straight minutes of smiling. At this rate, it would ache by the end of the night. But all the smiles and small talk would be worth it when she pictured the smiles of happy kids who had somewhere safe and productive to go after school.

"Josh, I'm so happy to see you. You look great," she said. And she meant it. He really did look fantastic, his bronze skin and gray eyes really popped against the black and white of his suit and shirt. However, seeing him didn't light her on fire.

It was part of the reason she knew what she felt for Teddy had been different. Josh had set the bar pretty high as far as first boyfriends go, both in looks and personality. But their chemistry hadn't been *wow*. At least now she knew what wow felt like.

She felt another pang in her chest for Teddy. She was trying hard not to imagine an alternate universe where it was Teddy instead of Josh escorting her. In that scenario, she'd dive into his arms, give him a light kiss so as not to leave her red lipstick on his cheek, inhale his spicy, woodsy cologne, and enjoy the tingle she felt every time he put his hand on her lower back. They'd make eyes throughout the night, enjoying the secret intimacy of lovers in a crowd.

"You are absolutely stunning," Josh said. Josh, whom she'd invited to the event, was standing right here in front of her.

Snap out of it.

She felt his eyes look her up and down, pause for a second on the bare pale skin between her breasts where the jeweled bows were holding her gown together. His gaze felt a tad bit more than friendly. But there was no time to think about that tonight, she'd have to deal with any lingering romantic intentions from Josh another time.

As the room filled with guests, Avery scanned the scene, her eyes darting back and forth between the entrance, the bars, and the silent auction tables.

Is there a line forming at the bar? She didn't want anyone to have to wait to be served.

Is anyone checking out or bidding on the auction items yet? Everything depended on it.

Are people moving quickly through the check-in process?

Her eyes searched and found Caroline, who was stationed at the entrance wearing high-waisted trousers and a headset, and her friend gave her a thumbs up. So far so good.

"You look tense, can I get you a drink?" *Oh, right. Josh is still here.*

"Yes, a glass of prosecco would be great."

He left to fetch it for her.

"Avery, just who I was looking for," her dad pounced the second he found her alone. "You remember my old business partner, Lenny?"

"Of course, so nice to see you again." Avery stuck her hand out to give Lenny a shake, but instead, the older, gray-haired gentleman leaned in and gave her a very damp kiss on the cheek.

Gross. She resisted the urge to wipe away the wetness. It would be both impolite, plus potentially smudge the makeup. Didn't this guy know that women in formal gowns wanted air kisses only?

"I understand you're the mastermind behind this beautiful party. That's one proud dad you have there," Lenny said.

Avery stood up a little straighter. *That* recognition was all she'd ever wanted from her parents.

By now, her dad had turned around to greet the next arrivals, the team principal of Mercedes and his wife (who was equally as successful and impressive in her own right), leaving Avery to entertain Lenny on her own.

"It's really all for the kids. All the proceeds from tonight are going to build the new Southside Youth Sports Complex. Did you know that we commissioned a study last year at UCLA that found that kids who participate in afterschool sports are three times less likely to get involved in gang violence?"

"Is that so? I played some basketball myself back in my day. Even got to play against Magic once when he was at Michigan State," he said expectantly as if he were waiting for Avery to fall over impressed.

"You must have been quite a player if you were up against Magic Johnson." Flattery never hurt when trying to get an older white guy to open up his wallet, "Say, did you see that we have a VIP Lakers experience including courtside seats up for auction later tonight?" Avery grabbed the program pamphlet from a nearby cocktail table and opened it to the page listing the live auction items.

As she was selling the other perks to Lenny, Josh returned with her prosecco.

"Lenny, meet Josh. He works in marketing for Archer," Avery introduced the two men.

"Not to mention, her dashing date tonight," Josh interjected.

She clocked the comment, but didn't respond.

"Josh, I was telling Lenny about the auction items. Now that I have my drink in hand, Lenny, I notice yours is empty. You really ought to go get something to drink," she nearly shoved the older gentleman in the direction of the bar.

"Yes, Lenny, do you like old fashioneds? Greg, the bartender, makes a fantastic one. Here let me introduce you," Josh added, whisking Lenny back to the bar.

Thank you, Avery silently mouthed to Josh. He winked back at her.

The rest of the cocktail hour proceeded in much the same fashion, with Avery's parents passing guests off to her to greet, and in turn, she gave them the elevator pitch about the causes and sent them on their way to the bar, or the auction tables. Josh continued to play his part beautifully, refilling her glass, interjecting during awkward pauses in conversation. He was a devoted date, but she was beginning to wonder whether inviting him in the first place had sent some mixed signals.

Finally, Caroline tapped on her shoulder. "Avery, it's time to start the program." She followed Caroline to one end of the tent, where a small stage and podium had been set up in front of a huge projection screen.

"Your dad is about to go on and give his welcome speech. You're up next with the video," Caroline informed her.

Right on cue, Avery's dad nearly hopped up onto the platform and grabbed the microphone from its spot on the lectern.

"Good evening, everyone, and welcome to the fifteenth annual Silver Foundation Gala. On behalf of Sharon and our whole family, including our chosen family at the Silver Formula One team, we thank you for being here tonight to help us raise money for worthy causes. Sharon and I are delighted to start the evening off by announcing that we will personally match the total raised tonight, so anything you give tonight will be doubled," he paused for applause, which the crowd offered thunderously.

Avery felt her mouth fall open. She knew, of course, that her parents would make a major personal contribution tonight. But she had no clue it was going to be a matching gift. Her mouth involuntarily formed a smile, the first one she hadn't forced all night. Seeing all of the heads around the room nod in approval and the hands vigorously clapping, reignited something in her. She felt a fire in her belly.

She knew that her dad was about to introduce her, that she was up next in the evening's line-up of speakers. While she felt the good kind of butterflies in her stomach that were only natural before speaking in front of hundreds of people, she'd always been a confident public speaker. Whether it was from the theater and improv class she'd taken in college or from always being in the quasi-public eye as a Silver, she wasn't sure, but for some reason giving a rehearsed speech to a crowd was far less scary to her than confronting someone one-on-one.

"Lipstick, please," she whispered to Caroline, who pulled Avery's tube from her cross-body bag. Caroline was carrying both Avery's and her mom's lipstick and phones in her purse, as neither of them wanted their hands tied up holding a clutch. They needed to be hands-free to shake hands, offer hugs, etc... A trick Sharon had passed down to Avery several years ago when she was old enough to start carrying a purse.

Avery swiped the creamy stick across her lips and pressed her lips firmly together a couple of times. She looked over at Caroline.

"Good?" she asked.

Caroline gave her a thumbs up. "Lookin' good, boss lady."

"And now, it is my honor and privilege to introduce the very talented woman who is responsible for bringing this incredible evening to life. She also happens to be my beautiful daughter," Michael's voice boomed from across the stage.

She cringed. He was never going to get it. *He'd never call another woman in the Silver organization beautiful by introduction.* She was finally getting some recognition for all her contributions, and they were made lesser when accompanied by mentions of her appearance. It wasn't fair.

She had to let the frustration fuel her because she had to go onstage *right now.* Her dad had teed it up for her with the matching gift and now she had to do *her* job—tug on the heartstrings. The video would do the job for her: adorable little kids and surprisingly eloquent teens speaking about what a new sports complex would mean for their community were far more powerful than her explanation.

She handed the tube of lipstick back to Caroline, who replaced it with her note cards. She hadn't needed to write down her speech word for word, but she wanted to make sure she didn't forget any of her major points or people she wanted to thank.

"Good evening, everyone, and thanks Dad, for that warm, albeit somewhat embarrassing introduction." She might as well lean into the awkwardness. It paid off, as she heard more than one person in the audience chuckle. She looked up from her notes to see her mom smiling at her. They made eye contact, and her mom nodded at her encouragingly.

"This beautiful event tonight would not have been possible without the hard work of some very important people. First, a huge thank you to my brother Ben, and my brother-in-law Adam for hosting all of us at their beautiful home." The crowd erupted into applause once again. She hadn't expected to pause there, but okay, this was good, the crowd was happy, feeling the celebratory atmosphere just as she had hoped they would. "And to Caroline Whitaker, my right-hand woman. Caroline, take a bow, please."

Avery gestured to where Caroline was standing on the ground next to the stage as the crowd clapped once again.

"And finally, thank you to everyone at the Silver Charitable Foundation, and the entire Silver team. From the drivers, Teddy and Zack, who went above and beyond with their auction contributions this year, to everyone at the factory who makes this organization what it is. I know Zack is here tonight repre-senting the team," She scanned the crowd, looking for Zack until she found him and grinned. He raised a hand and waved to the crowd, then blew Avery a kiss.

Avery looked back at him and froze.

It wasn't. No. It couldn't be.

She was hallucinating, surely. She could only see a sliver of the man behind Zack, hidden in his shadow—a brown flip of hair at the collar of the suit jacket, the slim fit of expertly tailored dress pants paired with pristine designer sneakers. It couldn't be Teddy standing in the back of the room behind Zack, *or could it?* She knew she had to wrap up her speech and cue up the video. But she felt completely breathless, unable to find the words.

She wanted to jump off the stage, elbow her way through the sea of people, and make sure her eyes weren't deceiving her. But she had a room full of people, with their eyes on her, waiting. She had to say something, anything, not just stand there staring like an idiot, frozen.

She cleared her throat, forcing her attention back to the microphone in her hand. "Right, thanks. With no further ado, please turn your attention to the video screen above me so you can learn the real reason we are all here tonight. To make sure our most vulnerable citizens have opportunities to pursue their dreams. Thank you."

The video came to life on the screen behind her, and Avery shot her eyes back to where Zack was seated, where she thought she had spotted Teddy, her heart pounding. *Where is he?* She squinted. Whoever that guy had been, he'd moved. Or maybe her overactive imagination had seen what it wanted to see, and projected Teddy's likeness onto some other guy? Maybe all these tall guys in dark suits looked the same from her vantage point on the stage.

Was he trying to be incognito? No, that would be seriously impossible for Teddy to try and blend in anonymously at this event. He'd be recognized instantly. She had to go find out if it was actually him.

She turned to step down, but felt one of her heels catch on the side of the stage, and stumbled. She was falling toward the grass below. *Please, God, don't let me eat shit right now.* Even with the lights dimmed and the focus on the adorable young-sters lighting up the video screen keeping her somewhat hidden, she really, really didn't want to be the girl who fell off the stage. Luckily, Caroline saw what was happening, and thrust her hand out, giving Avery something to grab onto while she righted herself.

"Are you okay? You look like you saw a ghost," Caroline asked with concern, her arm still on Avery's, steadying her.

"I... uh...think, I did see a ghost," Avery answered. "Teddy isn't here, is he? I mean, someone would have mentioned that to me. I would know that already," she said, trying to convince herself that it couldn't have been him. But she'd recognize those eyes anywhere (even if she only got a glimpse of one-quarter of his face) and the defined cheekbones underneath that meant he'd always have a backup career in modeling.

Caroline looked at her sheepishly. "Me too. I thought you knew."

"Knew, what? Caroline? Oh my god...Teddy's here? Teddy's here." Of course, Teddy was here, she didn't conjure him. Her eyes hadn't deceived her. She involuntarily shivered in delight. *Don't get too excited, he's probably here to be nice.*

She'd tried so hard to put him out of her mind, albeit unsuccessfully, and now he was here. *First the helmet, and now this? What does it all mean?* She needed a minute to collect herself.

"So you didn't know Teddy was here. Got it," Caroline nodded, pressing her lips together. "Do you need to sit? You look like you need to sit."

Sit? Seriously, it was taking every bit of willpower she had to not run in the direction she'd last seen Teddy. "No, I'm good," Avery tried to contain the energy bouncing around inside her.

"Are you sure? Because there's something else you may want to sit for. In fact, I need to tell your dad too," Caroline motioned to Michael to join their little huddle off to the side of the stage.

"What's up Caroline?" he asked.

"I hate to be the bearer of bad news, but we have a situation. Al Roker left. Snowmageddon is about to hit the East Coast, and he got called back immediately to the studio in New York. So... we don't have an MC for the auction."

Avery's head swam. Perhaps she should have sat down. "You have got to be kidding me," Avery said.

This was a lot to process. *Teddy is here. And their MC is not. Is Mercury in retrograde or something?*

"I've got this," Michael offered. "People love me, I have TV experience. I'll do it."

Oh my. Avery whipped her head around in Caroline's direction, trying to telepathically relay her emphatic opposition to her dad being the MC. *No, definitely not. Anything but that, in fact.* Her dad was not good without a script. He'd go rogue, say something that would embarrass her, mispronounce donors' names.

Luckily, Caroline caught her drift. She'd worked for the

Silvers long enough to not only pick up on Avery's non-verbal cues, but she probably also agreed with Avery's assessment of her dad's fitness as a fill-in auctioneer.

"Michael, you would be fantastic," Caroline said, stroking his ego. "But we need you to work the room at all times. Can't have you tied up on stage for too long."

Gosh, Caroline was a treasure.

"Yeah, Caroline is right, Dad. It can't be you, you'll, um, you'll be too intimidating up there?" Avery added, knowing it wasn't nearly as convincing as Caroline's reasons, but she piled on anyway.

"You girls might be right, I need to be doing some hustling on the side, egging these guys on to bid higher and higher. Any ideas who can fill Al's shoes at this hour? Think we can get that local guy over here from CBS? The young, handsome one who does sports scores?"

It wasn't a bad idea, but Avery knew there wasn't enough time for him to make it out to the valley. She knew the evening's program like the back of her hand. As soon as the video ended, the guests would be served their main course, and then as soon as the dishes were cleared, the auction was supposed to start. "I think it has to be someone already on site, given our time constraints."

She knew instantly who could do it, who would be an absolute smash.

She looked around the room for someone, anyone, else who could do it. It would have to be someone delightfully charming, polished, poised. Someone who could capture everyone's attention and had extensive media training.

There were exactly two men in the room who fit the bill.

She searched for Caroline's eyes again, and Caroline

nodded at her. They really were on the same wavelength tonight.

"Are you thinking what I'm thinking?" Avery asked her.

"Zack? Teddy?" Caroline looked at Avery nervously. "We could ask them to do it together."

"I like it. Let's do it. Are you comfortable with Teddy being up on stage?" her dad asked.

Avery appreciated her dad checking in with her. "Yes, I think it's our best option, really our only option at this point." And it would give her a *real* reason to go run after Teddy. She needed to look him in the eyes and try to figure out why he was here— whether her instinct that it was for her was on track.

"I'll go find them and ask," she told Caroline. "I'll be back in five. Hopefully with two handsome race car drivers in tow."

She suddenly felt like Cinderella at the ball. *Wait, no. Aren't I the prince in this scenario, chasing after the beautiful love interest who has taken off into the night? And what is the glass slipper, a glass helmet?*

Avery took a breath and tossed her waves over her shoulders instead before taking a big step in the direction where she'd seen Teddy and Zack from the stage. It was time to face her destiny, find her happily ever after, or at least find someone to save her ass and keep her dad as far away from the microphone as possible.

"Great job up there. What's going on?" Josh stepped into her path, interrupting her carpe diem moment. She'd forgotten Josh was even there the moment she'd seen Teddy out of the corner of her eye.

"Well, we are having a bit of an emergency. An MC situation. And I have to go take care of it. But we have a plan. Go enjoy your meal."

"Are you sure? I want to help. I am at your beck and call tonight," Josh offered, sweetly, but in a way that now irked her, too.

"Yes, I'm sure. This is something I have to do on my own," she leaned over and gave him her most chaste peck on the cheek.

"Go get 'em, tiger," he told her.

She suppressed the urge to roll her eyes.

Avery made a beeline to the back of the tented room, eyes down, avoiding eye contact with anyone who might get in her way. She couldn't afford any more interruptions.

She was on a mission, and the clock was ticking. She needed to find her man, *if she could call him that*, both for the success of the event and for her sanity.

Her best bet was Zack. Luckily, he had stayed put, and she found him exactly where she'd spotted him during her speech.

He gave her a warm smile and leaned in for a hug. His wife, Nora, looked beautiful by his side in a red bustier and matching pants suit.

"Congratulations, this is a beautiful party," Nora gave her the very European double air kiss on each cheek in greeting.

"Zack, I have a huge favor to ask you, that is, if Nora doesn't mind me stealing you away for a bit. Our auctioneer had an emergency, and the auction starts in a few minutes. We know the crowd would love to see you, and Teddy, up on stage," she explained. "Would you be willing to step in?"

"I'd be honored," Zack said sincerely in his warm accent, "Tell me what you need me to do and give me a few minutes to prepare."

"Thank you, thank you, thank you. You are a lifesaver. Seriously." If she couldn't find Teddy, or if he said no, at least the auction was taken care of. "Caroline will fill you in," she added, pointing to where Caroline was standing.

Auctioneer problem solved. Now onto her heart.

"Before you go. One more thing, do you know where Teddy went?" she asked, biting her lip. "I thought I saw him over here a few minutes ago. I'm hoping he will share the auctioneer duties with you."

Zack gave her a knowing look and smiled. "I'm sure he'd be happy to join me on stage. He said he needed some air. He probably stepped outside."

"Okay, I'm going to go try and find him outside. Thanks again, really," she hugged them both.

Avery left Zack and Nora and slipped outside. The sun had gone down since she'd entered the cozy confines of the heated tent hours earlier, and the December air was crisp. She shivered as both the winter chill and the nerves hit her.

She spotted him immediately and her heart leapt. He was leaning against the trunk of the juniper tree in Ben's garden, a few of its leaves scattered around him. Avery felt them crunch under the point of her heel as she approached.

He must have heard the crunch too because he looked up from his phone, which he had been staring at seriously.

"Teddy, you're here..." she said softly, her voice rising in a question mark.

"I couldn't stay away from your big night. From you," he looked at her fondly.

The golden flecks in his eyes focused on her, instantly warming her body from the inside out.

Maybe she was going to have her Cinderella moment after all. "I saw you from the stage, and in my heart I knew it was you, but then you ran off and I didn't trust my own eyes," she wanted to leap into his arms, nuzzle her head into the spot on his chest where she knew it would fit perfectly, let his strong arms surround her and hold her tight.

But she had an auction to save. There would be plenty of time for that after the event, or at least she thought there might be from the heat coming off his body, and the way his eyes had lit up as she walked toward him.

She stepped in closer to him, to his warmth. She was so close in fact that if he leaned in, and she tilted her head up, their lips could meet. But he stayed as still as a statue, and she still needed to ask him to go on stage.

"Listen, as much as I would rather stay outside with you all night under my favorite tree, I have a favor to ask of you first. The auctioneer had an emergency, and we are hoping you and Zack can fill in at the last minute. Zack already said yes." She cocked her head, looking at him pleadingly, hopefully. "I don't know if you are still trying to avoid the spotlight..." she added, offering him an out.

"You don't have to ask twice. I'll do anything for you. I want you to be happy, even if it's with Josh and not with me," he said, his voice earnest but flat.

What? "Josh? Wait..." *He thinks I'm with Josh?* Her stomach dropped. "No—"

"Avery! Teddy! There you are," Caroline barreled toward them, the tent canvas flapping behind her as a gust of wind blew through. "Zack said I'd find you out here."

Caroline's eyes darted back and forth between the couple. "Am I interrupting? Did he say yes?"

Yes, you are as a matter of fact. "He said yes to the auction," Avery whispered.

"Excellent, Teddy, here come inside and I can point out

which tables I want you to keep your eyes on," Caroline was off and running. "Your job will be to spot the bidders, Zack is going to pitch the items, I just went over the list with him..."

Teddy stepped back from her, breaking the magnetic pull. Avery felt dizzy as she struggled to get enough oxygen. She knew Teddy was used to completely focusing on the task at hand and could block out anything else, but she had to make it clear that she wasn't with Josh.

"Wait! Caroline, I need one second alone with Teddy." She *had* to set the record straight.

Caroline nodded and slipped back into the tent, leaving Teddy and Avery alone again.

"Josh is not... it's not what you think. I...I want to explain, please?" she pleaded.

"It's fine, Avery, truly. I've been watching you all night from afar, and I see how he dotes on you, takes care of you. You deserve that," Teddy said, looking down at his feet. "You deserve more than I was willing to give you. You don't need to explain anything. He seems like a good chap. I know you two have history and I'm glad you found what you were looking for."

Her mouth went dry. *I have to fix this. Now. How does he not know that my eyes only see him?* That she'd wanted more with *him*, a real partnership with *him*, and no one else.

"NO!" She practically shouted in frustration. "Teddy. I'm not *with* Josh, I invited him as a friend. I don't know what you think you saw, but absolutely nothing romantic is happening between us." She couldn't get the words out of her mouth fast enough. It was one thing if Teddy truly didn't want her or wasn't ready for the relationship that she wanted, needed, but it was quite another if he was holding back because of something he saw with Josh.

Teddy closed his eyes and exhaled. "Okay. Yeah, thanks for clearing that up."

She grabbed his hand. "Please, meet me back in the garden after the auction?" There was so much more she wanted to say, to ask.

"We'll talk then." He squeezed her hand back and leaned down, letting his forehead touch hers. She lifted her other hand and traced it along his jawline.

"But first, I'm going to raise a huge pile of money for your charity, bella." He grabbed her hand and pulled it from his jaw to his lips, pressing his mouth into her palm. He kissed her hand suggestively, licking one of the lines on her palm.

thirty-eight

LOS ANGELES, CA

Avery held her hand out and stared at it, her heart hammering in her chest. She imagined her whole face must be bright red, matching the shade of her lipstick. She lingered outside the tent for another minute, collecting her thoughts while the chilly air lowered her body temperature again.

The whole night felt surreal, every turn of events unexpected. She'd finally allowed herself to feel confident enough on her own, without depending on her parents or a boyfriend for validation at every turn. She'd thought tonight would be the culmination of all the hard work she'd done over the last months not only on the event, but on herself.

She had finally come to terms with having Teddy in her life as only a friend despite her ongoing attraction to him physically. She'd convinced herself that it would wane over time. But the moment with Teddy had left her reeling.

I'm getting ahead of myself, as per usual. Teddy hadn't said he wanted anything real. There was no way she was going to be able to resist him much longer, no matter how much it pained her to keep seeing him on his terms. *Can I handle a casual relationship and keep my self-worth intact?*

It was a lot, and she hadn't been expecting any of it tonight.

I can do this.

It had really been an emotional and professional roller coaster of a season. But every time a challenge had been thrown at her, she'd risen to the occasion, she reminded herself. *I can get through tonight, whatever happens next. I will be okay.*

She re-entered the tent, her eyes adjusting to the lights after being in the dimly lit garden. The guests had all been seated for dinner while she'd been outside and the volume had lowered considerably, chatter replaced by utensils scraping plates as everyone tucked into their salad course. She made her way toward the front, where Josh was seated with her parents and brothers at their reserved table.

"Josh, I could use your help with something," she caught him mid-bite and waited as he put down his fork and wiped his mouth with a crisp white cloth napkin. "Could you do me a favor and sit with Nora? She pointed to the empty chair at an adjacent table, where Zack should have been seated. "I had to steal Zack away from her, and she could use some company."

"Anything for you, beautiful," he answered, standing up from his seat immediately, like a soldier at attention.

She suppressed a shudder. The word, even in another language, felt wrong coming from Josh's mouth. *That's what Teddy calls me.* It felt contrived coming from Josh, and it confirmed her hunch that Josh's feelings for her were no longer strictly platonic. Time to nip that in the bud.

She didn't have more than a second, but she had to do this

now, so she could have a clear conscience before her impending rendezvous with Teddy.

She tugged on his arm, moving him a few feet away from the table. "Before you go, can I talk to you for a second?"

Josh looked at her, his blue-gray eyes shining. "Of course, what's up?"

Avery took a deep breath. She wished she didn't have to do this right here in the middle of all these people, but she couldn't have this hanging over her head when she finally had the chance to talk to Teddy later.

"I hope you didn't get the wrong impression when I invited you to be my date tonight. I treasure our friendship, and even though we dated when we first met, I thought we'd both agreed we were better as friends." She paused. "I just sensed that maybe you thought tonight was more. And I could totally be wrong, but I wanted to make sure we are on the same page."

Josh's face fell, but he quickly pulled himself together. "Aves, I enjoy being around you in any capacity. I admit I got a little carried away in the moment tonight, but we're good. Friends. Understood," he nodded his head solemnly a couple of times.

Avery bit her lip. Ugh, he was trying too hard to look unaffected. It didn't exactly convince her that he hadn't been hoping they'd be more than friends. Asking him for a favor and then casually, but unequivocally, friend-zoning him before he could go do that favor, left her feeling like she didn't quite fit in her own skin.

"Promise you're okay?" she raised her eyebrows.

"I promise," he confirmed, clearing his throat. *Of course, he'll be okay, he's a grown man.* Maybe he was feeling a sting of rejection, but Avery knew that he could handle it.

"Right, then. I'm going to switch tables," Josh pointed his fingers at Zack's now empty seat.

He walked away, leaving Avery entirely unconvinced that she hadn't cruelly rejected him in a room full of people, some of whom were his colleagues and important professional contacts. She felt a bit guilty for how she'd done it, but she still knew it was the right thing to do.

"Ladies and gentlemen," Zack announced from the stage, "We hope you are enjoying your meal. I'm Zack Maimon, driver for the Silver F1 team. Unfortunately, Al Roker was called back to New York due to the storms back east. I hope you won't mind if my teammate, Teddy Ross, and I fill in tonight as your auctioneers?"

The audience erupted in cheers and Avery thought she even heard catcalls and whistles from some of the ladies in the crowd. She felt a rush of satisfaction. *Yes, he really is that hot. And if they only knew the real him, well, they'd be as gone as I am.*

"Our first item up for bid tonight is this gorgeous yellow helmet signed by none other than our very own Teddy Ross, the second fastest driver on the team," Zack announced, roasting his teammate a bit. Luckily, the crowd was filled with F1 insiders who understood that it was good-natured ribbing between teammates and laughed. The rest of the crowd followed suit, and the atmosphere turned jovial.

Okay, this is promising. She scanned the tables—*who is going to bid?*

"Our starting bid for this helmet, the actual one Teddy wore last week during the race, is $1,000. Do we have $1,000?"

"Zack, we have $1,000 from the gentleman in the red suit,"

Teddy pointed to an NBA player whose hand shot up. You never knew who would be into memorabilia.

"How about $1,500? Do we have $1,500?" Zack sniffed the helmet. "Friends, I can verify officially that this is indeed the one he wore during the race. I'd know that smell anywhere." More laughter from the crowd.

Eau de Teddy? Yeah, I'd know that smell anywhere too.

Avery wished she could catch Teddy's eye, but he shrugged his shoulders and grinned at Zack, then turned to scan the crowd, looking for the next bidder.

They are adorable. Even better than Al Roker would have been. Avery wished having the two of them up there had been her idea to begin with. Maybe it would be the start of an annual tradition.

The helmet ended up going for a whopping $7,500. Avery had projected it would bring in around $5,000, and she was pleasantly surprised by the good-natured bidding war that had broken out between the NBA player in red and an older woman. The rest of the auction proceeded in much the same fashion, with lots of back and forth between bidders and light-hearted jokes from the drivers-turned-auctioneers.

"And that concludes our live auction. Thank you all so much for the support and generosity," Zack thanked the crowd.

Caroline leapt on the stage, tapped Teddy on the shoulder, and whispered something into his ear.

Teddy tapped his mic, "Zack, we have some breaking news. I was just informed that we raised a record-breaking one million dollars tonight. Yes, that's right everyone, never before has the

Silver end-of-season gala done this well. Big congratulations to all, the Silver family, especially Avery."

Avery's mouth went dry. *Holy shit. I've done it.*

She'd raised more than enough for the new gym and for the scholarships. Teddy's eyes finally found hers, and she got the eye contact she'd been craving. Avery felt her face dissolve into a full-on ear-to-ear grin. It was like she was in a movie, where everyone else disappeared, like she and Teddy were the only two people in the room. *I'm about to be a puddle on the floor. Record-breaking results the first year I'm in charge of the gala with Teddy the one to break that news to me.* She wished the moment would never end. Surely, life couldn't get any better than this.

Her heart pinged. *Ok, fine, there's one thing that would make life better than this.*

The crowd erupted in applause one more time as the waiters reappeared with platters of peppermint brownies and slices of sheet cake.

And that was it. Her work was done.

She thought she'd feel a tremendous sense of relief, like the weight of a million breaks had been lifted from her shoulders. Instead, it felt like someone had poked a teeny-tiny hole in a balloon in her chest, letting a fraction of tension seep out. The balloon hadn't popped.

Maybe after she finally had her chance to talk to Teddy. Yeah, it was going to pop alright, either exploding with heart-shaped confetti or gut-wrenching heartbreak.

"Avery, come sit down now and relax," Ben called to her from her family's table, breaking her near-euphoric reverie.

"I can't. There's one more thing I have to do," she replied as she looked around for Teddy. He was no longer on the stage.

Her mom smiled. "I see. Does it have something to do with our unexpected auctioneer?"

"How did you know?" Avery asked.

"Well, I didn't think he showed up tonight because he's crazy about charity events and making small talk. Go on, then," her mother waved her on, excusing her from the table.

She turned around to the tent entrance. Every fiber of her being wanted to take off the Cinderella heels and run outside to Teddy. But she knew she couldn't, that it would cause a scene.

"Excuse me," it was Lenny again.

Now, really?

Her toes curled in her shoes while she put on her best customer service face. "Thanks again for coming tonight, and enjoy those Lakers tickets. We so appreciate your support," she tried to end the conversation before it started. At least her salesmanship earlier in the night had paid off.

"That's what I wanted to talk to you about," he said, not letting her off the hook. "Do you know if there are any blackout dates? And if I can use the tickets during the playoffs, or is it good for a regular season game only?"

I do not have the time or patience to deal with this right now.

"Great questions," she replied brightly as if she were talking to Sadie or any other preschooler, "I don't know off the top of my head, but we will be sure to look at the fine print when we are back in the office. Caroline will follow up with you next week."

She turned her back to him, hoping a physical gesture might end the conversation since social cues were not going to work. *Deep breaths.*

Before she could take another small step, her aunt approached her. "Avery, I've been looking for you all night, but you've been so busy, busy. I haven't seen you since Austin, how have you been?"

Ha! How have I been since Austin? I've lived a whole life since Austin.

"Oh, you know, busy with the season and the gala," she tried to be as bland and generic as possible, even though she felt like she might scream if one more person interrupted her.

She'd thought Teddy'd be the one who would get mobbed on his way to meet her, leaving her waiting out in the cold, literally and figuratively. This gala was looking like the one instance where she was, shockingly, more in demand than an F1 star.

She excused herself from her aunt to scurry to the exit uninterrupted.

And there he was. Right under her tree.

* * *

He was pacing under her favorite tree. Teddy's hair was longer than when she'd last seen him in the hospital in Miami, curling up over his collar. It suited him.

She took a big gulp of air, and the cold nearly took her breath away; the rest of her body hadn't registered the temperature as she stepped outside, every fiber of her being focused on the handsome figure in the distance.

"Teddy!" she called out, moving as fast as her dress and high heels would allow.

"Thank goodness," he looked relieved as she got closer. "I was beginning to think you'd stood me up."

"Not in a million years. I just got stopped approximately one hundred times on my way out here. I think I got a taste of what it must be like for you all the time," she explained, the experience having brought her one step closer to truly under-standing his daily existence.

"Yes, rather frustrating, isn't it?" he empathized, his eyes twinkling.

Now what?

The silence hung in the air between them, as if words had been stilled by the damp air, the temperature seeming to have dropped ten degrees since they'd met at this same spot earlier.

"Thank you for..." Avery said, trying to put into words the immense gratitude she felt for his presence tonight. "I'm so sorry," he said at the exact same time, neither of them wanting to let the silence grow between them for even one second longer.

"Sorry. You go first," he said, smiling, gesturing with his arm that the floor was all hers, "I have a lot I want to say to you, now that I have the chance, but I'm more interested in your thoughts."

Avery exhaled, and her toes uncurled in her shoes. The chance to be heard, to be understood, for him to let her explain why she thought they would have been so good together, meant everything.

She took a deep breath, shivering as a cold breeze whipped the air.

"You're freezing. Here." Teddy said, peeling off his suit jacket.

"Thanks," she said, lifting her face to his like a sunflower towards the sun as he carefully slipped it over her shoulders. Her body relaxed as the jacket took the edge off the cold, and she felt her shoulders slide away from her ears.

He gently caressed her cheek with the back of his hand, before placing it in his pocket, but he didn't step away. The nearness of his body filled her with more warmth, maybe even a touch of heat. How she'd missed the feeling of his body near hers.

"You were saying," he prompted her.

"I'm just so happy you're here. I truly appreciate everything you did for the gala tonight, whether it was for me, or because you're a good person. It wouldn't have been nearly as successful without you," she spit it all out without coming up for air.

"Bella, it was for you. It's all for you," his eyes shone with tenderness.

She shivered again, whether it was from his words or the air, she couldn't be sure. Probably some combination.

It felt so right to be cozied up together, cocooned under his jacket, but Avery still didn't know where they stood. Now, more than ever, she knew she could never settle for picking up where they had left off. She knew for sure she didn't want to be a casual girlfriend, who just showed up at races as part of his cheering squad or hooked up when his schedule allowed.

It would be too hard on her heart, hanging around waiting for him to be ready for something more. She deserved more than that, and she believed he did too, but she couldn't force Teddy's hand. She knew she had to say something, to make her position clear, but she didn't want this moment to end. What if it was the last time she found herself in Teddy's arms? The thought of never feeling his embrace again made her knees wobble, so she pushed it out of her mind.

They stayed like that for a minute or two, Avery working up the courage to risk her heart breaking again by telling him how she felt. Teddy appeared to sense her slight discomfort.

"I had this whole speech planned, and now that you're here in my arms, I only want to enjoy the moment for a second," Teddy whispered into her ear.

Avery snuggled into him, inhaling his familiar woodsy scent. They clung to each other, not saying a word, the silence warm and pleasant, not frozen or full of anticipation.

"I don't want to break the spell either. I missed this," Avery whispered back, "But I really do want to hear that speech." She broke their warm embrace so that she could look him in the eye.

He stepped back and took her hands in his own.

"It sounded a lot more romantic in my head, but here goes. The bottom line is, I love you. I love you and I'll post it on Instagram if you want, or make a TikTok video, or we can keep it just for us. And I'm so sorry for not seeing it before, and for causing you pain because it took my emotionally stunted self a life-threatening car crash and time apart as friends to realize I don't want to live without you. I'm in, I'm all in. Nothing casual about it. That is, if you'll have me, if you feel the same?"

Avery felt warm tears fill her eyes in contrast to the chill of the air on her cheeks. She'd shed so many tears over him over the last several months: tears of hurt, anger, regret, and fear, but these tears were different. They were joy and relief.

Pop.

That balloon in her chest finally burst. She could breathe. It hadn't been the gala that had been taking up residence where her lungs were supposed to be. It had been her heart, puffy and swollen from the ache of being separated from Teddy. *No wonder I hadn't felt it burst when the auction ended.*

Teddy released one of her hands and used the pad of his thumb to wipe away the tears that had spilled out onto her cheek. "I hope those are happy tears."

"They are," she smiled through the tears. "I've wanted to hear those words from you for so long. I just didn't think you were on the same page."

"I was. *And* I wasn't, to be honest. I was completely smitten with you from our first meeting. I'd never met a woman like you. I didn't know what would happen when I suggested we fake date back in London, but I knew that I wanted a reason to spend more time with you, to be around you."

He caressed her cheek, running the same thumb that had wiped her tears down her jawline. "I knew that I was attracted to you, but I had no idea I was going to fall for you the way I did. I had spent so much time convincing myself that I couldn't have a real romance until I had made it, had secured my motorsport legacy, and set my mom and brother up for life financially. But it was all fear. I know that now. Everything I was afraid of, my family history getting out, a crash... it all happened anyway."

Avery pressed her cheek into his hand silently urging him to keep going. She hung on his every word, taking in every detail of what had been going on in that beautiful head of his while they'd been oceans apart.

"And I'm still standing. And I have you to thank for that. If you hadn't come into my life this year, I'd still be operating out of fear. Going through everything I, we, have gone through this season has made me realize I don't have to do this alone. I don't want to do this alone. I want to do all of it with *you*, specifically."

She took a breath and tried to memorize the subtle ever-green smell of the garden in winter. She wanted to remember this moment forever. She'd known all along he had this in him, that the real Teddy had the capacity to live a full life—career, family, and love and not just exist as a perfect cardboard cutout of what he thought an F1 driver was supposed to be. It warmed her heart to the point where she could no longer feel the cold. *I love him more than I ever have before.* Her chest swelled with pride and joy for him, but she wasn't the same person she was when they met either.

"Avery, say something" he blinked. "Please, anything,"

"I love you too. And I'm so proud of you. I'm so excited for you, for us," she answered.

"Why do I sense a but coming on?" Teddy breathed.

"Because I want nothing more than to live happily ever after with you. But how are we going to make this work?" Avery paused.

She needed to make her dreams a priority too if they wanted a shot at making this work for real.

"You're based in Europe, not to mention that you crisscross the globe more than half the year. And I've learned a lot about myself this year too. For the first time in a long time, maybe ever, I feel like an important part of my family's work. And I know that I can truly contribute, not only to the charity side of things, but maybe to the actual family business. And I want to see where my career takes me."

Teddy considered her words carefully for a moment, knitting his brow as he formulated his response. "It will be hard, complicated, and messy. But I know you. I know what I'm doing here. I'm never going to expect you to be the type of partner who accompanies me race-to-race, whose sole role in life is my sidekick. I want you, the ambitious, capable, woman you are."

Finally.

"You're the only one for me, Avery Silver. And I'll do whatever it takes. I can live in LA in the off-season, and I can fly you out for as many or as few races as you want. Okay?"

"Okay," she nodded. "I trust you."

"I trust you too. We will make it work. I promise," he whispered.

"Can I kiss you now, please?" he pleaded.

"Nope," she said, lifting herself up on her tip-toes and grabbing his crisp white shirt. "I'm going to kiss you."

He leaned down letting her pull him in, and their lips found each other, tender and sweet. She parted her lips for him. The warmth she had felt in her heart morphed into a fire, making her burn in a straight line from her mouth to her navel, in stark contrast with the wet drop that fell softly on her head.

Avery broke their contact and looked up. "It's raining. It never rains in LA," she said as a soft drizzle dusted the broad shoulders of Teddy's coat that she was still wearing.

Teddy hugged her tight and grinned. "Rare indeed. Should I pull out my camera so we can post this rare phenomenon later? Or should we go live?" he teased.

"No," Avery replied, "I need my hands for this, not for a camera." She wrapped her arms around his neck, pulling his face back to hers.

The drizzle of rain came down harder, the sound of big, fat drops pounding on the tent's roof, drowning out the DJ who had taken the stage inside. Avery felt her sleek waves go limp, water dripping off them down her back and legs, water squishing into her shoes.

It was perfect.

epilogue

MONTE CARLO, MONACO
Six Months Later

"God Save The King" blared from the speakers above Avery's head. She felt goosebumps on her arms as she stood next to Stacey amid the Silver employees who had gathered beneath the stage. She squeezed her friend's hand. "This is your win too, I'm so proud of you."

Avery looked up at the podium, where both Teddy and her dad, who was representing the team, were standing, both men beaming with pride as they waved to the crowd below, the champagne bottles at their feet begging to be sprayed. So much in her life had changed over the last year, but that feeling of pride when she saw silver and blue on the podium—that would never change.

Avery felt a lightness throughout her body as she caught Teddy's unabashed grin beaming from beneath his Pirelli Tires cap. Finally, the world was able to see how he lit up, how his eyes sparkled when his joy wasn't rehearsed, and wasn't manufactured on cue. Avery grinned too. Had this win happened a year ago, he probably would have used his practiced smile, or would have stood there frowning, already thinking about the next race. But during the off-season, once Teddy had more-or-less moved in with her in LA, he'd started seeing a therapist regularly and working on mindfulness. He'd been trying to stay in the present and not ruminate quite so much on his past trauma or future goals.

Today the hard work he'd undertaken on and off the track had paid off. Teddy had won his first F1 race. *The storied Monaco Grand Prix, no less.*

She turned to Teddy's mom, Margaret, who was standing on the other side of her, and winked. The lithe, silver-haired woman smiled back, the twinkle in Margaret's hazel eyes so similar to her son's.

"I'm so happy you're here to see his first win. He wouldn't be here without you," Avery shouted in her ear to be heard over the deafening cheers. While Teddy was slowly coming to terms with his past, letting go of his instinct to protect his family from publicity was proving to be a bit harder. This was only the second race his mom had come to this season, and it couldn't have worked out better.

"I don't think he could have done it without you either. I've never seen him so settled, so grounded as he has been since you entered his life," Margaret shouted back.

Avery gave her a little side hug as a steady, calm washed over her. Celebrating this moment beside Teddy's mom while Teddy was celebrating with her father up on the podium felt so natural, like they were on their way to being one, big happy family.

She put her other arm around Stacey, who had literally been

bouncing on her toes since the final ten laps of the race when it seemed like Teddy might really be able to win. Stacey deserved to enjoy this win as much as any of Teddy's loved ones. She had spent her off-season in LA working with Teddy so he could stay in peak shape. It had been a win-win for Avery; she loved having her best friend around the corner.

The national anthem ended, and the crown Prince of Monaco handed Teddy his sparkling trophy. *Stunning.* Teddy triumphantly lifted it over his head to the roar of the crowd. The Prince of Monaco had commissioned Louis Vuitton to hand-craft the bespoke trophies, which were hand-painted with the fashion brand's famous logo in the red and white colors of the Monegasque flag.

Teddy and the others put their trophies down and grabbed the champagne bottles at their feet, spraying one another with abandon. Drops of sticky, sweet bubbly drizzled onto Avery's dark hair.

"I wish I had an umbrella right about now," Stacey moaned, shielding her eyes. But Avery didn't mind, tipping her head upward to see if she could catch a drop on her tongue, savoring the taste of victory. It was part of the fun of winning. Besides, she was going back to their hotel to shower and get dressed up before what was sure to be a wild night out at the Casino de Monte-Carlo.

Cody, the Archer driver who had caused Teddy's crash last year, had come in third. He was merciless, draining his magnum-sized bottle over Teddy's head. Teddy looked positively giddy trying to nail Cody right back. Avery shook her head, grinning. *No different than eight-year-old boys with water guns.*

Teddy turned away from Cody's onslaught and toward

Klaus Erikkson, who had come in second and was stationed on Teddy's other side. Teddy sprayed him, enticing him to join the fray. Cody, seeing Teddy momentarily distracted, stepped off his podium to go nail Teddy from behind.

But Cody's toe clipped Teddy's porcelain trophy as he stepped up onto Teddy's first-place platform to douse Teddy from above. Avery bit her lip as the trophy wobbled precariously on the edge. It almost happened in slow motion, eventually toppling over and breaking into multiple pieces.

Cody looked down, mouth agape, until Teddy clapped him on the back, laughing. There were clearly no hard feelings between the racers.

"Oh no, oh my," Teddy's mom gasped in horror.

Avery shook her head and turned to console Margaret. "Don't fret, they will fix it or make him a new one." Broken first-place trophy? It was a good problem to have. You couldn't have a broken first-place trophy without winning first place.

Margaret looked doubtful.

"Seriously, Mrs. Ross," Chloe, a team engineer and a member of Teddy's pit crew, chimed in. "It's not the first time an over-exuberant driver has broken a trophy. Heck, it's not the first time Cody has broken a trophy." She rolled her eyes.

Chloe was one of Avery's first hires in her new role as Silver Racing Director of Equality and Sustainability. Brandon, the team principal, had been so impressed with Avery's work at the gala and her commitment to creating more equality and opportunities in sports, that he'd offered her the newly created position.

With each additional day at work at the team factory, instead of the family office in Santa Monica, she felt herself grow more confident in her new role, knowing she had a real part in shaping the future of the team like she'd always dreamed. While it had been hard to relinquish control of the foundation, she knew that Caroline would do an excellent job. And she couldn't pass up an opportunity to make a real difference within the Silver organization. Her first order of business had been to recruit top female engineering talent. She was working to build a pipeline of opportunities, starting at the karting level, for youth from all socioeconomic backgrounds to get involved in the sport. She hoped that other teams would follow suit.

Avery looked up one last time at the podium before her gaze wandered to the crowds around her, which were noticeably thinning as fans returned back to their real lives.

Avery was happy that she too, had a real life to return to once the race was over. Racing was a huge part of her life and always would be. But she loved that it was now a part of the life she was building with Teddy, and not their whole life.

The team reconvened in the pit lane in front of Silver for hugs and photos before going their separate ways. Avery stood on the periphery of the small crowd that had formed in front of Teddy's garage, content to watch Teddy accept the never-ending congratulations and well wishes from a distance. She intended to let him shine; *I'll get my time with him later*. But as soon as he spotted her, he jogged over to where she was standing, pulling her close and lifting her up for another celebratory kiss.

It reminded her of their first kiss in Austin, the euphoria, the way his lips felt soft and full, yet firm. But the similarities ended there. Gone was the uncertainty about his motivations. There was no holding back, no hiding her feelings. She didn't wonder if it was for the cameras, or who had captured the moment.

They'd tried to keep their private life private for a few months after the gala, but their friends and family had all known they were together. And while they'd never made a public declaration that they were back together, their coupledom was old news by now, even on the internet.

She pulled her lips off his, reluctantly. She could have gotten lost in his embrace, his broad shoulders so familiar they felt like home. "You did it. Teddy Ross, F1 race winner. Congratulations, handsome," she said, beaming. "I can't wait to celebrate with you tonight."

"No, *we* did it, and I can't wait for tonight either," he said, eyes shining at her.

* * *

Avery grabbed Teddy's hand to still it as they walked through the restaurant where they'd celebrate Teddy's win with the team over dinner before going to the casino. He'd been fidgety the whole way there, buttoning and unbuttoning the top button of his crisp white dress shirt, tugging at the sleeves of his blazer.

"Hey, the hard part is over. This is the fun part," she encouraged him. "I know all eyes will be on you, but let loose tonight. For once."

He nodded, but didn't say a word. Tugged on his sleeve again.

"Is the jacket too small?" she asked.

He shook his head.

"It looks great," she added. "You look great."

"And you are the most beautiful woman I've ever seen," he said, one-upping her compliment. "I love that dress."

She ran her hands down the smooth blue silk. She knew she

looked great. And her mom was right, she'd found an occasion to wear the sexy, summery gown.

"I don't know how I'm going to keep my hands off you in front of everyone." His hand lingered.

Her cheeks heated.

Teddy held the door open to the private room at the back, where candles were lit, casting a romantic glow over a table set for ten. They were the last two to arrive, and the room went silent at their entrance.

Avery stopped in her tracks. What was her mom doing here? She hadn't come to the race.

Avery paused and turned her head, looking at the rest of the faces around the table one-by-one.

Her Dad. Teddy's mom. Expected.

Stacey. *Of course.*

James. *Made sense.*

Ben and Adam. *What on earth?*

Caroline. *She hadn't been at the race.*

Her pulse ticked up and she turned her head toward Teddy, eyes wide.

He cleared his throat. "Everyone, if I could have your attention, please?" He turned to her, and their eyes locked.

"Avery Silver. My bella. Months ago, as the rain was pouring down on us in your brother's garden, I made a vow to myself that I would spend the rest of my days on this earth showing you how much I love you. From the moment we met in the paddock, we were inevitable. And while it wasn't the easiest path to get here, I don't regret a single thing that happened over the last fifteen months because it led us here to this moment."

He lowered himself to one knee.

Her hands flew to her lips in utter disbelief as she gasped.

I've dreamt of this moment. Someday in the distant future. Avery's eyes filled with tears. *Of course.*

"Happy tears?" Teddy asked, stopping himself.

She nodded through her tears and fanned herself, trying to dry them. "Keep going!"

The gentle laughter of everyone she loved most in the world filled her ears

"I told you then, the night of the gala, that I wanted to experience all that life has to offer with you by my side. And I don't want to wait another day to make it official. Avery Silver, will you marry me?"

His hands reached into his shirt poached and he pulled out the world's most perfect ring - a single, oval shaped diamond on a platinum band.

"Yes. Of course, yes," she couldn't hold back the tears anymore. They fell down her cheeks as he slipped the ring on her finger.

THE END

DID YOU ENJOY *PODIUM PERFECT*?

Please feel free to write a book review.

A few sentences on Amazon or Goodreads helps a lot.

Thank you for supporting independent artists!

acknowledgments

I've dreamed of becoming an author for as long as I can remember. I'm fortunate to have many wonderful people in my life who have helped make this dream come true.

First, a huge thank you to my writing coach and editor, Britta Jensen, for your guidance, enthusiasm, and spot-on feedback. I have learned so much from you and truly enjoy working with you.

Thank you to my fabulous cover design team, Sam & Deb | Ink & Velvet Designs, for bringing my vision to life. You knocked it out of the park.

Thank you to my early readers, Ali, Laurie, Jenn, Pam, Alyse, and Jess for your honest opinions and feedback. Thank you for also being the best friends and confidantes a girl could ask for. And to Nili, for being my fresh eyes before print.

To my ATX Write-In crew, thank you for making me feel like a real writer. Thank you to Hannah Hembree-Bell, Chandler Baker, and Alex Kiester for bringing us all together. And a very special thank you to Erin Quinn-Kong and Debra Doliner for being my writing besties and holding my hand throughout the entire process.

Thank you to all my other amazing friends, extended family, and Austin neighbors who have checked in with me and cheered me on throughout the writing and editing process. I'm so excited for you to finally read my book.

To Dana Dovitch, I wouldn't have finished writing this without you, and I wouldn't be the person I am today without you.

To Ms. Pfau at Chaparral Elementary School, for being the first person to tell me I was a good writer and could write a book someday.

To my parents and sisters, thank you for being my biggest cheerleaders and for always being my safe place to land. I love you. Mom, Taylor, and Cayla thank you for your thoughtful opinions on every piece of the puzzle along the way. There's no one I trust more.

Thank you to Finn and Archie for being yourselves, for your big hearts, and for inspiring me. I hope I make you proud. You both make me proud every day.

Thank you to my husband, Yoni. You are my true partner in every way, including writing this book. Your faith in me and your unwavering support have made this possible. Thank you for taking me seriously, always believing in me, and for making **all** my dreams come true. It's a really nice life.

And finally, thank YOU, my dear reader, for giving my book a chance. Whether you're a longtime F1 fan, a romance reader who knows nothing about F1, or you just picked it up by chance, I hope that you laughed, that your heart skipped a beat, and that it made you smile. And I hope it took you less time to read *Podium Perfect* than it did for me to write it.

about the author

Photo by Paige Newton

Lexi Richards is a debut author who writes flirty, fast-paced contemporary romance. Before focusing on swoony book boyfriends, she spent years crafting speeches, newsletters, and press releases for elected officials and nonprofits.

A proud graduate of Duke University and the University of Southern California, she now lives in Austin, Texas, with her husband and two sons, who share her love of Formula One and good storytelling. Her family's Sunday morning tradition of watching F1 Grands Prix inspired her debut novel, *Podium Perfect*, which reimagines a classic romance trope at 200 miles per hour.

Podium Perfect was a finalist in the 2023 Writers' League of Texas Manuscript Contest (Romance category). **Learn more about Lexi's books and sign up for her newsletter at lexirichardsauthor.com.**

instagram.com/lexirauthor